Satisfy Me

D1528925

Books by Renée Alexis

GOTTA HAVE IT

HE'S ALL THAT

Books by Fiona Zedde

BLISS

A TASTE OF SIN

Published by Kensington Publishing Corporation

Satisfy Me

Renée Alexis
Sydney Molare
Fiona Zedde

APHRODISIA
KENSINGTON BOOKS
http://www.kensingtonbooks.com

Aphrodisia Books are published by

Kensington Publishing Corp.
850 Third Avenue
New York, NY 10022

All Kensington Titles, Imprints, and Distributed Lines are available at special quantity discounts for bulk purchases for sales promotions, premiums, fund- raising, and educational or institutional use.

Special book excerpts or customized printings can also be created to fit specific needs. For details, write or phone the office of the Kensington special sales manager: Kensington Publishing Corp., 850 Third Avenue, New York, NY, 10022, attn: Special Sales Department, Phone: 1-800-221-2647.

Aphrodisia and the A logo Reg. U.S. Pat & TM Off

ISBN 0-7582-1565-7

First Kensington Trade Paperback Printing: January 2007

10 9 8 7 6 5 4 3 2 1

Printed in the United States of America

Contents

Still the One

Renée Alexis

October 30

10:00 A.M. Mr. Ellery looked like an undertaker, but he was much more than that. He was the finder of lost loves, or, in this case, the finder of wanted-to-be loves. He sat his jet-black briefcase on the table in front of the gentleman who hired him and said, "I found her."

A calmly excited voice responded. "Really? Where?"

"She owns several pharmacies in the metro area but mainly works out of the one at 906 Dayton Street; Stuart's Pharmacy."

"A pharmacist?"

"Correct. She's been one for almost ten years now."

"Here in Cleveland, you say?"

"Yes, sir."

"She was always a smart, pretty young thing. I knew she'd make it big one day. Christ. She's been under my nose all this time, and I didn't know it."

"She's been here for only two years. I traced her from work records in California."

"Still, two years—I should have seen her." The client slid the envelope of money across the table to Mr. Ellery. "Job well done. I appreciate your time."

"I appreciate your business." Mr. Ellery took a card from his wallet and handed it over. "Pass the word. My prices are fair, and I can negotiate."

"What you just did for me is worth a mint. And if she's open to seeing me, I'll be glad to endorse your ad in the *Metro Times*, free of charge, naturally."

"That's what I call spreading the word."

The client watched as Mr. Ellery walked from the office, and then called directory assistance to get the number for Stuart's Pharmacy. "Hello?" The voice on the other end was definitely that of Ms. Beverly Stuart. Her voice hadn't changed in almost twenty years, and he relished the sound of it. He tried to sound rational as he spoke. "Can you tell me what your store hours are? . . . And that is 906 Dayton Street, correct? . . . Thank you."

At 7:30 that evening, the man approached Stuart's Pharmacy and stared at the building covered with garish Halloween decorations. She had always been the festive type—it fit so well with her personality: bubbly. He smiled at the talking Dracula. *"Never steal a drop without your Blue Cross identification card. It could save your life!"* Cute, real cute. He walked in.

Behind the counter, Beverly kept her eyes on the exact dosages to get her customers' prescriptions right and ready for tomorrow-morning pickups. Fresh out of a terrible relationship, working like crazy to keep her mind occupied was the only thing left to do.

As she worked, she thought over her life, wondering if she did the right thing by putting Tony out a few weeks ago. He was good for curing the loneliness for a hot minute, but that was it. Other than that, he wasn't worth the dime in his pocket.

As usual, her next set of doubts set up camp in her mind: would she have had a happier life in San Diego if she hadn't moved back to Cleveland? Living in California was fine, but she missed her family, friends. One in particular came to mind: Debbie Jacobs. They'd been pals years ago, despite the constant presence of Debbie's kid brother and all-around monster, Ethan Jacobs. Ethan had always been cute in his way, but he was a pest.

When you're fourteen, you for sure don't want a snotty-nosed little chump tagging along. She and Debbie were at the age where they had the hots for boys and any X-rated film they could sneak in to. That ended when Debbie's mother went to work in the ER of Oakland Medical and was on call most nights. Ethan was practically forced on them, and even at the tender age of eight, the little snot was sizing Beverly up. Yes, the cute little tyke wanted her; as if he knew something about sex. Frankly, it grossed her out to think Ethan was smiling at her.

Sure, she was considered pretty, with satin-brown skin, long ginger hair, and dark brown eyes, but she didn't want a kid drooling over her. Yuck! As it always happened, Ethan was around because she and Debbie were inseparable. They were mad about the boys and were going to get to them, come hell or high water—even if they had to have Ethan right behind them.

That was many stories and lifetimes ago. She had lost contact with Debbie, who had gotten married right out of high school to one of those boys they were hot over. Beverly went on to college to become a pharmacist. As far as Ethan was concerned, she hadn't any idea what happened to him. She just assumed he got hauled off to some institution for the sexually insane. Good for his little butt. Other than right now, she hadn't actually thought about him too much.

The last thing she wanted to be doing on Devil's Night was working late doing the books. Her idea of a cozy, haunted night was to be in front of her television watching anything scary featuring her favorite, Mr. Vincent Price. Weirdos and slashers were her thing, for some reason. Maybe it stemmed from wanting to do away with Ethan years ago.

Nonetheless, her work night was to be a long one—at least for another hour. She owned several pharmacies in the metro area and had to make sure everything was right before opening the following morning to sell packets of alcohol chasers to late-night partyers. Yes, Halloween would be a big night—her pharmacy would make a mint on inebriation fixers and keep Cleveland hangover free.

It wasn't quite closing time, and there were a few customers left to serve, plus another employee who hadn't left yet. Beverly was about to let her off early when another customer came in. She watched other customers leave and told her employee to take off, that she could handle the last guy who'd just come in.

Carol really didn't seem to want to leave Beverly in there alone with a strange man on that particular evening—either that or Carol was checking out how fine his ass was and wanted to hook up with him later. No matter, Beverly made her leave so *she* could size him up instead.

This gentleman was just browsing, and she didn't know if he'd come in for a prescription or what. After a few more minutes of staring his delicious ass down, Beverly decided it was time for him to either buy something or leave. She was tired and wanted to get back to the comfort of her own queen-size bed—alone. This man was cute though, cute enough to share that big bed with. She couldn't help checking him out. Something about him made her stare, stare, stare. There was something more than an instant attraction, something familiar about him, but what?

She noticed how his eyes would search her, then dart away like he was shy. Maybe it was a male thing—checking out the action. That was cool with her, because he was the sexiest thing that had ever stepped foot in there. Her usual customers were men in their seventies and eighties, humped over and trying their best to flirt while flashing a toothless grin. That wasn't about to happen, not for her. If she was to take up with a man ever again, it would be the long, lean, sexy type, the type that was walking her way. The gentleman was definitely an attention getter, and she hated the fact that his very persona was close to flooring her. He was stacked, had dark curly/straight hair, and looked like the baseball player Alex Rodriguez (A-Rod), who was as fine as a needle in a haystack; a welcome sight!

Beverly was actually a little nervous about speaking to him, for fear of mumbling gibberish. She cleared her throat. "Sir, we're about to close. Is there something I can help you with?"

He walked up to the counter, and her legs got weak. He smiled and skyrocketed her straight to the moon. Even his teeth were pretty—straight, with no gaps or missing teeth, just perfect. He was *damn* fine walking DNA. Beverly was used to primates or single-celled organisms like Tony or her ex-husband, BJ, because that was all that approached her. She knew she was lovely—why couldn't she get the handsome ones? Even this man, she thought, was going to buy whatever he needed and then leave the store.

As he approached her, he looked straight into her eyes. At first he didn't say anything, but she encouraged him a little. "Sir, are you okay? Can I get you anything? We *are* about to close."

He leaned in to her with that delicious smile. "You sure the hell can get something for me, Beverly Stuart."

That floored her. How did this stranger know her name? Her lab coat was thrown across the chair, and he couldn't see the name on it. Again she cleared her throat, "Excuse me? Who are you?"

"You don't remember?" he added with a wrinkling of his forehead.

Beverly stood there as patiently as possible, hoping he wasn't just a cute pervert. "I haven't any idea who you are, and to be frank, again, it's closing time."

"Then I'll be frank with you. I'm Ethan Jacobs. Debbie Jacobs's brother. Do you remember me now?"

Before she could even think to control her words, it came out. "Ethan? You can't be serious! That little chump that used to try to lift my skirt? For real, are you him?"

"Don't I look like him? Mom says I haven't changed a bit."

She walked through the swinging pharmacy door while saying, "For Christ's sake, Ethan. How the hell are you? I was just thinking about you."

"You were thinking about me? The girl I thought hated my very soul!"

"Well, you were a downright pest, but so are most little boys."

He looked himself up and down. "I've changed a bit."

"I'll say! Get over here and give me a hug." She delivered the biggest hug, something she never thought she'd give Ethan Jacobs. He was so tall and sexy, and he smelled so good—Gucci aftershave. His muscles showed even under the tweed blazer he was sporting, and she could just about feel everything on him. Yes, he was definitely better than that little snot who worshipped the panties she walked in.

He'd grown up nicely from head to toe. He used to be so skinny, but he was perfect now, tight, taut, and in all the right places. Beverly couldn't believe her eyes. It was the one and only Ethan Jacobs. Her fingers smoothed across his warm cheeks. "How have you been? Where have you been?"

"I'm doing great, got my own business here in town. I never left. I own a Lexus dealership on Montcalm Avenue; doing the paperwork for another one. You know I always loved tinkering with cars—and with you."

She wanted to melt right in front of him, but she managed a

little self-control somehow. He kept talking while she tried not to be obvious in scouring him down to his very nucleus.

He continued. "I have a little girl I just got custody of, and I've bought a new house."

She had managed somehow to hear what he was saying but was still in dreamland imagining the size of his erection and how it would feel plowing into her. "Really? How old is she?"

"Five and driving me crazy."

"I remember just how insane you were as a kid. You couldn't keep still, and everywhere Debbie and I went, you were sure to go, like Mary's little lamb or something. I didn't even know how you found us most of the time, because we used to hide from you. Remember?"

"I remember, but I was determined to find you, Bev, just like tonight. I didn't need anything in here but you." He smiled like something wild and sexy was inside him. That's what he was, wild and sexy, always had been—probably always would be. She was surprised he'd had only one child.

Ethan took her hand and kissed it. "I've always wondered what happened to you. You were, and still are, the prettiest thing I've ever seen in my life. The only thing was, I just didn't know if I'd ever have a chance with you. Yes, I know I was eight the first time I met you, but—"

"Actually, you were five when I first met you, and you always had a runny nose."

He grinned. "You have an excellent memory, but this is all about you, now. Even when I was ten, I wanted you. When I was thirteen, you were still the best game in town. When I turned fifteen, I thought you were so super-hot, I broke into hives just hearing your name. And believe me, men were calling your name a lot."

"Really? How's that? I was never the precocious type."

"Girl, all I can say is when a man sees you, he never forgets you. I sure remembered."

"I see that. What took you so long?"

"Fear, skepticism. Believe it or not, once I grew up, I got shy. But only around you. You'd speak to me when you saw me and actually treated me as if you really liked me. That set me off. I felt like I was human to you. I wanted to make my move on you then, but you moved away."

She smiled and shook her head. "I simply can't believe you had that much of a thing for me. I thought it was just some silly crush that would go away the minute you hit middle school."

"It went deeper than that, way deeper. You see, I found you after all these years. You just disappeared one day. What happened?"

"I transferred to another university in southern California to get my degree. Your sister and I were out of contact by the time I returned to Cleveland, my other friends were either married or moved away. Back then I just figured I'd leave, too; start over somewhere else. I didn't think anything was left here for me." She smiled into his eyes. "Apparently that wasn't the case."

"It certainly wasn't. Had I known, I'd have searched the city to try and convince you of how I really felt."

She wanted to tell him that she was here for him now, but wasn't that forward? She didn't *really* know if he was still that attracted to her. Maybe he only wanted to see her for sentimental reasons. His next sentence changed her mind.

"I'm still going crazy over you, Beverly. I just can't help myself. You consume me." He looked down at his Rolex, and then back at her. "Look, I know it's late, and you're probably very tired, but would you join me for a drink? My buddy Tad owns the new pub on Lexington."

After all these years. . . . She couldn't get over the fact that she was accepting a drink with Debbie's younger brother. But she wanted to be with him now—though that was the last thing she thought she would ever admit to. Ethan was different now, a man—apparently a man who had a lot going for him. It wasn't an everyday occurrence for a black man to be an owner of a Lexus dealership, and on Montcalm Avenue at that. That was the ritzy part of town.

"Sure, I'd love a drink about now. It's been pretty busy around here—you know, end-of-the-month hell, getting prescriptions filled before the prices raise for the following month. I try to give my elderly clients every thinkable discount, because they deserve it. They've lived long enough to get respect from someone. The government sure doesn't do it."

He smiled and kissed her cheek, feeling the glory of her soft skin against his hungry lips. "You always had a way of caring about others. Even me. I was a pain in the ass, but you and Debbie looked out for me once I found you."

"Someone had to do it. God only knew you were stupid enough to run in front of cars."

"The car would have gotten the worst end of the deal."

"Maybe so. I'd hate to see anything happen to you now." She slowly released his hand. "Let me grab my coat."

Ethan watched the love of his life whisk to the back and lock up. He looked at her pharmacy, realizing she'd done really well for herself. Somehow he'd known she would, but he was even more impressed with her: Beverly was a raving beauty with just as much brains as loveliness. He was so thankful that she seemed happy to see him again.

Beverly came out wrapping the belt of her leather jacket around her trim frame and laced her fingers around his again. "I'm ready to have that drink with Debbie's kid brother." Even she had to smile at the sound of it. So did he.

"Kid brother, huh? How I'd love to show you how much of a 'kid brother' I no longer am."

"One step at a time, Ethan. I'm still amazed at how tall

you've gotten." She looked into his face with a lighthearted expression. "The second thing I can't get over is that you own a dealership."

"Actually, in about two weeks I'll be the proud owner of a Mercedes dealership."

"Unbelievable!"

Once they were out in the unusually warm October air, she automatically headed for her Cadillac. "You deal with cars all day; let me drive. I know where Tad's pub is. Remember, he was a little pest just like you were. When you weren't trying to put Debbie and me into the nut ward, you were out being a menace to society with him."

"You remember Tad well. He's still a hell-raiser." Ethan pulled her arm. "Ride with me. My Lexus is just over there. I'll bring you back to yours later—much later." There was that sexy grin again, ready, willing, and definitely able to melt her heart and a whole lot more. From the feeling between her warm thighs, she knew there was a new Ethan in town, and in such a sensuous body.

It was warm and cozy inside his car, and he took off his suit jacket. He was wearing a smooth silk shirt and matching tie. Just watching him take off that tie made her panties super-wet. He leaned against the seat and started the engine. Years ago, she couldn't imagine the likes of Ethan Jacobs behind the wheel of anything but a Tonka truck. Times sure were different.

He took her hand. "It's been a long time, Bev. What's been going on with you?"

"Not a lot, just working for a living."

"How long have you been in Cleveland without me even knowing it?"

"Long enough to buy myself a couple of pharmacies, end a relationship, and try to live my life."

"Then you're still single?"

"Yes, divorced two years."

"Who would divorce you?"

"I divorced him. We weren't right for one another. I wanted monogamy; he wanted a harem. Plain and simple."

He pulled into the street. "It sounds like he had the 'simple' part down to a science. What man in his right mind would want more than you? You'd be enough for any man—certainly enough for me, always have been."

She smiled into his sensual eyes. "You have a way with words. It's working."

"Hmm. How well are they working?"

"Perfectly, Ethan." She didn't know what else to say because her emotions and libido were on overdrive. They drove to Tad's in silence, with hands joined and hearts growing warmer with fondness and anticipation.

Minutes into listening to smooth jazz on WCLV, the oversize neon sign of Tad's pub came up on the right. Ethan smiled at the sign. "He was always into *big*. Big fights, big women, and big drinks."

"All except for him. He's still the same size he was eighteen years ago."

"Yeah, all five foot five inches of him. For a little dude, he sure leads a big life." He leaned over and kissed Beverly's cheek again, coming so close to the corner of her mouth that he had to actually stop himself before he felt he'd get slapped. "Come on, let's get that drink."

They walked into the dimly lit pub with country music playing in the background. Ethan wrapped his arm around her as he looked around for Tad.

"Why in hell would a short, loud-mouthed black dude be playing Charlie Daniels's, 'The Devil Went Down to Georgia'?," she asked.

"Because he can, and because he's weird that way." Ethan looked across the room and saw Tad running their way. "He'll give us a table in the back. Is that OK with you?"

"Sure."

Tad reached and pulled Ethan's hand. "Dude! Where you been lately?" Tad looked over and spied Beverly. A smile appeared on his face that stretched from ear to ear. "I see you've been taking in the action."

"Don't you know who this is, Tad?"

He took Beverly's hand in his. "Who the hell wouldn't know the queen of Cleveland? Bev, so good to see you. By the way, the article in *People's Monthly* was outstanding. It really did you and your pharmacies justice."

"Thank you, Tad. Glad someone actually read that."

Ethan broke in, needing Beverly back in his corner. "I didn't. But I will. Tad, got a table somewhere in the back?"

"You want some alone time with the beautiful Ms. Beverly Stuart, huh?"

She blushed at the insinuation but followed along as Tad led them to a secluded spot in back.

Tad pulled out her chair. "Secluded enough?"

Ethan slid in close to Beverly. "Perfect. Just perfect. What do you want to start off with? Anything you want, you got. Tonight is yours."

"Tonight is ours, Ethan." She thought for a second. "I'll have a glass of sherry."

"Cutty Sark on the rocks for me."

They both watched as the neighborhood loudmouth rushed off to fulfill their order, but within moments their eyes locked, and the air around them stood still.

Beverly was first to break the silence. "What made you want to be a business owner? I figured you'd be a construction worker type who whistled at the first miniskirt that passed you."

"You were the only woman I wanted to whistle at, but after you left I decided to go to school, do something with my life. I got my MA in business administration, and bought my first dealership two years later."

"Hmm, cute and smart."

"Is that what I am to you now?"

"Every step of the way."

"I wish I had been that to you before you left town. I could have been the reason you stayed."

"Frankly, the only thing on my mind was finishing my doctoral degree. Then came BJ, who at the time was the love of my life. That lasted a quick minute."

"Right, the polygamy man. What a creep. All the better for me, though." He kissed her perfectly manicured fingers as the drinks came. With her hand still in his, he sipped his whiskey. "If I had been old enough to land you, you'd be my wife right now. No other woman does it for me, Bev."

"What about your daughter's mother? What happened with that?"

"Just about everything was my fault in the destruction of our relationship."

"Why?"

"Because she wasn't you, plain and simple."

That one compliment filled her heart with more warmth than her nine-year marriage to BJ ever supplied. "It couldn't have been just you. There are always two sides to any failed relationship."

"True. She wasn't ready to be a wife . . . or a mother. I'm ready to settle down, live with someone who absolutely takes me apart every time I look at her."

She didn't know how to handle that. Ethan Jacobs was actually making her nervous, but in all the right ways. Beverly changed the subject in fear of him finding out that she was now a willing pawn in any chess game he wanted to play. "What's your daughter's name?"

"Danica. The second love of my life."

"And the first one is, let me guess, that gorgeous car in the parking lot."

"Wrong. I'm looking at her. Beverly, I know you don't believe me, but I had to find you again. I was determined to see you once more, even if you blew me off."

"Why would I blow you off? You're a perfect gentleman."

"Maybe because when I want something, I never think I'm worthy of it."

"You are worthy, Ethan, and I'm enjoying your company."

"Enough to have another exciting evening with me?"

"Sure. Besides, I want to meet Danica."

Ethan nodded. "She asked me who you were when I mentioned your name once or twice. You stayed on my mind all this time."

"Really?"

"Absolutely, girl! That's why I'd love to take you out tomorrow night. What time do you close for the holiday?"

"Depends on where you want to take me."

He swallowed the rest of his drink. "I've got a great idea, something I've always wanted to do with you—a haunted house. Tomorrow is Halloween, you know."

She moved closer to him, feeling the heat of his thighs against hers. "I am aware of that. I haven't done one of those in years."

"I've got the perfect one, if you're game. It's out a little ways, but it's creepy enough."

"A monster behind every corner?"

"Better! Get this, Hideous Harry's Hellish Hayride and Haunted Haven. Sound fun?"

"What in the world? That sounds like a place you'd come up with. It's a hayride, too?"

"Yep! We can dressup, sit in the back of the hayride, and make out!"

"No kids?"

"None. It's strictly adults."

"I've always wanted to go on a hayride."

"Then let me take you on one. Say, about nine?"

She sipped the last of her sherry. "Let's do it. Funny thing," she rubbed the back of his warm hands, wishing they were sliding up her thigh and into her panties, "I never thought I'd be on a date with Debbie's baby brother."

"It'll be a hell of a date, too, like tonight. If only it could last longer." He looked at his watch. "I have to get Danica from her mom in about an hour or so."

"We have until then, don't we?"

He slowly reached over and took a chance on kissing the most delectable lips he'd ever seen. The very impact of her lips on his stiffened an already super-stiff erection. He nibbled her top lip in long, succulent caresses, doing the same to her lower lip. The fact that Beverly was finally kissing him back loosened his body, made him relax to her overtures. His soft voice filled her ears. "God, Bev, I've wanted this so much. I used to dream of you, dream of doing this with you, taking you into my arms and making love to you all night. Is this real? Am I really with you?"

She smoothed the front of his shirt, feeling his rippling muscles, glorying in the touch and aroma of an all-grown-up Ethan. "It's hard to believe, but this is real, Ethan." She kissed his lips again before pulling back, staring into his dark eyes. "This is so amazing."

"Isn't it just? Come on, let's take a drive. Tonight is such a beautiful evening. Let's go to a park I know, take in the night air, sit and talk, get to know one another for a few minutes. Would you like that?"

"No one's ever asked me that before. They usually led, and I followed."

"Tonight is going to be different."

His car smelled just as good as he did, like smooth, rich leather—a new-car smell. "How long have you had this?"

"Oh, not long. I had it shipped in about a month ago. You like it?"

"It's beautiful."

"Like you." He put his hand over hers and kept it there for what seemed to be minutes, but was only seconds. The thing was, she didn't want him to move it. His skin felt good on hers, and she liked it—a lot. He took a deep breath. "We'd better get going before I get us in trouble. We're all alone here and I could get us in a lot of trouble, Bev—you know how crazy I am."

The way he said that made her want to say, *Forget the park. Let's get naked.* Then she actually did say it, and didn't even realize it at first. She was so taken by how fine and gentle he'd become.

That took him by surprise. "I thought I'd never hear you say that to me." He brought her hand to his mouth and started sucking her fingers, every single one of them, nice and slow. Ethan excited her like no man ever had before, especially considering her marriage and dates with Pleistocene men. He was so different. What he was doing to her fingers put her in a trance. She took her other hand and caressed his cheek. Before long, her fingernails were tracing a line down his perfect nose to his lip line. All along, her quivering voice was saying his name over and over again. "I can't believe I didn't recognize you at first, Ethan."

"Maybe I have changed."

"No, you're still gorgeous."

"You thought I was gorgeous?"

"By the time you were in your teens, yeah. But I'd never have told you that. I should have recognized you, though. Do you remember those staring contests we used to have? I knew every inch of your face, right down to those small freckles on your cheeks."

"Sure I remember, and I never lost."

"I wonder why that was. Better control than me?"

"It was because I couldn't take my eyes from you, Beverly. I still can't. I know every part of your beautiful face, and it's even more beautiful each time I look at you."

He placed her fingers on his chest. His urgent movements beckoned her fingers to work those buttons. She couldn't wait to unleash him. His body heat was radiating through his silk shirt already, and she could feel how finely chiseled his chest was; she couldn't wait to see it, taste it. Ethan, Ethan, Ethan. She was drowning in him.

She pulled back the unbuttoned shirt and raked her nails gently up and down his chest. "You aren't cold, are you?"

"I've never been hotter."

That was just fine because her lips went right to his erect nipples. Nothing had ever tasted that wickedly fantastic to her. The warm intensity of her tongue made him tense with each lick and she made sure to leave lavish wet streaks across his beautiful bronze chest. He was smooth and sweet, like human honey.

He let the seat back and placed her hand over his erection, rocking it up and down with such friction, watching Beverly as she stared into his incredibly handsome face.

"Ethan, let me—let me experience you."

"It's right here for you, sugar. It belongs to you, always did."

It was so hard and thick, practically touching his stomach. She really got to work on him after feeling all of that. Tender tongue massages continued to lap his chest while her fingers played with his navel and zipper, inching it down. It was practically splitting apart from the size of him, and when she reached in, she pulled it out—all of it, all nine inches. The man was packing!

Ethan barely pulled away, needing to ask a question that needed an immediate answer. "Have you really thought of me before now?"

She toyed with his lower lip, saying, "Every once in a while, but I never expected this." He wanted to say something else, but her fingers covered his mouth.

"We can talk later. Now, we make love." The decadence ensued as her tongue moved way down his chest, tickled his navel with sweet torture. Moments later she was experiencing what she knew he owned, taking what she knew was her destiny. She heard the click of the seat reclining, smiled in complete satisfaction, and then went all the way live on him. The very minute her lips made contact with his tip, she knew he'd be a habit, much harder to break than smoking or chocolate.

Her lips covered him, getting almost all of him in, and slowly moved up and down, giving him the pleasure he deserved, the pleasure *she* yearned for. He'd waited so long, and it had been so unnecessary. Had he just found her sooner, her lonely life would have been so complete. That was then, and this was now. Ethan, Ethan—what a man, and what a world he was in.

Beverly could hear his sexy voice just about howling, fogging up the windows. Man, he even tasted like heaven and she wondered then how good he'd feel inside of her. The very thought made her want to slide out of everything she had on.

He was thinking the same thing. His hand slid up her skirt, feasting on the feel of her silk hip panties, relishing in the moisture her body emitted, knowing for damn sure what was to come. There was no stopping those two long fingers. He continued prodding, poking, pleasing her, taking her to that point, that magical point they could both share in with quivering waves of unbridled ecstasy. He was pleasing her in every possible way. His low voice murmured, "God, I knew you were wet and juicy like this."

"Then don't stop," she breathed.

He played her insides so expertly she could hear his fingers making contact with her nectar, a sound so incredible she did come by the sound alone. Her muscles gripped his fingers and held on tight. The deeper he went into her, the more her tongue circled the underside of his erection. She moaned, "Ethan, take me there. Take me there."

He slowly moved his fingers out and took her face into his hands. "My place or yours? I've gotta have you, Bev. I am so losing it over you."

"Right here, right now." No words; he just followed her command. He faced her, slid off her jacket, then the blouse and bra, kissing each nipple and circling them with a slow, wet tongue . . . driving her to drink, but from his well only. He licked and sucked them so hard that she thought *she* was going to lose her mind. Then she wriggled out of her panties somehow.

Within seconds the seat was reclined to its lowest position, exactly the position Ethan ached for, and he slid her onto his erection. Her core contracted around him, and it felt out of this world. He filled her inch by glorious inch as they wrapped their tongues around one another's. He kissed so sensually, lapping her into a frenzy while blowing the bottom out of her tenderness. He was rocking her so hard the car was bouncing.

Beverly thought the guy was going to have to get new shocks for the car the next day. He didn't look like he cared and neither did she. Hell, she'd be happy to buy the shocks for him.

Her fingers twisted around the strands of his hair while his strong arms held on to her. She could feel those tight muscles. He was strong enough to hold her forever, and she loved it. She never wanted to let him go. The more he pounded into her, the more she was pulled toward the ultimate release, a sexual vortex. It was as though she were racing into oblivion, but she wanted to make it last. Beverly held on for as long as possible, giving him all he needed. But the feeling was too hard to subdue—that wonderfully insane tension was draining her, making her want to come with this man like never before. When his rocking motion spread her like an eagle's wings, she let go, rode the wave, and never looked back.

He stared at her as her orgasm showed upon her face. The sight of watching her in that tremendous moment almost left him speechless, other than what *had* to be said. "You're so beautiful. You're so incredibly gorgeous, and I love every part of you. Always have—ohhh—" At that, he came, spilling all of God's rain into her tight spot. He pumped so much cum into her small body it flowed from her.

She screamed in excitement again, rocked by another orgasm simply from watching him. She thought she was going to break his windows, having never wailed on a guy like that before.

When they finished, she looked into his flushed brown face and kissed him again. Her body was still twitching and squirming because of him, and it felt so good. He was still inside her, slowly pumping, getting the last bit of sex before they both collapsed. He rubbed his hands up and down her back. "Let me take you home with me tonight, every night for the rest of our lives. I've waited long enough now, Beverly. I have to have you."

She didn't reply right away, just looked for her clothes, slowly coming back to reality. "What about your daughter?"

"She can stay with her mother a little longer. You'll love Danica."

"I can't wait to meet her." She straightened in his lap and looked at him seriously. "I hope I wasn't too forward tonight. Should I have waited?"

He brushed the hair from her face and smiled. "Too forward! Baby, I've waited my entire life for you. No, you were right on time; don't ever think otherwise."

Beverly kissed the tip of his nose. "We'd better go. I want more of you, but in a bed where I can *see* everything, and on a night when we can be totally alone without you having to rush back. You promised Danica, so you should go to her."

"Can you wait another night? Because I know it'll be damn hard for me."

"Of course I can. Your child comes first." She sat down and helped him put all the goodies back in order, both his and hers. She began to get dressed, an awkward process inside a car, smiling to herself. Ethan had gotten her clothes off a lot faster than she could get them on. "How's Debbie doing? I haven't seen her in ages."

"Great. She and Ward live in Nevada with their five kids."

"Five kids? Wow! Why aren't you in Nevada with them?"

"I wanted to stay here."

"Was it worth the wait?"

"After what we just did, what do you think?"

"I think I've been missing out on something really wonderful, and that includes the man himself, not just the body. It proves that silly baby brothers grow into sensual, smart men." She finished buttoning her blouse as Ethan watched. She could feel his eyes scanning her, watching every move. "You really have a flame for me, don't you?"

"More like a five-alarm fire."

"Is Ward still head-over-heels in love with Debbie?"

"Those two make out whenever they get a chance. Of course, who's to say I won't do the same with you?"

"Then Debbie must still be the knockout she was before."

"She's still pretty and tall, but she has gained thirty pounds. She said getting pregnant will do that."

"I guess so, after five kids."

Ethan kissed her hand. "You ever thought about having your own little angels?"

"I used to think about it, but the marriage was all wrong. I unfortunately married a man whose grandfather created the revolving door."

"What?"

"I'm serious. BJ's grandfather Willis created the first working revolving door, and the talent stayed in the family, apparently. BJ turned the door of my house into just that, a revolving door. Bitches galore were flying in and out of there, spinning that door so fast it made even his head spin."

"Didn't he see that he had the best thing in town?"

"I was good to him, really good. Probably too good."

Ethan turned her face to meet his, their lips barely apart. "You can be good to me, and believe me I'll more than appreciate it."

Beverly felt her insides warming again as he kissed the corners of her mouth in tiny nibbles. "Ummm, Ethan, we'd better stop before we end up in bed."

"That's my plan, girl. That sweet nectar you gave me a little while ago can't sustain me for long. I've waited my life for you, and nothing but all of you will suffice. I'm hooked, have been for years, and now that I've truly tasted the forbidden fruit—well, if you thought I was a pest back in the day, you haven't really seen anything yet."

What she saw in his eyes was total sincerity, unlike the other men she'd been with, Ethan kept it real. For tonight, she told herself, not quite willing to believe it could be forever. She had to think this through.

"Ethan, I would love to spend more time with you, but I know you have to get Danica."

"You would love to spend more time with me?"

"Amazing, but true."

Ethan laughed. "If I keep hanging with you, I'll go plum mad from desire. However, you're right. I did promise my baby . . . that is, my little baby . . . that she could spend time with Dad before her grandma takes her from me tomorrow."

"So, who's your '*big baby*'?" Pretending as if she hadn't a clue.

"You! Is that what you wanted to hear?"

She rolled her eyes, and then looked at him. "Yes, actually. I do enjoy hearing that from you, Ethan Jacobs. Christ! I still can't believe this. I'm here with Ethan, making love, wanting to make more love, and enjoying every part of you."

He cranked the engine. "Get used to it. I plan to hang around forever."

They turned into the parking lot of Stuart's Pharmacy, and Ethan kissed her again, hating to let her go, itching to get back into her love as soon as he could. "You know I'm trailing you home, Beverly. It's late, and I wouldn't want anything happening to you now that I *really* have you."

"You don't have to. I get home by myself every night."

"Not now that I'm in the picture. Give me your number so I can call and kiss you good night with loving words."

She scribbled on the back of a business card. "I'll put the phone in bed with me."

"I'd rather it was me."

"I don't think you have to worry about that."

Ethan opened her car door and secured her inside before he returned to his car. When she drove off, he sat there shaking his head, thanking God again that he had found her—and wondering what would happen next. Being with Beverly made him think of down home, blue-lights-in-the-basement parties, and slow dancing . . . very slow dancing. It also made him think of the downright dirty lyrics that James Brown screamed into the mic. He turned on his CD player and selected number eighteen. Automatically James screamed out, "Please, Please, Please," his second favorite song by the famous artist, second only to "Papa's Got a Brand New Bag." Yes, Ethan knew he had a brand-new bag, and it came in the form of a five-foot-seven inch, dark brown-haired beauty named Beverly.

* * *

There were no James Brown tunes in Beverly's head, but there was an incredible feeling in her heart . . . and in her body. The thought of Ethan's lips covering hers made the churning in her core almost unbearable. Remembering how Ethan's hands had slid between her thighs, making her sex so super-hot made her twist and turn in her bed. Never in a million years did she think the likes of Ethan Jacobs would turn her body into a quivering mass ready to detonate at his very command. After two years of nonstop work to establish her pharmacies, she was ready to experience life again.

Her evening with him had been way too short. Ethan, coming back to her out of the blue, was everything she wanted a man to be: attentive, sweet, and handsome as the dickens. He took sex to an entirely new level. Fantasizing his body moving swiftly in and out of hers made her react, react to the point that her fingers moved to her still-moist core, feeling where he had played until his satisfaction erupted all over her. Her tempo increased, making her fingers slide between her wet folds with almost as much precision as his. Sexual satisfaction was but seconds away, and her mind's eye could only conceive of one thing; Ethan's bare chest, and how his tight, hard nipples felt against her tongue. A sweet sensation exploded inside her as she imagined Ethan hovering over her, pumping inch after inch of his hot, stiff cock into her. In her mind, she could see herself reaching for and smoothing his raging shaft, guiding it deeper into her, pumping her, teasing her, heaving up and down as he thrilled every part of her.

Her body jerked, and her soft, smooth voice called to a man who was there only in memory—but what a memory he was. The sheets fell from the bed; her legs parted farther and farther as her make-believe lover turned her out. She felt like the freak of the week, and for once, was glad to have that daunting title.

When she returned to herself, she looked around the room in a haze. The moon shone brightly into her window, casting

eerie shadows of a nearby tree. Her gown was bunched between her thighs, and she knew her hair was a fright, but the
dream was well worth it. *Was that what it was, a damn dream?
Was Ethan simply a dream? If so, why him?*

She bounced from bed and looked into her mirror. The
hicky he'd given her was still on the side of her neck. It looked
sexy for some reason, and she delicately rubbed it, making sure
it was really there instead of something manufactured by an
overactive mind. She smiled at the tender bruise, liking the fact
that it was real and that he had given it with such passion.

She returned to her bed and pulled the scattered covers
above her still-heaving chest. Within minutes Beverly slipped
into sleep with one thing on her mind—seeing Ethan again the
next night.

Halloween . . .

At Beverly's pharmacies, she and the other employees gave
out goodies to all the little monsters, witches, ghosts, and
wrestling stars. But not the candy they expected. She preferred
to hand out toothbrushes, fruit-flavored toothpaste, and other
cute cavity reduction items.

There was a feeling in the air, one that brought a sense of
pleasure and fun. Whether in California or Ohio, she had always thought of Halloween as just another holiday and would
sit at home alone and watch every Vincent Price movie she could
rent. This time was different. All Beverly knew was that it took
one thing to change her perspective—the love and feel of a delicious man. She hadn't had that feeling in years, not since she
threw the last of BJ's girlfriends out of her house over a year
ago. Ethan Jacobs was now her man of the year, and she couldn't
wait to close shop and get to him. The last of her scary little
darlings left, and she locked up early and flipped the door sign
to the CLOSED side, heading for a place to purchase a scandalous
costume.

Halloween Town's glowing neon sign could be seen from a block away as she turned onto Lexington Avenue. Surely, she could find the perfect costume. She checked her watch—she had a little more than an hour before Ethan showed up to take her on an excursion she'd never forget. And the hayride would be fun too.

By nine that night, Beverly stood before her mirror, making sure the costume she had selected fit perfectly, hugging every curve. The barely black stockings and three-inch black heels added to the appeal of the suit. Once satisfied with how she looked, she checked her makeup, making sure the sparkling red on her luscious lips shone enticingly. She brushed her long silky strands and put them up in a sexy French twist, retrieved her trench coat, and awaited her mysterious night stalker.

On the dot, Ethan rang her bell and awaited with a smile. Beverly opened the door to see him in a costume she really hadn't expected. She took his hand, pulled him inside, and landed a hungry kiss on his waiting lips. Their long, lavish kiss slowly ended. Her voice echoed in a whisper. "I've been waiting for this since I left you last night."

"Really? You actually thought about me after you took me to heaven and back?"

"More than I thought possible."

"Yeah? What were your thoughts?"

She didn't answer. His costume finally got her attention. "Ethan, what the hell kind of a costume is that?"

"You like it?"

"I don't exactly know." She raised her arms in the air and gave him a baffled look. "What are you?"

"I'm a condom!"

"A condom! You can't be serious!"

"Very. I thought you'd get a kick out of it."

She looked at the plastic-feeling, neon-black material covering him from his knees to his neck, with a white body suit underneath. He actually wore a hat that resembled the mushroomed tip of a phallus. Automatically she moved back into his arms. "That answers one of your questions."

"What was that?"

"What I was thinking about in my bed last night. I fell asleep thinking about how you plowed every single inch into a woman who was so sex-starved, though I never wanted to admit that to myself. You touched me in such delicious ways, Ethan. It was amazing. After making love with you, I realized that I have never really been made love to before."

"I aim to please."

"And your aim was on the money, with every stroke."

"I put out your fire?"

"It's still burning."

"I can take care of that now, if you like."

"No way, sir. I went through a lot to get this costume just the way I want it."

He slowly loosened the belt of her coat and spread it apart. His eyes widened to a black and silver Playboy Bunny outfit and heels. "You are out of this fucking world, Bev. Do you have the fluffy bunny tail?"

"Reach behind me and find out, smart mouth!"

He definitely felt the fluff of cotton, but it wasn't exactly the tail that molded to his hot hands. He groaned and pulled her closer, massaging a tight derriere that filled the costume to perfection. "How many times have I wished I could see you in an outfit like this?"

"I knew you'd like it."

"Like it! You don't know the half of it." He took her hand and smoothed it across his already engorged shaft. "See how hot it is for you? How about we stay here and do the bunny hop?"

Her smooth, black-gloved hand caressed the stiff-as-metal cock. "Tempting, but you mentioned Hideous Harry's, and that's where I want to go. We can play later; that secluded hayride sounds like fun. I looked it up on the Internet."

His nose nuzzled hers. "It sure can be, if we sit in the back. And plan on that playing around, girl, because I am so ready for you."

"That's my plan, Mr. Ethan." She checked out his costume again and shook her head. "Sure hope this is for adults only."

"Don't you worry your lovely head about that. I've got some very adult plans for us when we get into that haunted house."

"Like what?"

"You'll just have to see. You know me, it's a mad fucking minute every step of the way."

She felt the top of her head. "Wait! I forgot my bunny ears. You can't be a Playboy Bunny without the entire costume."

Beverly returned to the room wearing a headband with white satin pointy ears. Ethan took her hand and proudly walked his succulent playmate to the car.

As usual, the minute he got into the car, he flipped the CD player to his favorite. James Brown's "Sex Machine" automatically came on. "I hope you like James, because he reminds me of you."

Beverly stared at him, confused. "I don't think that's a compliment, Ethan. I'd rather not be known around town as the King of Soul."

He leaned over, nibbling her lower earlobe. "Every song he sings reminds me of how we used to dance in our basement to him. I envied my sister because the two of you used to slow dance together. About two feet apart," he added hastily.

"It beat dancing slow with you—then. Now is another story." The tips of her fingers slowly moved down the condom fabric, stopping at his tight abs. "Hmm, suddenly Mr. Brown is sounding awfully good."

"I promise you a dance when we get back, but definitely not in your basement. I always wanted to see your bedroom." Ethan reached into the backseat and handed her a Hallmark bag. "Got you a little Halloween surprise."

"That was sweet. Thank you." She opened it and pulled out a stuffed bear in a witch's costume, holding a bag of goodies in its paws. She looked up and smiled. "This is so cute, and it's got my favorite candies inside—Reese's peanut butter cups. How did you manage to remember that?"

"Like I've told you, I remember everything about Beverly Stuart." He saw the saddened expression on her face. "What's wrong?"

"I didn't get you anything."

He licked his lips at the hint of black stocking peeking from her coat. "Believe me, I've got mine and plan on getting more. Ready for Hideous Harry?"

Her hand covered his free one. "I've been ready for a long time, but not for Hideous Harry."

By the time they got to the farm, it was almost dark. The trees in the distance were brilliant hues of orange and gold and the setting sun cast an autumnal glow on the rest of the land-scape. There were pumpkins scattered about, with many more in the pumpkin patch, and apple trees all over the place. Beverly stared through her window. "This is so beautiful, and peaceful."

He pointed ahead. "See that big house? That's where all the freaky shit will happen."

"And you know this because . . . ?"

"I've been here before, but it wasn't any fun."

"Why?"

"I wasn't here with you."

Her grip tightened on his hand. "Well, you're with the right person now." She looked at the spooky, dilapidated farmhouse again. "It looks like something out of *The Texas Chainsaw Massacre.*"

"That's the effect they were going for."

"Well, it scared the shit out of me at the movies, and it's scaring me now."

"Too scared to go inside?"

"I'm not that scared. Besides, didn't you say the freaky stuff was in there?"

"Yeah. Most of it."

"Then I want to go in and be scared right into your arms."

"Then let's do it."

At the front gate was a large wagon loaded with hay and several other customers in various costumes waiting for it to leave.

Ethan escorted her from the car and pointed to several large wagons in the middle of a cornfield. "Prepare for all your fantasies to come to life. Your chariot awaits."

Beverly took his hand and walked toward the first wagon. "My fantasies started last night. I could hardly sleep for thinking of you. Far cry from that little girl who used to stick out her foot just to see you trip."

"I'd fall for you any day."

He gladly trailed behind her as she led him to the wagon. Before boarding, he stopped her. "This isn't our wagon."

"Aren't they all the same?"

An uneasy look crossed his face. "Not exactly. You see, Harry picked out a special wagon for a few of his close friends."

"Would you be one of those 'close' friends?"

"Absolutely!"

She tugged on his costume. "So what's so special about our wagon?"

"Not as many people, for one thing. Ten tons of hay to hide in. It gives us room to explore things, if you get my drift."

"Oh, I get it! A haunted orgy."

"Yeah, an orgy of many, but with two stars—you and I."

"Look but don't touch, for everyone else?"

"You got it."

"Can't wait."

Ethan helped her aboard the wagon. Once he hopped on, he found a secluded space in the back behind hay bales stacked high enough to conceal them both. He sat her on his lap. "This is good already, isn't it?"

She smiled and kissed his lips. "I like sitting on your lap. I can feel all the added perks already."

Several more customers arrived before Hideous Harry jumped on, looking like a farmer who was run over by his own tractor. He grinned a toothless grin at everyone, moved long strands of blond hair from his dirty face, and then screamed out, "You ready to get the daylights scared out of you?" He cracked his whip, and the horses jolted into step, following the other wagon. Harry added, "The first of you to spot ten of my dead relatives gets free admission to the haunted haven. Ready!"

Ethan leaned against a bale of hay, whispering into Beverly's ear. "I have other things to search for besides dead relatives."

Beverly shifted on his lap, making his erection higher, tighter and ready to plunge into her crotchless costume—another added feature Ethan hadn't known about until they pulled over on the side of the road to make out on their way up to the haunted house.

The wagon slowly carried the load of customers deep into the pumpkin patches and cornfields. Beverly looked around, expecting a dead relative to jump out at any time. Her voice quivered, "Toto, I don't think we're in Kansas anymore."

"Scared yet?"

"A little, but it's fun."

A few figures jumped out at the wagon, forcing Beverly

deeper into Ethan's arms. He took advantage and calmed her nerves by moving his hand into her trench coat, sliding it off.

She stopped his hand. "Are you sure this is OK?"

"No one cares about us back here. Look around, if you can see over all the hay. Those who aren't making out are listening to Harry's stupid ghost story. Come on, face me, and let's start cooking."

"Well, if you're sure."

"Hideous Harry's is known for couples doing their thing, so long as they stay quiet. We don't want to scare the horses, do we?"

"I don't care about the horses." She unsnapped the buttons in the crotch of his costume, reached in his underwear, and smoothed an already pulsating erection. "You ready to get singed, boy?"

He shifted on the hay and patted his thighs. "I might smoke the place out after messing around with you."

Beverly carefully sat on his lap, positioned his tip above her opening, and slowly sank onto it. Ethan held her in place as her hips began a slow grind. She put her trench coat over her shoulders and wrapped it around as his phallus continued to invade her walls. She rocked up and down, matching the rhythm of the rickety wagon.

The sex-charged atmosphere invigorated her. Deep, loving, erotically sexual sounds of nearby couples dressed as wacky monster and gory ghouls made her inhibitions dissolve. Having Ethan inside of her set her body on fire. She pressed him to take her to total satisfaction in the midst of everything happening in that wagon. It was love, it was sex, it was wild, it was spooky, chilling and so thrilling. It was everything erotic that the mind of a mere mortal could fathom. She'd gone from being a buttoned-down pharmacist to spending Halloween night in the arms of a devil of a lover.

The deeper he moved into her, the harder she kissed him, pressing her body into him. She was as quiet, at first, but there was something about having Ethan inside her that made her want to scream with passion. But she didn't. Beverly let loose on Ethan, dominating him, silent but aggressive making him writhe beneath her.

Ethan saw the expression on her face, loved it, loved the look of love and total satisfaction. It was his honor to serve and please, and Ethan did any and all jobs well, especially when it came to satisfying the only woman who ever mattered to him.

As he watched his delicious Beverly get closer to her personal heaven, he knew she'd be ready to blow at any minute. His smooth fingers caressed her lips as he whispered to her, "Stay quiet, baby."

"But it's so damn good," she whispered back.

He smiled and continued to rock back and forth with her in slow motion. "You like it slow and scandalous, don't you?"

"I like it forbidden."

He pumped a little harder. "Like this?"

"Do it to me."

His rod ascended deeper inside of her as he increased his thrusts. He moaned softly, hardly able to breathe as he spilled cum slowly into her.

Beverly nipped at his lips as the sound of Hideous Harry's voice scared those few who were still listening to him. She smiled and stroked Ethan's cheeks. "I can't get enough. Pump more into me, and let me ride."

His cock bumped against her G-spot and made contact with her clit, making it sing hymns. Within seconds, he felt his lover tighten around him, and circle her hips in smooth, small motions while she whispered his name. He came again. To hell with waiting, so long as the sex was the way she wanted it to be. Aiming to please was his game.

His hot, rigid phallus erupted again, pulling at her sex as he milked her. Her thrusts finally quieted, and he slowly pulled out, feeling naked without her nectar keeping him warm. Their lips met again in heated fusion before a large bump in the road separated them. Ethan took her hand. "Was it good, sugar?" he murmured. "I mean, was it super-good, out of this world, magnificent—"

"It was a mad fucking minute, quoting your own words. Outstanding."

Ethan gave her a proud smile, happy he'd satisfied his sensual playmate. "Wait until we get to the haunted house."

"I know we'll have to pay, because I wasn't concentrating on any dead relatives."

"I'll gladly pay for us to get in, Bev. That way I can *get in again*. Know what I mean?"

"All too well."

"There's a room in that place that no one knows about but me. I found it purely by mistake and took sole advantage of it with someone about two years ago."

"Was whoever she was worthy of such an erotic experience?"

"I'm here with you, aren't I? So what does that say?"

"Everything!" She pulled his hand tighter around her hips and enjoyed the rest of the hayride.

Twenty minutes later the wagon pulled in front of Mutilation Mansion, and Hideous Harry smiled that same disgusting, toothless grin. "I know many of us were too preoccupied to find my dead relatives, so get your money out and pay dearly to have the bejeebies scared out of you." He broke into a deafening, frightful laugh and tied the horses to the hitch near the house.

The house was a guided tour, but Ethan had his own plan once they got to the second floor. To get to Mutilation Mansion, the crowd had to walk through a dilapidated graveyard. Broken tombstones, purely fabricated, greeted them, set amid bumpy grass and dirt. For Beverly, wearing three-inch Playboy Bunny heels with white pompoms at her ankles, that was no joke. But her only thought was how incredible it felt to have Ethan's arms around her.

Once Ethan paid the ten-dollar cover charge at the main entrance, Beverly stepped inside and looked around at the crudely decorated interior. Definitely a great place for a murder, she decided as she held on to Ethan's arm. Investigators would be too scared to try and find the body. It was all so classic, with decrepit chandeliers barely hanging from roundels; ripped, dark curtains; pictures of weirdo relatives dating from the eighteenth century . . . definitely something out of Vincent Price's *House of Usher*. Creepy, but that was the point. Beverly had her limits when it came to Halloween-type things, but she'd do anything to be with Ethan.

As the crowd of people ascended the rickety, winding staircase, noises were heard: distant screams, windows shattering, slashing knives. Sound effects from hell. She clutched her lover with determination.

Ethan looked down at her, smiling at a barely existent profile due to light. "You scared, girl?"

"You could say that."

"You wanna leave? I could always plan something spooky in the comfort of your own bed—or mine."

"It's just a bunch of rigged contraptions, but they look so real. No, lets stay. I'm anxious to see exactly what you have planned for me."

"Good girl." Purposely Ethan lagged behind, letting another couple get in front so they could be the last in a long line of scared yet sexually intoxicated individuals.

Beverly yanked his arm. "Why are we last?"

Instead of saying anything, he found what he was looking for and quickly opened one of the bedroom doors, pulling her inside. With her back flush against the door and his lips so ready to engulf her, he answered. "This is why we're last. This room is the plan, baby, the plan that will be executed so well by the time I finish with you."

Her pliable body relaxed against the hard wood door, weakening to him, weakening to the idea of what he could do to her in the dark. That's what she liked about the dark—though its hue was pitch black, everything was illuminated. As his hands roamed her feverish body, she realized exactly why Ethan was in her life again—to give her something no other man had been able to deliver. He was raw, so was she, and she liked being that way. There was something about Ethan that brought out the bona fide animal in her. She needed that after many affairs that had gone absolutely nowhere. The only thing was that she didn't want to fall for him. Beverly wanted her nice, hot, secret affair and nothing more, especially with the baby brother of her best friend back in the day. But who was this man making insane love to her? That snaggle-toothed boy had grown into something she knew she needed one way or another, one love or another. That was the burden she had to bear.

She relaxed to the idea of wanting him for what he could give her and what she could give back in return. Thus, feelings of raged heat engulfed her, making her aid him in his frenzied plight to disrobe her. She broke from him and looked around, seeing a room most unlikely to make love in. Skeleton props shadowed the room, some clothed, some bare and hanging. Fake cobwebs crowded corners, bloodstained walls added to the special effects as Beverly's eyes scanned everything. That was nothing. The real sight was before her in an outrageous dick-protection costume, looking sexier than humanly possible, if one could believe that!

A calmness took over as she felt Ethan delicately squeezing her breasts until the tips of her darkly hued nipples teased the garment. He unzipped the back of her outfit with her help and slid it down her slender frame. And she moaned like never before, overtaken by pure, unbridled desire for a man she hadn't a clue she'd ever touch again. But she was, and touching him in spirals of fury—hungry for the main dish.

That silly mushroom tip of a hat made her smile as she knocked it from his jet-black hair. His curls were so soft and silky between her fingers; she loved the feel, needed to feel and rub soft hair in so many other places. With that in mind more than breathing itself, she unzipped his costume and slid it from his taut frame. God, the muscles on him, flexing to every move he made, slick, hot muscles so ready to be drenched with her liquid love. Fuck everything! Fuck how she felt about him being a kid brother to a long-ago friend. Fuck the fact that he was younger by six years. What she wanted was action. Now.

His costume dropped to the splintered floor with a thud, and before her stood perfection in a white bodysuit with an erection bulging to monumental heights. Her jittery hand smoothed across his tight chest and stomach. "How do we get this off, Ethan?"

"You really want it off?"

She stared into his eyes, seeing his expression through the darkness. Shadows of light illuminated him in streaks, and she held to that serious stare. "I want it off now before my whistle blows. I'm caving in, weakening." Her hand slowly traveled, feathering his flat stomach and inching down to an erection so livid it wet the white suit in drops of fire.

His back arched to the intense pleasure her fingernails delivered to his thick scrotum. His shaft squirmed to be free as he covered her hand, rocking it to a tempo that could only be Ethan Jacobs. A masculine yet almost trembling voice erupted. "Once this suit is off, Bev, there is no going back. There's only one way to go from here—complete nakedness, complete closeness, something so intimate it's never been written about, sung about, discussed. Is this what you want?"

"I had it last night."

"What you had last night was safe, inhibited, clothed. What

I'm talking about now is raw, sinful, unbridled, Ms. Stuart, mistress of my soul."

His words called her. His soliloquy demanded her in every aspect, from her body wanting to be bare with his, to her mind saying, *Yes, God, yes!* So, it was done. "I want it, Ethan. I suffer because I need it. I want it bare, raw, and every way you can hand it to me. Don't make me wait. . . . Where's the release?"

He reached behind, pulled his zippered back down midway, and took her hand. "You do the rest."

She moved into him, found the rest of the zipper, and pulled until it stopped at his derriere. Firm, hot buns graced her palms, and she squeezed. The ripeness of his male anatomy brought that oh-so-familiar flutter across her body, one that shook her, one that made her quivering sex dance for him. Her eyes sleepily closed from maddening desire, and a single tear rolled down her satin honey-brown skin.

Ethan tipped her face to his. "I love it when you come. It's the most sensuous thing I've ever seen."

"Then make me do it again, only longer, harder, so hard it takes control of me. I don't want control, Ethan. I want fire and ice, every thick inch of it."

He flipped a switch, and a dim row of electric Halloween candles barely lit the room. Yes, it was everything he had expected, everything he had planned and had paid Harry quite well to make perfectly haunting for them. What was worth the money and that much more was pleasing the woman he had with him, watching her dance in utter delight of anticipation.

For seconds only, Beverly scanned the room and saw a bottle of something scrumptious sitting on ice. Next to it was a blanket already spread and waiting for body-to-body contact to christen it. Her eyes twinkled as one of her favorite smiles lit his face. "Why am I not surprised you would do something like this?"

"Because I'm not typical, and you know that. I want it perfect but odd. Now disrobe me, and let me get what I need, girl."

Loaded words. True words. Beverly removed the white spandex from around his shoulders and slowly exposed him. With each tug, his body was visible, showing her hints of such perfection. Glazed bronze was the only term she could use to describe him. He had been hidden before. In his car the sex was incredible, but nothing was seen. Now it was. Her mouth watered at the sight of his bare chest, his dark nipples, the delicious six-pack of his stomach. Her new state of mind was uncontrollable, and her lips ached for the delivery of feathery kisses upon him. Yet he stopped her.

"Not yet. Take everything off me."

"Ethan!"

"Please. I wanna be so raw and naked with you I can barely take it."

It was either his words that made her obey or that insatiable shaft poking its way closer to her. She wanted to believe it was both, but this time she knew it was a hell of a cock ready, willing, and able to split her in half and ride her into the atmosphere of the full moon. She slid the suit down quickly, and he plunged out.

She'd never seen it before, not truly. The night before was more feel, feel, feel, letting her imagination bring it to sight. It made its presence on the hayride, yet, still, sight was the very damn key!

His sex glistened, and weakness contorted her body, making her almost drop to her knees. Ethan stopped her. "No. Start at the top. Work me while I work you." Their lips met in fusion. Tongues coiled; lips, wet with desire, burned for one another. For Ethan, it wasn't the fact that she was nipping and tugging on every pleasure principle his body contained, it was simply the fact that his soul mate was doing it. The minute he saw her lovely face at the tender age of five, he grew up, knew what he wanted, and set out to get it, hook or crook. There she was.

He removed the rest of her bunny suit and stroked her majestically perky nipples, rubbing the pads of his thumbs across them. Her back arched, and he took full advantage. Ethan dipped into the curve of her body, bracing her back with his strong hands, and sucked each hot bud until they were slippery from his saliva. The feel of her hair dancing across his wrists emitted pheromones he didn't know he had. Just the feel of her hair, for Christ's sake, almost took him to his peak.

The rest of her body needed him. She ached within his grasp, and it was so evident, due to her skin trembling. His lips left her breasts and made a streak from her collarbone to her navel, dipping inside the small pucker, and licking. That wasn't enough for him; thus his descent continued to the cotton-covered mound of her sex, kissing before lowering to her slick folds. *Christ! Where am I? Have I finally reached my eternal resting place?* Ethan knew he could live his life between her thighs and not have another thought about anything else.

His tongue devoured her, and the hammering began again, a stiff, deep, sweltering orgasm that made her legs weak. Words caught in her throat as he pulled on her clit, rocking it, nailing it, making it submit to him. "Ethan! Ethan! Lay me down. I need to be wrapped around you."

Quickly he stepped from the rest of the spandex, tossed away what was left of her Playboy Bunny costume, and lifted her into his arms. Glee carried him from the door to the blanket. Just looking at her excited face took him where he needed to be. He didn't have to hide his emotions from her, for fear of being called a five-year-old snake in the damn grass, a warthog, or anything her then-eleven-year-old mind could concoct. They were now on the same page.

Ethan carefully laid her upon the blanket and instructed her to lay back. "No! I have to taste my man again, get everything from him I couldn't get last night due to cramped quarters."

He stood to his knees and watched as she enjoyed her early Thanksgiving. The idea of Beverly pulling on his joint, making it longer, licking the underside until he could barely stand, did wonders for his mind. He was lucid, free, ready to enjoy the ultimate release with the ultimate woman—his Beverly. Finally.

For her, it wasn't just an erection filling her mouth, it was *this particular erection*; its owner was a king, though it had been a long road for him to achieve that honor. He had definitely come a long way from being a snotty-nosed little turkey who made her and Debbie's life a living hell every summer, winter, spring, and fall. She had taken the literal fall, and the more she sucked him into mental intoxication, the more she found herself falling for Mr. Unlikely.

Lips almost raw from an erection the height of the sky nibbled his tip once more before she looked up at him. "I'm ready to be personalized!"

"You are, indeed." He knelt to her, placed her lacy-stockinged legs around his hips, and leaned over her. The one thing Ethan had visualized since he was old enough to know what sex was was looking down at Beverly while making love to her. His dream was finally coming true. An angel was beneath him, and nothing could tear his eyes from her, not even sex that could and would shake the planet.

With his arms on either side of her head, he positioned himself parallel and poked at her oozing sex. Marvelous! With each thrust, his eyes remained on his treasure. With each rock and gyration, his stare was penetrating.

They climbed their steep hill and rolled down together, nonstop, in unison. Their waves joined as he rocked her harder and harder, moving both of them from the blanket, landing in front of a skeleton in a rocking chair. They didn't care about that because what they had was unbreakable. If his life had depended on it, he couldn't have pulled from her.

Beverly could feel him in her soul. And as he banged mercifully into her, crushing her G-spot, clit, and everything willing to get banged by the famous Ethan Jacobs, the more she was falling for him. When the intense feeling started spiraling within her, she grabbed his forearms, dug into them, and screamed. Her tempered yells mixed with other frightful sounds throughout the house, but only she and Ethan knew they were from total satisfaction. Electric satisfaction!

That was all Ethan needed to start his own chain reaction. He looked down on the beautiful sex-stained face of his lover and could barely control himself. Venom shot through him like liquid fire, draining him, making him tremble. Something no other woman had managed to do for him with such velocity. As was his saying, "It takes the right woman to make me react the right way." Beverly was definitely that woman, had been his entire life. He had had to find her because nothing in his life, other than his daughter, was real until Beverly was at his side.

He smiled down into her flushed face, seeing her excitement over him. Yeah, that was love, and he'd finally found it. His body tiredly lowered onto hers, and he lay there, happily listening to a heartbeat he hoped beat for only him now. Whispers of her soft voice lit him, mellowed him to the sounds only an angel could possess.

"Ethan, did I please you? Did I really please you the way you needed to be pleased?"

He smoothed the softness of her bare flesh below his, strumming her satin breasts with the back of his hands, and smiled to her words. "It was amazing, just the way I knew it would be. More amazing than all the daydreams I had of you, more amazing than the first time I was inside you." He looked at her, smiling the most infectious, loving smile he could possess. "You've completed my life, Bev. This is all there is to life, making love to the one woman you know you're destined to be with. The idea of you being in my life is what makes me breathe."

Her fingers gently massaged his damp scalp, fingering the feathery curls she used to have to brush so his sister could finish getting ready for school years ago. It was a drag then, having to hold a little monster still while she unsnarled curls from the night before, but now it was a slice of heaven, a thick slice.

The more she played with his gentle curls, the more she started falling harder for him, wondering how in the world it could be that the two came face-to-face and could hardly keep their bodies from one another. Lives changed; so did the times. Of all the men she thought she was meant for, he was not the one—until a day ago. The others were mere unreasonable facsimiles, something to butter her up for the ultimate in male entertainment . . . but he was so much more than that.

Ethan looked at his watch, dangling from his wrist due to perspiration, and groaned. "As much as I'd like to stay in this one place for the rest of my life, we'd better get going before they close." Before they clad themselves with silly costumes again, he reached for the bottle and uncorked it.

Beverly watched as he filled the goblets full of champagne, not having remembered such a romantic time, even though it was in a creepy haunted house. That's what added to the entire effect, however. It would take a man like Ethan to concoct a plan this sinfully . . . irresistible!

Willingly she took the filled goblet and joined him in a toast. "To a woman so unforgettable she makes my head swim." He wrapped his arm around hers, and they each sipped from the other's goblet. Champagne had never tasted so sweet as it did to both of them that evening. Sex-tainted lips, satisfied bodies, and warm hearts accounted for a glow and aroma that ordinary champagne didn't house.

Ethan slowly put the bunny costume onto a sumptuous

body that hardly needed clothing. Before he covered her breasts with the frilly bustier, he kissed them, paying exceptional attention to nipples still so excited from the best lovemaking a woman had known. As his lips slowly withdrew from the perky buds, he quickly kissed their tips once more. "I'd better cover these before Hideous Harry walks in on us and wants his share of them."

At that, she helped him with her top. "No way. These belong to you only. A man with no teeth just doesn't do it for me."

"That's makeup. Believe me, he's got plenty of teeth; sharks usually do. He's a corporate lawyer."

"What? That disgusting bunch of shaggy hair with red eyes and ripped overalls from hell is a lawyer?"

"A good one, too. How else can he afford to own haunted houses all over Ohio and Indiana, along with coffee shops and pumpkin patches?"

"He's a damn Monopoly board, isn't he? Does he also own Boardwalk and Park Place?"

"Almost. He's a cool dude, though."

He pulled her to her feet, and they both finished attaching his condom outfit, making sure it fit in all the right places—snap seat, mushroomed hat, and all.

They both ran from the room in hysterics over just how simply disgusting they both looked after putting on wrinkled suits, smelling like flaming-hot sex. What stopped them in their tracks was Hideous Harry leaning against a rail in front of their door. His toothless grin did nothing to help calm their hysterics. Ethan had to basically kiss Beverly to subdue her hysteria over how stupid Harry actually looked. *Rich! Ha, what a kicker!* Only her thoughts could temporarily stop the gaity of the evening.

Ethan grabbed his old buddy. "Harry, this is the lady you

have been hearing about for years. Beverly Stuart. Bev, this is my college buddy, though usually he looks better than this."

The scarecrow of a man was eager to take her hand and finally meet the only woman who made Ethan smile from the mere mention of her name. "The wonderful Ms. Beverly! It's an honor to meet you. You sure make this man's life, you know that?"

Shy for the first time over a compliment. "And I'm glad to meet the owner of this . . . for lack of better words . . . fine establishment. It was awfully sweet of you to allow us to occupy—and I say the word loosely—one of your rooms for so long."

"Anything for my man Ethan. He's a good guy. He'll make you happy."

Beverly slowly released Harry's hand. "He already has."

Ethan stepped in, recovering what was to be his for the rest of his life. "I'd better get this little lady home so she can get her rest. Lots of prescriptions to fill in the morning. I told him how smart you are, Bev, owning pharmacies and all."

"Keep her happy, then," Harry added, "or she'll give you someone's Viagra medicine in a cup of coffee."

As they walked down the winding staircase, Ethan looked back at Harry and grinned a sly grin. "Don't think I need the Viagra; this chick keeps me pumping well enough."

Beverly pinched him over the comment. "Don't tell him that."

"He can see it on my face anyway." He latched on to her hand, and they walked the dark road back to his car.

At a nearby cider café, Ethan bought her a glittering terracotta pumpkin with a whimsical face, and they sat at a table sipping piping-hot cider with cinnamon sticks and doughnuts. Beverly looked around the spooky decorated place and smiled. "This place even looks like something Hideous Harry would own. It's cute, very cute, quaint. How can something so out in the middle of nowhere be so popular?"

"Like I said, Hideous Harry is a lawyer. He has contacts, helps a lot of people who are more than happy to get the news around town about his Halloween extravaganzas. I'm one of them."

"What have you done?"

"I decorate my dealership for the occasion and pass out fliers to his haunted houses. Friends do that."

"Is that why Harry gave you back your admission after leaving Mutilation Mansion?"

"Exactly, but he didn't have to. I always have a good time at his places." He took her hand and kissed it. "So, Ms. Playboy Bunny, did you have a good time as well?"

She hazily looked up to the ghost decorations dangling from the ceiling and then back to him. "It was nothing short of amazing. I've never had a Halloween like this before. Usually I just hand out candy, pop popcorn, and watch a movie with some of my girlfriends. Nothing to write home about. I look forward to watching horror movies, even if I'm alone. The last few years in Pasadena, I was definitely alone, having thrown out Tony."

"I just can't get with that. Didn't he know he had the best thing a man could have? He did me a favor, though, and took a hike so I could move right in. Do you think that's possible, on a permanent basis? You wouldn't have to watch *House on Haunted Hill* by yourself and get scared. I'd be there with you, every inch of the mile, and I mean every word of that, Beverly." He sat back in his chair, staring at her, waiting for an answer. "So, are you and I possible?"

"I'd love to say yes, but I'm not as easygoing as you may think."

"I know you're not, and that's what I like. You've always

been your own woman, even as a girl. You made me do what you wanted me to do, and I'm still doing that." He rubbed her hand against his cheek. "Bev, don't you know I'd do anything for you, be anything you want me to be? I just want you in my life. I don't want to be a casual bystander when it comes to you."

"You know you're more than that to me, Ethan. In a way you always have been. You made me pay attention to you—always did, and you eventually got what you wanted from me."

"Do I still have it?"

"I think so, but, Ethan, I've been alone for a while and I needed to be. My life hasn't been easy with men, and I'm, well, a little skittish."

"I'd never hurt you, sweetheart."

"I know that, and I don't want to hurt you."

"Do you think you would?"

"Not intentionally. I just don't want you to feel you have something that may not really be there until I want it to be. In other words, I don't want to hold you back from loving someone else."

"I don't want anyone else. I've waited this long, and I'll wait until you're ready. I know you care about me. You're not the type to waste your time on someone if you aren't interested."

"This is true. I do care about you, Ethan—a lot. That's why I couldn't bear it if I did anything to hurt you. My feelings about everything these days are so scattered my head is still spinning."

"The only thing you could do to hurt me is keep me out of your life. Do you want that?"

"You've always been a part of me since I was eleven years old. Now that I know *this*, Ethan, I know I want you around, but can we take things slowly?"

"As slow as you want."

"I know that's stupid of me to want, because I've practically gone hog wild over you, but maybe slower would be better. Can you deal with that?"

"Beverly, I want anything I can get from you, and I want to give you anything you want and need. I'm the one that's grateful for even sharing five minutes with you." He moved his chair next to hers and briefly kissed her lips. "I want Beverly, and I want her for the long haul, problems or no problems. We're all afflicted with a past. I want to be the one to prove to you that not all men are stupid and willing to act like an ass to the one woman they need to prove everything to."

"You won't have to prove a thing, Ethan. But there is one thing I need you to answer."

"Anything. Just ask."

She looked at him with a smile in her eyes. "Tell me the truth. Were you the one who took my Barbie hair-design doll and put a GI Joe on top of her, hugging her? Your sister and I found it under some blankets in your parents' basement."

He held his hands in the air as if under arrest. "True, I did that, and I remember doing it. Even back then, to me that was us."

She tightened her hand around his, teasing. "So to you I'm a Barbie head with a bouffant hairdo."

"No, but you have the 'doll' part down to a science."

Nothing could stop her from leaning and kissing lips warm enough to let go of all her inhibitions and make him her live-in lover from that point on. He definitely was the lover, but her inhibitions were determined to linger. She pulled away from his lips and sipped more of her hot cider. "Well, Mr. GI Joe, since you're willing to take it slow with me, why not agree to another date? Have Thanksgiving dinner with me. I'm cooking for my family because my sister Ruby is going to be out of town. She usually makes most of the dinner, but I can cook also."

"I know you can, girl."

"Silly boy, that's not what I mean. Mom would love to see you."

"Hopefully we'll have our next date way before Thanksgiving, but I actually had something else in mind. Debbie always invites me to Nevada for Thanksgiving, sometimes Christmas. Why not come with me? You can see Debbie that way."

There was that panicky feeling again. The kind that awakened the rest of her inhibitions, the ones that said, *Do you really want his family to see you dating the kid brother that always got on your nerves, the kid brother that's a good six years younger? Wouldn't Debbie just stab you right in your back for that? She'd want to know about your past lives with men, and she would find that out, one way or another. She doesn't want that for her only brother. No, keep him a secret, and make him keep you one.* That terrible, terrible inner voice, that was so right most of the time, wouldn't leave her alone.

His voice brought her back to reality. "You zoned out on me."

"Did I?"

"Yeah, and you didn't answer me. Come with me to Nevada, see Debbie for the first time in years, meet all those kids they have."

"I don't know. Let me think about it."

"What's there to think about? I know Debbie wants to see you. Her face lights up when I mention you."

"You haven't told her about us already, have you?"

That concerned him, made him answer slowly. "No, but I'd like to. Are you reluctant about that?"

"What would she think—"

"About me dating one of her girlfriends? She'd like it, especially if she knew it was you."

"She might think otherwise."

"She wants me happy, and you make me happy. She saw

how miserable I was with Elaine. I could never be that with you." He continued eyeing her, hating to ask the next question, but was compelled to. Concern showed in his voice as well. "Bev, are you embarrassed about liking me?"

"Ethan! No, not at all."

"Then why is that gloomy look on that perfect face of yours?"

"I just don't know what people would think about us. After all, we have a past."

"That was years ago, and we were both kids. Besides, fuck everyone else, this is our life, not theirs—if you want one with me."

"I do. I just don't want to cause you any turmoil."

"Turmoil for me is not being with you. We can take it slow, Bev, like I said. I'm so willing to do anything to be with you. Please believe me."

"I do believe you, and you know I'm crazy about you."

A smile lit his incredibly handsome face. "I do know that, and I'm ecstatic about that, but do me one favor, think about Thanksgiving. I want you to be with me. I just want to share my happiness over you with the family. They already love you. If not, Mom wouldn't have had you over for dinner three out of seven nights a week."

"Yeah, Debbie and I practically ODed over being constantly in one another's faces."

"Now you know how I feel about you. Hell, I was the one who set your plate setting. Debbie and I used to fight over doing that."

"Really?"

He took her hand. "Come on, let's get outta Dodge and take a slow ride home. I know you're tired."

"A little, but I had an amazing time."

"Then my job is done. I can rest my cape for the evening."

"You're not done, superhero. Just keep satisfying me."

*　*　*

An hour later, they pulled to the front of Beverly's house, and he walked her to the door. He walked her inside and pulled her into him, delivering the best good-night kiss a girl could ever ask for. It was hard pulling away from Ethan Jacobs, the man who gave her a Halloween she'd never forget. "You'd better get going if you plan on taking your daughter that filled pumpkin. She'll enjoy seeing that the minute she steps out of bed."

"Yeah, I'd better leave, but it would be so easy to spend the night here with you."

"Soon, real soon."

Ethan kissed the tip of her nose. "I sure hope so. Um, by the way, after work I'd like to take you to dinner and then show you my house. We could take a moonlight stroll after we get back. It's supposed to be warm again tomorrow night. Besides, I love this tree-lined street. It would be perfect. Can we do that?"

"I'd love that. Say, six?"

"You're on, baby, and thank you for accompanying me to Hideous Harry's. It was a blast!" He kissed her again and then was off.

Beverly watched as his car drove out of sight, and then she retired to her bedroom to undress. As she slid into bed, sounds of "It's the Great Pumpkin, Charlie Brown" on the television lulled her. As she drifted to sleep, she thought about being with Ethan on Thanksgiving, wanted to be with him all the time now, but the same old questions continued to loom heavily over her head, *What would they think of me? Would they hate me for loving a man that much younger than I am? Am I even ready for love? What to do, what to do?*

All day at work, Beverly's mind was on one thing: Ethan Jacobs. Soon after having the most delicious thoughts of him, her next set of boggling mind tricks made themselves apparent: what his family would think of her. To her, what people thought was very important, despite the hard-shell personality she'd become accustomed to, having dealt with the world alone for so long. This situation was not *the world,* however, it was *her* world in which suddenly she didn't know what to do or how to act. With just Ethan, life was easy; their heads were in all the right places—along with their hearts. When it came to including others, however, that was the tricky part.

As had become their custom over the past two and a half weeks, that night they had dinner together and took in a good stroll somewhere, making every minute of the unseasonable weather last for as long as possible—making out like banshees in the park. The evening was still so young, and Ethan, as usual, hadn't had his fill of her. His hand slipped around hers. "What's up for the rest of the evening?"

"Well, since it is a weekend in which I don't make medication deliveries to seniors, I can stay up for as long as I wish."

"You sure can, but doing what?"

"How about you let me into the rest of your life, Ethan?"

"You are in my life. You're as in to me as any woman could ever get."

"Then let's take it further. Let me see your inner workings, what gets you cranked, what drives you."

"I'm looking at what does that, darling."

"What I meant was, take me to your dealership. Let me see the other less romantic side of Ethan Jacobs. I saw your parents, your daughter, other parts of you, but not this. I want it all."

"You really want to see where I get buried under paperwork, huh?"

"Sure, that's a part of you."

"Anything Beverly Stuart wants, she gets. I'll show you the new one."

"There's more than the Lexus and BMW dealerships?"

"I own three, just like you. A conglomerate!"

She delicately tapped on his forehead. "I knew brains would one day inhabit that head of yours—once you got out of the sex asylum."

"Sex asylum! Girl, after being with you, I know I need to be in a place like that. An ounce of you isn't enough, but what *is* enough when it comes to you?"

Within minutes they pulled in front of Jacobs' on Fifth, and Beverly smiled. "This place is yours? I pass this place two days a week getting to my other pharmacy."

"Wasn't the name a dead giveaway?"

"Not really. I thought about Debbie once or twice when I first saw your last name scrawled across the front of the building, but I didn't really connect anything. I know Debbie and your parents are so proud of you. Your mother's face lights up with nothing but smiles when she speaks of you."

"Too bad she wasn't smiling back when she used to whip my ass over some stupid thing I had done."

"A woman can't smile that often, Ethan."

He pulled her into his arms. "Are you trying to say something, Ms. Stuart?"

Her nose nuzzled his. "Yeah, that I'm now the contented one who whips that delicious ass of yours."

"And you do it so damn well. The really good thing is, Mom thinks we are a good match."

"We are."

"Then come with me to Nevada, and let's show Debbie how good we are together."

"Ethannn."

"I know I promised not to bring that up again and to let you make up your own mind about it, but, baby, I just want you with me. I want to show people what kind of a man you have made me in almost three short weeks. Will you at least keep thinking about it?"

"I promise."

"Good enough for now." He got out and opened her car door. "Come on, let me show you the jewel of the Nile . . . well, at least the jewel of Fifth Street, my third dream come true."

"What was your second?"

"My BMW dealership."

"And the first?"

"I think you know the answer to that. You, and my daughter."

"You should put her first, Ethan."

"OK, you both share first place. Satisfied?"

She ran her hand up and down his arm. "Absolutely."

The showroom was gorgeous, decorated with subtle autumn decorations. But the best decoration was a room filled with every Mercedes model a salivating woman could dream of. Immediately Beverly walked to a lapis-blue M-Class and smoothed her hand across the hood. "Where in the world did you get the clout to actually be the owner of a Mercedes dealership? I thought you specialized in Lexuses and BMWs."

He moved in behind her, nibbling her earlobe. "Variety is the spice of life. Don't you know that?"

She wrapped her arms around his neck. "I do know that, and the more I'm around you, the more I find that out."

"Then I'm pleasing to your senses?"

"You're pleasing to every inch of my being. You nourish me, Mr. Ethan, man of my wildest dreams, and I do mean wildest!"

He delivered a faint kiss on her full lips. "Well, then, Ms. Stuart, I've got more pleasing to do." He motioned to the showroom. "Pick one."

A quaint smile crossed her puzzled face. "What?"

"Go on, pick one. Let's have some fun here."

"You're . . . telling me to . . . pick a Mercedes. This is not 'Wheel of Fortune,' and I'm certainly not Vanna White, ready, willing, and able to turn over letters for a million dollars a year."

"I do resemble Alex Trebek about the eyes, don't you think?"

"Not at all. Now what do you mean, 'pick a car,' Ethan?"

"Exactly that. Point one out, and let's get busy."

"You can't be serious! You want to *make out* in a car you would sell to someone?"

"Baby, the car can be cleaned, although if a man bought it and got one whiff of your succulent aroma inside it, I'd have to bottle your fragrance and sell it along with the car. I'd make a mint! Pick the car, Bev."

He watched as she walked about the showroom, stopping briefly at different models and then moving on reluctantly. Finally she stopped at a red two-door model. "This one! It's luxurious, roomy in the back, and the new-car aroma is awfully sultry. Makes a woman simply want to strip in front of it, with a sexy-ass man to boot! All the ingredients are here."

Ethan took the keys from behind the counter and walked to her as he undid his tie. He moved into her arms. "I knew you'd pick the red one."

"How?"

"It looks like you—your style, flashy, and sexy beyond the imagination." He clicked the locks and held open the back door. "Your chariot awaits."

Beverly slid in and was taken by the plush leather and new-car smell. Her hands slid across the tight new leather, reminding her of how her lover felt against her skin, like smooth satin, flawless. "This is so beautiful. I've never been in a Benz before. A BMW, yes, but never something this plush."

"Then get prepared for a real ride." He slid her onto his lap. "Does this remind you of the night we met?"

"Yeah, let's relive it together. I relive it enough on my own."

His voice lowered to a seductive drawl, moaning against her ear. "We can't have that, now, can we?"

Her lips feverishly brushed his, her voice hushed with anticipation. "No." Her hunger for him took over, wanting, needing, dying to mate with him in any way possible. She nipped his lips feverishly, taking in his aroma, letting her senses drive her wilder than wild. He was delicious, more so than a man had ever been. This awesome entity controlled her heart, mind, and body with just one kiss. One thing was now a proven point in her mind: that little snotty-nosed boys had so much potential—and *potential* filled her arms with such a strong force. He was amazing; he was . . . Ethan, and there was no way to successfully hide her love from him.

As her fingers played in his hair, her lips moved to his neck, gently licking and sucking his Adam's apple, feeling his throat as it bobbed in ecstasy. He smelled so good, so much like a man, so natural, so intoxicating. What made the heavens open up and thrust him upon her once again? Fate? Yes, fate. They were meant to be there, in that time and place, in this life!

Her lips mellowed in the crook of his neck as he slid down his zipper. His low, lingering voice moaned in her ear. "Be with me, Bev. Be with me in every way a woman can be with a man—totally, freely." His arms wrapped tight around her slim hips. "I love you so much. Don't let anything get in the way of this incredible love I have for you—the love I know you have for me. I can feel it in your body. Don't stop it. Don't be ashamed to be with me."

She slowly raised her head to his words, staring unbelievably into his dark eyes. "Is that what you think, Ethan? You think I'm ashamed of you around Debbie?"

"I didn't mention Debbie. You did. I don't want to embarrass you around anyone. You didn't feel that way around my parents the other day. Why Debbie? I know it's her you're apprehensive about."

He was so right. What the hell was she thinking? Debbie was not the god of accountants who could cancel her out if her numbers didn't exactly match Ethan's. Debbie was just another woman. Then why was Debbie still so important to Beverly after sixteen years?

"Be—because Debbie had the power back then to make or break me. Everything we did was because she wanted to do it."

"But you were the stronger one. *You* were all she talked about, all I talked about. She wanted to be you but loved you too much to be jealous of you. She told me that one day about ten years ago. And, frankly speaking, you were the beautiful one. Even as a child you were outstanding, with long cinnamon hair, honey-colored skin, and shapely—quite shapely, for your age. She wanted to look like you but had to suffice with being your friend and staying in control."

"Really? Was that it?"

"Afraid so."

"She was beautiful, too."

"But not like you. Her looks came from my father's side. I got Mom's, with the light brown skin. She envied you; I wanted to make love to you—whatever I thought love was back then. Beyond that, Beverly, I'm still in love with you, and that's all I care about. I know what it is now and know how to take care of it, treat it right." He took her hand, kissed it. "I love you way beyond the physical, way beyond how much you make me feel like a man when I'm inside you. When I hear your voice, I'm that man again whether we're touching or not. Love me back, please."

"I do love you, Ethan."

"Show me. Show me now, and show me in three days when I leave for Nevada."

At that moment in time, the *now* was of utmost importance. She had to show him she could conquer Debbie. But dealing with Nevada was still something different and something she would think about later . . . much later.

She raised above him as he removed his erection from his pants. Anticipation welled within her body, because each time they made love, it was different, better. The fact that she loved him was the special part, the part that made everything fit together.

As she lowered her body onto his, that incredible pressure filled her, the type of pressure that came from a shaft that was beyond all others. She rocked with him, to him, on top of him, spinning her wheels to total ecstasy. Nothing mattered but that moment with a loving man in her arms. Debbie, Thanksgiving, her exes—all were a blur, as everything was when it came to Ethan making love to her. That's what it was—love, unconditional love that was proven to her within a matter of three weeks. It was young but strong.

She climaxed for the third time as Ethan teased her nipples with tongue swirls, wetting her breasts, wetting her sex as he pumped ferociously inside her. When Ethan reared back and squirmed within her arms, his juices billowed out, saturating her, staining her, marking her for life. He was it, the real one, the master of her soul, and she had to find a way within her fear of life to please him in every possible way.

Beverly lay against his wet chest, stroking his muscles, feeling his still-hard shaft invading her. She was at peace, mind and body. They kissed again, and then she slid to the other seat quickly just to get a glimpse of him. There was nothing more attractive to her than Ethan's erection. It was exciting, erogenous, and she had to put her hands on it. Her quick, hard strokes made him see stars; so did she as he came again. The feel of his nectar on her hands was what made her. The salty taste of the underside of his shaft was what completed her. She was

Ethan, and he was her. That was the bottom line to it, and nothing more.

After the dealership was locked, the car ready to be sent to the car wash the following morning, and a quiet ride home, he made sure her coat was fastened and her fur scarf tucked snugly around her neck before opening her car door. "Can't have my baby getting cold out here."

"Am I still your baby even though I haven't given you an answer to Nevada?"

"You'll always be my baby. I'd like it if you felt freer with me, but with you, I'd be glad to accept the crumbs if I had to." He slipped his arm around her. "Beverly, I'd be glad to be your slave. I want you in any possible way I can get you. If you want me to simply be your Ohio man, us sharing our little world, that'll be fine. If you want to share me with the family, mine and yours, that's great, too. Just let me be in your life for the rest of our lives."

His words were so touching she couldn't help but stroke his cheek. "I've never understood love like that, because I've never had it. My ex-husband was a jerk, my past lovers selfish. All I've truly had was, well . . . me."

"How does it feel, now that you have a man who really loves you for everything you are?"

"Like silk and diamonds wrapped around a bed of pearls."

"That good?"

"That good, Ethan."

"I can give you that, plus more."

"I have what I want." They kissed tenderly yet heatedly— velvety smooth. Ethan pulled away slowly, shaking his head. "I'd better get you in the house before I force you to have sex in a car again."

"It wasn't hard to convince me before. What makes you think it would be this time?"

"Just the same, we'd better go. I've got a long day ahead of me tomorrow. By the way, I have to take Danny to a birthday party by noon. Care to come along?"

"Can't. Reports to complete even though I'm not making deliveries tomorrow. You know how it is when you own your own business. It's more work than ever before."

"Amen to that."

As they walked to her house, they pulled their coats closer together due to stronger mid–November winds. When they stopped at the door, Ethan patiently watched her unlock the door and then took her face in his hands for the last time that evening. "I love you, Beverly, just know that no matter what. I leave in three days for Nevada. Let me know something before then. Three days, baby. Can you do that for me?"

A slow, "Yes."

Ethan kissed her cool cheeks one last time and then was off. As he drove off, he pushed number four on his CD player, and, automatically, his main man, James Brown, blasted the speakers loud and clear with, "I Guess I'll Have To Cry, Cry, Cry." It was the first time he didn't want a James Brown song to remind him of Beverly. He didn't want to cry, yet leaving her house each night without the promise of a lasting love made him cry inside. Still he listened to the song as he left her block to travel the long, cold night roads to his empty home.

With her back pressed against her front door, Beverly's heart felt heavy, preventing her from walking toward her bedroom. That was the one place that reminded her of Ethan. He'd conquered her there, too, on an earlier chilly November night. It would be colder that night as well . . . colder than most but for all the wrong reasons.

In bed, there was no Charlie Brown music to lull her to sleep, there were only thoughts of Ethan . . . and of Debbie. That was the real nemesis. For the life of her, she couldn't remember having been intimidated by Debbie before, or by anyone, for that matter. They were the best of friends until Debbie got married. They parted, but, apparently, the feelings still lasted for Beverly. Now the only problem was how Debbie would accept her. Years ago, Beverly's last fear was dating her best friend's baby brother—a brother who definitely was no longer a baby. Would she be able to make that final step to prove that nothing was more important than her love for him? She always hated tricky questions.

Thanksgiving eve, and Beverly was helping her mother make dressing for the turkey. Plenty of thought had been given to the Nevada trip, yet not one bag had been packed. Her mind had stayed constantly on Ethan since the day he had left. She knew the minute, hour, and second his plane left Hopkins International Airport. Last time she saw him he was gloomy over the fact that she wasn't joining him for the big family celebration but was making the best of it for her sake. Everything he did was always for her, even when he was a child, and Beverly knew that. Was it wasted sentiment? Not really, more like fear over what *others* expected of her. It still haunted her way beyond any haunted house ever could—even Hideous Harry's.

Once her family's pre–Thanksgiving celebrating was over and all questions about Ethan answered, she slowly walked to her car. The snowy November sky reminded her of what she could be having, a nice, warm evening by the fireplace with the love of her life in her arms. Instead she cranked a cold Cadillac and drove home listening to a station that played continuous Christmas songs. What awaited her at home: a cold bed and an empty suitcase longing for a lightweight Christmas dress and an elegant nightgown for him to remove from her. That, unfortunately, wasn't about to happen, and it would be a long night, simply due to her inhibitions.

*   *   *

Playing in the background on his sister's new audio system was his favorite Christmas song, Bing Crosby's "Jingle Bells," with the Andrews Sisters. It had always put him in good spirits in the past, but this time was different. There was no joy on Ethan's face even though he was sitting at a table fit for a king. His queen hadn't shown up, and that canceled out all his fun on the spot.

He watched as Debbie and her husband finished cooking all the holiday favorites while other relatives ran behind loads of children. Then there were others sitting around the fireplace sipping spiked eggnog. Certainly it was too warm in Nevada to have an actual fire, but the effect was what the guests were striving for. All of that did nothing for Ethan. What gave him a little glee was watching Danica playing with her cousins. God only knew Debbie and Ward had enough children for a nursery school. That sure kept Danica busy while her father continued to sulk in front of roasted turkey and cranberry sauce.

Debbie and Ward walked in with the rest of the fixings and placed them where they needed to be. Ward saw the expression on Ethan's face and nudged his wife, whispering. "What's with him?"

"His pilot light is out."

"What?"

"I told you he fell for an old buddy of mine in Cleveland, and she chose not to show up here tonight. He's in the dumps."

Ward quickly kissed his elegantly clad wife. "I'd be in the dumps if my lover wasn't with me on Thanksgiving."

"That statement had better be about me." She teased him with a quick kiss and resumed decorating her table for a Thanksgiving not soon to be forgotten.

Ethan saw the exchange between his very happy sister and Ward, wishing he had fallen for someone willing to show him love in the open instead of in the privacy and safety of her own home—or in his Lexus, for that matter.

Debbie placed a cup of eggnog before him and sat at his side. "Ethan, you're going to have to get over the fact that she's a no-show. I know that's hard, but—"

"You don't know how hard. You've had Ward constantly for over fourteen years. You don't know what it's like to lay in a cold bed while your warm heart beats for a distant lover."

"You really fell hard, didn't you?"

He sighed and toyed with his glass. "I fell hard for her over twenty years ago."

"She was beautiful and a lot of fun. Can't blame you."

"She still is." That brought a semismile to his face. Just one remembrance of how Beverly's smile lit any room she was in lit his fire.

"Are you going to be OK?"

"Yeah, once I get back to Cleveland. I should probably leave late tonight."

"You really miss her, don't you?"

"Yeah. Funny thing, I've only had her back in my life for a little more than three weeks, but, Debbie, she's the one, even though she's too shy to be seen around me in front of you. She's the one who brings out the wildness in me, though. I'm primal when I'm around her, always have been."

"You were born primal. Hit the scene scratching and clawing at everything." She poked at him playfully. "Another thing: you always stunk! You cried, and you stunk—two things you were good at."

"Come on, Deb, I'm serious. I'm in the dumps, and you're dogging me."

"I'm only trying to brighten my brother's spirits. Is that so wrong to want to do?"

"I guess not." He took her hand. "Thanks, sis. Wish it was working, though."

She shrugged her shoulders. "It will, eventually. At least hang around for dinner. Uncle Craig and Aunt Emma are due to show up in about ten minutes."

"I'm not leaving, not yet. You haven't visited with your niece nearly long enough. All Danica talks about is her Aunt Debbie."

"That's what five-year-olds do. I remember someone you talked about constantly when you were five."

"Yeah, who?"

"Someone you still talk about, and when you do, your entire face lights up like a Christmas wreath."

He got the message, but that wasn't helping his cause. The thing he needed to do was *not* think about Beverly. Yet the only thing on his mind was getting back to her and playing by her rules.

As he sat there tinkering with his drink, he thought about the good times she was probably having with her family, probably not even thinking about him. His heart shifted in his chest. Minutes later, when Debbie decided not to wait for Uncle Craig and his overtly slow wife (slow dressing and slow-witted), and to start the Thanksgiving prayer, his mind was still on being with Beverly.

Minutes into the dinner, the front bell rang, and Debbie jumped up to answer it. After all, Uncle Craig had the green-bean casserole. Ethan was contented to sit there and play with his food while pretending to be interested in his cousin Phil's boring conversation on sprocket manufacturing. It made him feel like George Jetson's boy, Elroy.

He and everyone else jumped when he heard Debbie shriek with high-pitched laughter. Everyone around the table looked at each other as Ward went to see about his wife. Again Ethan returned to his food and made sure Danica wasn't throwing hers.

His mind had begun to play tricks on him, hearing Beverly's distinctive laugh. In actuality he knew she was celebrating with her family back in Cleveland, probably seeing him as a mere thought that would no doubt return to reality days later. What made him look up was seeing his sister return to the room smiling from ear to ear saying, "Everyone! Look!"

His only thought: *Damn! Is the bean casserole good enough to have its own introduction?*

Debbie cast her arm aside and made a path for a queen. Beverly steped inside with her eyes dead set on Ethan. Her red coat gapped open to reveal a navy-blue, sequined dress and matching silver jewelry. Her hair was in a loose bun with ringlets of curls circling her face.

Ethan stood in a trance, not believing what he was seeing. He almost spilled the eggnog as Debbie spoke. "Don't just stand there like a zombie, though that is what you do best. Get your behind over here, and introduce your lady."

The world disappeared and left Beverly in its place. With a spring to his step, he walked across the room, took Beverly immediately into his arms, and kissed her lavishly in front of everyone. Debbie had to clear her throat to get their attention. After all, they were embarrassing the guests. The children were staring and laughing; the older family members were oohing and aahing, saying things like, "Oh, isn't that just sweet. That boy deserves to be loved the right way after what that *other* girl did to him." Ethan heard nothing but the sounds of his lips making love to hers.

Beverly forgot her embarrassment and took Ethan for all he had, entertaining an audience of people she had never seen before, other than Debbie and their parents. She didn't care, either. The world was gone. There was no roomful of people with faces full of turkey and any inebriating drink they could get their hands on. No, there was just Ethan and the fact that she overcame fear of herself to actually leave her family and join him.

Debbie nudged the kissing couple. "You guys!!"

Both Ethan and Bev slowly parted and smiled a sheepish smile. Silence was broken as he wrapped his arm around her and introduced her. "Everyone, this is my lady, Ms. Beverly Nicole Stuart."

After everyone said their hellos, Beverly smiled and spoke to the clan of happy faces dotted with whiskey and cranberry sauce. The only things missing on their faces were the beans that had yet to arrive.

Debbie broke in. "She's also my old buddy from the Cleveland days. Ethan fell in love with her when he was five." Debbie loved embarrassing him, but at that point, he didn't care. He had every holiday wrapped up in one, and it was wearing a blue dress for him to peal off later that night.

Before the excited chatter subsided, he whisked Beverly into the living room, pulling her into him before she could speak. The way her body felt crushed next to his was unbelievable. His lips nibbled hers, his tongue danced within her, awakening crevices even she thought were completely sealed due to lack of her lover. His mind danced in whirlwinds of passion as he held her for dear life. His heated chest felt her hardened nipples graciously greeting him. In other words, he wallowed in the mere thought of her.

Slowly he broke the kiss and stared at Beverly with stars in his eyes. Before him stood a lover he thought was going to stay with her family for Thanksgiving dinner, and dance to golden oldies with her sisters. His lips parted, words cracked with emotion. "Unbelievable!"

"So, are you pleasantly surprised?"

"Baby, 'pleasantly surprised' isn't exactly the physical response I had in mind. Look at the front of my pants, and tell me if I'm excited over seeing you."

"I don't have to look at your pants for that. I can see it in your eyes." Her hand caressed his cheek smoothly and seductively. "I've never had a man react to me like this. No one has ever lit up like the Fourth of July over me."

"Is that what you love about me, the way I react when you're around?"

"What I love about you is . . . you! For the first time in my life, I wasn't comfortable in my own house, knowing I should be here with you."

"What about your family?"

"They helped me pack."

"Smart people, but how . . . when . . ."

"I took the red eye at ten thirty last night, landed here at two this morning, grabbed a motel room, and got some sleep. After all, I knew I'd need energy to be with you because, boy, you wipe me out!"

"Why didn't you call me? I'd have gladly met you anywhere."

"I know that, Ethan, but I wanted to surprise you, let you know in my way that it was time to stop living in the past and face the world. Let the world see how much I love you."

He pulled her warm, beautiful body into his again, his face barely inches from hers, smiling the usual Ethan Jacobs sensual smile. "And you *do* love me, don't you?"

"I'm here, aren't I?"

"Bevvvv?"

"Yes! Yes, Ethan, I'm in love with you, and it feels so unimaginable."

He kissed the tip of her nose. "You know, on television and in books it always seems like it takes forever to fall in love. Not for me, though. I've been in love all my life."

"One thing puzzles me about that. I can't remember doing

anything to make you love me. I used to hit you, trip you, push you down, jump out of corners to scare you, and . . ."

"Beverly, you were being you, and that's what did it. You were a child, too." He wrapped his arms tighter around her hips. "I've always liked the rough-and-tough girls. You were beautiful and rugged."

His eyes danced with a sparkle of glee, definitely catching Beverly's attention. "What are you thinking about?" she asked.

"I actually remember when I fell for you."

"Yeah, when?"

"Me, Debbie, you, and your sister Evie were in my parents' basement dancing and singing to your dad's new James Brown record. You took my hands, and we twirled in circles, singing and laughing. You were the only one who would dance with me."

"I was paid."

"You weren't."

"I remember that day also. You learned every word to 'Sex Machine.'"

"And now I have a real one, the one I've always wanted. Maybe that's why I love James Brown so much." Their lips tenderly met, soon engulfing in a kiss that was so bittersweet they both felt weak. He slid her coat off her shoulders, letting it hit the floor with a thud. He embraced and seduced skin he'd ached to touch since the last day he'd seen her. The low dip of her dress made access to her bare skin so much more attainable, making him forget he was in his sister's house. Her mere touch was earth shattering, making his pants poke in the front like a rocket leaving the galaxy. He whispered, "The bedroom is upstairs. Wanna go with me?"

"And miss your sister's Thanksgiving dinner?"

"She understands."

"Maybe we shouldn't—"

His lips covered hers again, licking, sucking, hungering for so much more, trying to convince her while nibbling insatiable lips. . . . Then a voice cleared from the entrance. "You two gonna stay out here, or should the turkey walk out to you?"

Ethan slowly turned to see Debbie smiling at the lovers. His caddish grin returned while trying to hide an erection the height of Mt. Fuji. "We're coming. I just wanted to—"

"I know what you were 'just' trying to do. You've always been good at taking off girls' dresses, including my Skipper doll years ago. You eventually lost her clothes and mashed her boobs in." Debbie hiked her thumb in the direction of the dining room. "Get a move on, you two."

As the three walked, she pulled Beverly aside, whispering, "Tell me, is my brother a good lover to you?"

"Are you kidding? He's the best in three states!"

"Seriously!"

"Debbie, no man has ever taken me where Ethan has. He's amazing."

"Should be; he's been practicing enough. You deserve the good things in life, Bev."

"And your brother is it!"

After eating his third slice of homemade pumpkin pie, Ethan slid a piece of paper into Beverly's hand.

She quickly read it and looked up at him in surprise. "What? You aren't serious."

"I'm very serious."

She looked at the car-wash receipt again, a reminder of when she'd insisted on paying for the red Mercedes in his dealership to be cleaned. But her eyes narrowed in on the small handwriting. *Paid in full, you are now the new owner of an X-Class Mercedes LI*. Her eyes widened to the size of saucers. "You're giving me a car, Ethan?"

"That and more."

"More? What else do you have up your sleeve?"

"You'll have to see later when we're upstairs. Do you like your car?"

She willingly kissed his lips in front of everyone again. "I love the car, but I love you more."

"Exactly the words I've always wanted to hear."

"So, what's it like dating Ethan?"

Beverly looked around the elaborately decorated kitchen, trying to think of the perfect response. There was only one when it came to him. "Incredible!"

"Really? Are we talking about the same Ethan Jacobs?"

"Sure. Don't you know your own brother by now? He's really quite the man, something I never would have expected from him years ago. I could just see him impregnating half of Ohio and working his way west to Indiana." She smiled a coy smile. "Actually I was surprised to find out he had only one child. He's really something."

Debbie enthusiastically plopped her elbows atop the table. "Really? How? I want details, girl, from the day you first saw him grown to now."

"You won't believe this, but he actually hired someone to find me."

"He *has* always been a basket case over you, so that doesn't surprise me. Believe me, he's got the money to have anyone found. How'd he do it, though?"

Same old Debbie, always the one to dig for information, down to the very nucleus of the situation, but that's what made them friends—they complimented one another, and they still did. "Ethan just walked into my pharmacy on Devil's Night and—"

"Devil's Night, huh? Yeah, that sounds like the kind of night he would show up on."

"It was perfect though. I didn't recognize him at first. I actually thought he was a pervert, a cute one, and I was about ready to call the cops. Then he told me his name, and everything kicked in place. The minute he smiled, there was Ethan all over again, but taller, sexier. I couldn't believe my eyes."

"I'll admit, Ethan turned out to be a hottie." Debbie took a sip from her hot cider. "I knew he'd find you one day. Every time he comes out here, the second thing out of his mouth is about you. He really wanted to find you, girl, and I knew he'd be relentless in his endeavors."

"I'm glad he was."

"Me, too. I've often wondered about you, and here you are, a big-time pharmacist."

"I don't know about the 'big time' part. In a way, I wish I had your life. I've always wanted a husband and children. I had the husband and the child—unfortunately they were in the same body."

"Girl, you are so crazy, just like old times." Debbie took Beverly by the hand. "I hope this means I'll see you again before another twenty or more years pass. Besides, I think Ethan is more than willing to be that perfect husband and father. He's great with Danica. You should see him out there playing with all those kids, and believe me, it's a lot of them out there. All are mine and Ward's but three."

Ethan ducked his head into the kitchen door with a smile lighting his scrumptious face. "Did I hear my name being called?"

"You did indeed. Beverly and I were discussing the lack of brain mass you possess."

"No, we weren't. You're such a tease." Beverly turned in her chair, reaching for Ethan's hand. "I told her about the best night of my life."

"Was I in it?"

"You made the night, buddy boy."

Ethan immediately bent over to land a sweet kiss on her lips. "Mmm, I could and will do that all night tonight. How about I tuck Danica into bed with April, read them both a story, and then curl up with you?"

"Sounds great."

"Give me twenty minutes, and then come up to the second guest room, the one on the left."

"How many are there?"

"A lot. My main man Ward designs amusement parks. Funny thing, he was a dope in school, from what I can remember hearing."

Debbie eagerly cut in. "Yeah, and you weren't?"

He kissed Beverly's soft cheek. "Remember, twenty minutes, girl. Don't be late."

After he walked out, the overly anxious Debbie nudged her friend in a giddy manner. "That boy is really planning something. What in the world have you done to him?"

Beverly took the last sip from her cider. "Not nearly enough, and I'd better not be late tonight, right?"

"Apparently not."

Twenty-five minutes passed, and Beverly was eagerly on her way to the second guest bedroom. Giving a man five extra minutes of anticipation was always so worth it, and with Ethan, the rewards could be astronomical.

As she walked the rest of the upper floor, she saw just how well Debbie and Ward were doing. Sure, she was doing fine with her two-story house in one of the more affluent areas of Cleveland, but nothing like this. Ethan's house wasn't even this fabulous, even though he had the cash to live like a rap star. He was her rap star, and she was happy to be a duo with him.

When she entered the luxurious bedroom, she automatically heard splashing in the bathroom. What really got her was the big bed; she and Ethan could play all night on something that huge. Yeah, that was the real deal. At that, she turned the knob to the private bathroom and saw Ethan sitting in a sunken bathtub filled with bubbles. His only words: "Take those clothes off, girl. Right now."

He enjoyed watching her perform her slow striptease, tossing away clothing like crazy and exposing hints of honey-brown skin soft and smooth enough for him to spray his very fluids at the mere thought of her. When she was down to the last few pieces, he stared at her plump breasts in amazement. "Take off your bra, and squeeze them together for me. You know I like it when you do that."

She eagerly did it, taking the tender mounds into her hands, massaging them to the point where both nipples almost met. His expression almost made her come. His seductively low voice called again. "Slide from the panties."

She did one better by moving the garment to her hips and sliding a hand inside, stroking her own dripping-wet sex just for his benefit. The way he watched her made her come hard that time. What added to the tension was how he stroked himself while watching her. Her eyes peered into the tub, wishing, hoping that even a part of his luscious tip would poke from the water.

"Get in with me, baby. Take me to another world."

No words, no nothing, just lots and lots of oozing action. The minute she stepped into the warm, soothing water, she knew there was only one move to make. His hands braced her as she lowered herself onto his erection. The deeper she lowered onto him, the more she could feel her muscles constricting, accommodating him, taking him all in until she felt so full and solid—full of solid, hot cock, and it was ready to be driven.

Before he got into action mode, he kissed her, kissed her long and hard, making her moan and call to him just by one kiss. He was good like that, and she loved it like that. All of it put together was cool like that!

As their lips met, Ethan heard the distant sounds of the Christmas music—another one of his favorites, Bing Crosby's Hawaiian Carol, "Mele Kalikimaka." He definitely was in the literal tropics each time his lips met Beverly's. And to add to his delight, he strategically placed the bubbles around her nipples, making the tender, pointed buds reach out to him. With a quick rinse, the darkly hued nipples were again in licking distance. He devoured them, one after the other, playing with one while sucking decadently on the other.

Everything Ethan touched on her gave her goose bumps, but her breasts were especially sensitive to him. The harder he pulled and nipped at the heightened peaks, the more she rode him. At first, her thrusts were gentle, rhythmic, quickly becoming more rugged, faster, moving so hard up and down on him water was splashing from the circular tub. The hell she cared—she'd come a long way to be with a lover way beyond no other, and she planned on taking it and him to the ultimate max. The harder she moved on him, the more she could feel her sex tightening around his. He felt like a mountain within her, one that was ready to release heat in eruptions that were totally outrageous. But not yet.

Complete lovemaking had to last, and as she danced upon him, listening to all that lovely Christmas music, the more she had to feel him. His smooth, hard body mixing with the heat from the water made that winding feeling within her core return with a fury. All she wanted to do was let it go, let it pour from her in sheets of melted passion, yet there was still more.

Ethan edged her on by holding her sides as she pounded him. The look on his face as he watched the only woman he ever really loved making love back to him was way more than a

Kodak moment, it was a portrait waiting to happen. Love danced in his eyes, and seeing that love returned made him take her to that ultimate moment faster and faster. His hands wrapped around her hips and held her in place as he rocked ferociously backward and forward. He knew she loved it rough, and giving it to her in the harshest yet most arousing ways was all he planned to do for the rest of his life. Adding additional pressure to her sex made him see stars, lightning, rain, fireworks—everything. Yet *he* still needed more.

His mouth covered hers again as he moved two fingers into her alongside his shaft. Double duty, and Beverly's muscles relaxed enough to accommodate every inch of him. What made him rock to the ends of the earth was hearing her scream out those terribly sexy moans and screams. That was another thing about Beverly: her lustful screams triggered every reaction in him. No woman had ever made the great and powerful Oz scream in utter mania, yet she had accomplished that by being with him the first time.

They came together in powerful thrusts, wetting everything in the vicinity, including Debbie's marbled dark-red-and-cream tiled floor. What the hell—everything else was wet, why not that? As Ethan watched his lover squirm from a monster of an orgasm, he quickly made her stand, parted her legs and felt the rest of her climax as he sucked it from her. That was a feeling he'd never forget, how her body quivered all over his lips. The best part, her cream was so sweet, so moist and alive, just like the rest of her.

Out of breath and lovin' it, Beverly relaxed against him, feeling the still-warm water tickling her breasts as she returned to a seated position between his thighs. Her hands smoothed his muscular thighs. "I've never done it in a tub before."

"Did you like it?"

"Out-fucking-standing!"

"Good, because we did everything else but bathe. Perhaps we should do that."

"Bathing you is another one of my fantasies. However, this isn't the first time I've seen you in a tub. You took my baby sister's plastic tugboat and was in the tub with it. Naturally I was over and had to use the potty. I stepped in and saw you with Christy's boat, and I took it! Your naked butt chased me all over the house, and I got the biggest kick out of watching those spindly legs of yours."

He smoothed her cheek. "Are they still spindly?"

"No. Neither is anything else on you, for that matter."

"Now you can take anything I have and give me a good sudsing down, to boot! I'm still a filthy son of a—"

"No, you're not, but a good bath would be a bittersweet end to this glorious evening. Where's the bath gel?"

Ethan reached behind him and retrieved a container, handing it to her with sudsy hands. "I think you'll like this soap. It's scented."

She opened the box only to see another box inside it—a midnight-blue satiny box. Her eyes bugged. "What is this?"

"Soap! Open it, and get busy on me."

"Ethan! What have you done?"

"Just open it. Always questioning with that empirical mind of yours."

Beverly slowly opened the box, listening as it creaked open. Revealing itself to her was a diamond cluster engagement ring. Her fingers delicately touched it as if it would break. Her voice was a quivering mass of happiness. "Ethan, is this what I think it is?"

"I sure hope so, baby." He slid the ring from the box and onto her finger. "I've always wanted to say this to you, but you were either not around or busy thinking I was still a kid—which I was at the time. I love you, Beverly. I love you more than I love the air I breathe, and nothing would make my life more complete other than you marrying me. So will you marry me? Be my full-time baby and my lifetime mistress?"

Her watery eyes stared into his as he spilled his feelings to her. She stopped him in midsentence. "Yes, Ethan!"

He blinked, not believing the words he thought he heard. "Did you say yes to me?"

She strummed his smiling cheeks. "I said yes to you. I said yes to Debbie's baby brother."

"You will?" He pulled her body into his, kissing her lips in lavish form. "I'll finally have the wife I've always wanted."

"And me the husband I've always wanted."

Instead of towel drying every portion of her, he licked her in all the delicate areas, starting with her lips, working his way down. Her still-throbbing, warm core was so ready for his re-visitation. When his tongue entered her, flicking around her clit, a smile came to her face, a thought to her mind. *I can have this forever.* Forever it would be, because once Ethan Jacobs got his clutches into anything he wanted, it was for a lifetime.

The scent of peaches and cream filled the guest bedroom. Awaiting her was a sunken bed large enough for her and Ethan to do anything they wanted for however long it took. That's what she liked, a bed big enough to live a lifetime on—and with a loving husband she knew would take care of her for the rest of her life. The days of the revolving door were gone; no more of the man who operated on his own rules solely without a second thought to the woman he married. Ethan was a man, a real man, though she could still see that darling little face of a kid who had the perpetual terrible-twos syndrome. Now he was bad in other ways . . . superbad!

Mr. Super Bad now awaited her on the fresh silk sheets, patting the space next to him. His hand reached for hers and pulled her on top. "This is the first night you and I can really act like man and wife." His eyes gleefully looked to the ceiling. "Hmmm, man and wife. I like the sound of that."

"I *love* the sound of that. And I swear to you I'll make the best wife a man could ever want."

"You've done that already. The minute you took that damn tugboat from me, I knew you were everything. I've worked hard for what I have—the house, my dealerships, Danica. I just want my life to be something I can be proud of, for someone to be proud of me. I was always that kid everyone thought was nothing but a walking sperm bank; everyone thought my life would be nothing but one useless relationship after another. When Elaine and I broke up, hell, I thought the same things myself. But in the back of my mind, I knew I was more than that. Somehow or another, you were always a part of it."

She leaned over him and tenderly kissed the tip of his pointed nose. "I'm proud of you, if that counts for anything."

"It counts for everything. I just want to be good for you, for us."

A shriek of devilment illuminated her eyes. "Let me be good to you." She lowered his cotton boxers and glorified over how his maleness jumped out at her, all nine inches of him, steaming hot and ready to get fulfilled.

He was still damp from the bath and smelling like sex-and sage bath gel. The mixture suited him; the taste of it satisfied her as her tongue played with his tip, circling its middle. Her hot lips soon covered it, drawing on it slowly over and over as his eyes rolled in his head. His fingers tangled in her hair, massaging her scalp with the same intensity with which she was adorning him.

She took in his length completely, slowly moving him in and out as his hands massaged her back and sides. "I could do this with you twenty-four-seven, girl. You know that?"

No verbal response, just the continuance of her attack upon his scrotum, dragging her tongue across it and circling his base. He felt so good and hard, smelled like the luscious man he was. Nothing in her past life had ever been that good; no man had ever pleased her the way Ethan had. *They* had not been men, and it took a real man to point out a boy.

He awakened the next morning to find himself lying on top of her. They'd made love so hard and for so long the previous night they fell asleep in the process. They were still in the same position he remembered, doggy style. That was Beverly's favorite position, and being a man into cars the way he was, he was more than happy to "rear end" her any time she wanted him to.

When he slid from her, she automatically awakened, yawning with smiling eyes. "Wow, what time is it?"

"Still early."

"Did we do it all night long?"

"Last I looked at the clock, it was after three A.M. So, yeah, we did it all night, and it was mind-blowing. Each time with you is different, each position is a course in sensuality." He kissed her hand. "You didn't give me an answer to my question last night."

"What? About marrying you?"

"No, believe me, I remember that answer. The other question, you know . . . when we should make it legal."

She moved back into his arms. "As soon as possible. I've always wanted a New Year's Eve wedding. We can wed in the day, and let the reception last until just after midnight. That way, everyone can kiss us into a new year and a new life together. How's that sound?"

"Absolutely perfect. Let's go home and get started."

"On what, the wedding plans?"

"We can do that, too."

"You're a mess, Ethan. Haven't I worn you out enough?"

"Not hardly. I have a lifetime to go."

They descended the winding staircase with Danica behind them. The first to meet them were Debbie's two pit bulls who were literal cream puffs in every sense of the word—Pork Chop and Chrysanthemum. Their flowery barks brought Debbie from the kitchen. Her eyes widened to the sight of both Ethan and Beverly carrying suitcases. "What's going on here? I thought you two were staying a few days."

"No, we've got to get back. Things to do."

"Oh, right. You have to get Danica back to school. I forgot about that."

"Debbie, she's in kindergarten. What's she going to miss, nuclear science?"

"Cute, real cute, but I wanted to visit more with Bev." Debbie reached for her old buddy's hand. "Am I going to see you again?"

"That's a distinct possibility." She nudged Ethan's shoulder. "Should we tell her now?"

Debbie's eyes widened. "Tell me what? Come on, you guys!"

Ethan's arm tightened around his soon-to-be bride's waist. "I've asked Beverly to marry me, and she—"

"I said yes."

Debbie screamed her typical high-pitched scream that set off the dogs again. Everyone upstairs jumped out of bed and came tumbling downstairs as Debbie's words echoed in their ears. "They're getting married! They're getting married!"

Ethan and Beverly stood in the middle of the floor kissing as the crowd gathered.

As planned, Ethan and Beverly became Mr. and Mrs. Jacobs late on the day of December 31 and kissed their way into undeniable love at the stroke of twelve. They have been married for two years, and he's the best thing that could ever have happened to her. They have a nine-month-old daughter named Eden, who they are raising alongside Danica. Funny thing, Beverly never thought Ethan would produce girls; he looked more like the kind who would have a slew of rusty-butt boys.

The point to this story is simply this: girls, don't mistreat your friend's baby brothers. They may be bigger than you think!

Her Wildest Fantasy

Sydney Molare

1

_____

Present day

I pushed open the bar door with something akin to relief. I'd
had the bitch to end all bitches of a day! On top of that, I
needed some relief from my cell phone blowing up. Shoot, I'd
left that sucker in the car. Let them call away, 'cause ain't nobody gonna answer shit till tomorrow.

See, I quit both of my boyfriends today. Yeah, I woke up
and realized that I was dating two single men, yet I'm alone
every holiday and special occasion, like they're married or
something. Did they accept the new status quo, and leave it
alone? No. Hence the phone ringing every, and I do mean ev-e-ry,
few seconds. Dang, what is it about men that makes them lose
their minds when you end the relationship? I mean, they're always losing interest, moving on, or needing space. But when I
say I need the same thing . . . World War III, IV, and V are initi-
ated. Shit!

I eased myself onto a stool and looked around the half-filled
room. There were plenty of men present, but I didn't give them

more than a cursory glance. I'd had enough man drama to last me a lifetime.

The bartender stopped in front of me. "What would you like?"

I looked him over—earrings (blah!), tight-assed T-shirt, and a bald dome. Not bad, just not interested. "Got a Singapore Sling up in here?" I asked quietly.

"Nope."

"Sex on the Beach?" I offered.

"Nope."

Shit, that was my entire repertoire of drinks I liked. I shook my head slowly and said, "OK, what do you have sweet?"

He leaned closer to the countertop. "We've got Romper Room, Incredible Hulk, and a new one I call Fuck Till Sunrise." He winked seductively.

"Give me the Fuck Till Sunrise!" I was betting the drink was as delicious as the name.

"Coming up."

While he mixed the drink, my mind moved back to my ex-boyfriends. Tommy was a tall dark drink of water. His lanky body was true poetry in motion. Even though we didn't see each other nearly as much as I wanted, I loved the way he focused totally on me when we were together. This brother gave a Swedish deep-tissue massage that was an out-of-body experience! He used these massage lotions that got hot when he rubbed . . . oh! Everything was limp and pliable once his capable hands had roamed my body. Now, he was a little slim in the dick department, but his lightning tongue made me forget that. Shit, he ate pussy like he was in competition for the King of Cunnilingus title. I ain't mad about it, either. But still, seeing him once a week—maybe—just wasn't enough. And after a year, I guess he didn't see fit to increase the time we spent together, so I bounced.

Now, Felix was just the opposite of Tommy—golden and

thick. As a matter of fact, everything on this brother was thick—feet, dick, neck, thighs . . . The list goes on and on. This brother was a true roughneck. He spanked that ass, bucked me like a bronco, and tied bows in my tongue. He was a wild roller-coaster ride, and I willingly rode his ass without a seat-belt. But again, seeing him every psychedelic moon wasn't working. I mean, yeah, he worked late, but stop by on your way home, and toss this ass sometimes. I got tired of waiting until his day off. I think he teared up or something when I broke it off. His voice trembled, got low. I felt kind of bad . . . but like I said, don't wait until I'm out the door to let me know what I mean to you!

The bartender slid my drink in front of me. "Ah, sexy lady, I get off at two o'clock."

I glanced at the clock and saw it was only seven thirty. "Thanks for the info, but I'll be deep in dreamland by that time. I'll keep it in mind for another time, though." Right.

I gathered my drink and found a table. The music was an eclectic mix—Top 40, reggae, R & B with some slow jams every now and then. I leaned back and watched the other dancers, hoping the "somer teeth" men I always attracted didn't come breathing on my neck.

I was halfway through my drink when the chair next to me was pulled out and a familiar body sat in it—Felix. Neither of us said a word for a few minutes. His eyes devoured me. I wished I could say I felt uncomfortable, but, shit, let him look at what he let get away.

Finally, "Why?"

I sighed. "You know why."

He looked down and then back at me. "If you'd give us an-other chance, it won't be the same way."

"Yeah, right."

Felix leaned closer. "I mean it. Just give me another chance, baby."

I skipped replying, took another sip of my drink, and looked around the room. You know how you get that feeling that someone is staring at you? I felt the hair on the back of neck rise and knew someone was staring me down. My eyes filtered through the darkness and settled on two eyes boring into me three tables over. Tommy.

Shit!

What's the likelihood of both ex-boyfriends showing up at the same place and same time I'm at? Slim. These jokers must have a tracking device on my phone or something.

My hand trembled as I took a long gulp of my drink. The deejay put on a slow reggae song, and Felix gave me a smile. "This is our kind of music, girl." And he was correct. He'd always made mad love to slow reggae. "Let's dance."

I wanted to refuse but needed to delay the inevitable encounter with Tommy, so I took the proffered hand and walked onto the dance floor. He gyrated his hips, and I followed suit. His hands grazed up and down my waist as they always had. The music moved me, and I relaxed. I began dancing like an island girl—all pelvis, no upper body. Felix licked his tongue out and blew me a kiss. I blushed in spite of myself.

The song finally ended. I turned to walk off the floor, when the opening strains of R. Kelly's "You Made Me Love You" came on. Felix grabbed my waist from behind, and his minty breath said in my ear, "One more . . . for old time's sake."

I should have walked off the floor, but something in me just . . . couldn't. I leaned back onto that massive chest and grooved with his groove. His hand encircled my waist, pulled me forcefully backward. My ass met his hard dick. He shifted and allowed it to settle between my cheeks. I closed my eyes, willed myself to be strong . . . somehow.

When I opened my eyes, Tommy was still staring me down. I could make out the angry glint in his eyes from a distance of twenty feet. Felix's lips pressed into the back of my neck, and his breath floated down and tickled my chest. His hands slipped up and down my flat belly, pressing, releasing. I felt my nether lips begin to weep in ecstasy. I never broke eye contact with Tommy as Felix slowly massaged my ass with his dick, around and around, side to side. Lawd! How the beat held me hostage.

Tommy rose suddenly and strode toward the dance floor. I knew this could be some cemetery shit, but something told me it wasn't. Tommy stopped six inches from me. Felix never hesitated in his groove. I could see hell in Tommy's eyes, and, sure enough, the devil came out.

Tommy took a step closer, body now touching mine, before he began rocking to the beat himself. His hands reached around and cupped my ass cheeks, squeezing momentarily, as he molded his pelvis to mine. His dick was rock hard.

Aw, shit!

Tommy rubbed his dick up and down my clit, creating mini-sparks that caused me to jerk. My pussy sobbed.

Felix began nibbling on the left ear. Tommy took the right. Talk about a mind-blowing experience!

Felix kissed along the left shoulder. Tommy nipped along the right. Felix cupped my breasts and squeezed. My nipples were like diamonds. I'm sure they were etching FUCK ME into Tommy's chest.

Tommy nipped back to my ear and whispered, "Let me love you like you know I can," before he captured my lower lip in a teasing bite.

Not to be outdone, Felix pulled my head back and deep-throated me. He kissed my eyes, cheeks, and then whispered, "Nobody can love you like I will tonight."

Now, I don't care what they say about R. Kelly, but that was the right song, for the right occasion, played at the right time tonight! Dry-humped by two brothers I liked, and nobody complaining? Hell, I was doing some shit I'd only heard about, and I wasn't about to back down. Besides, my coochie was hysterical 'cause it was so horny.

I closed my eyes again as twin lips traced love notes on my skin, pelvises sizzled through fabric, and hands made promises I damn sure wanted them to keep. Fingers stroked, slid, pinched my waist, breasts, ass, hair . . . shit!

I don't know how long the song was, but it wasn't long enough. I was sad to hear it ending. As we broke apart, I noticed that people were standing and staring at us. I guessed we'd been the show. That's all right. If they'd had the chance, they would have done the same thing.

They both stepped back, and each offered me their hand. My skin tingled as I watched them stare at me. Make-up sex was definitely in the air . . . but which one?

Suddenly my fantasy of two men popped into the forefront of my mind. I imagined twin lips, hips, thighs intertwined with mine. Two sets of hands stoking my fires, two sets of cocks stroking me deep. . . . But, no, that was a fantasy, not reality.

Or could it be?

2

***

One year before

It was one of those warm, muggy summer nights in which the sky lay on my back and the stars shined like a marquee board. I'd wandered outside, nursing a glass of now-warm red wine, as I tried to find some relief from the smoke, loud music, and the usual suspects—the married, the separated-but-the-wife-doesn't-know-it, the have-a-live-in-girlfriend-who-didn't-understand-him, and the obviously gay.

I swatted at the mosquitoes feeding on my exposed arms while I stared at the moon and pondered the mysteries of relationships, or, rather, why I couldn't seem to stay in one, when—

"Have you ever danced with the devil in the pale moonlight?" a male voice said so near I could feel his breath in my mane.

The hair rose on my neck; the glass slipped from my fingers, shattering momentarily. I turned quickly, elbow connecting with the abdomen just at my back.

"Oomph!" The figure bent over.

I skirted the man and broken glass, intent on running for help. He must have noticed because he stretched out his hand to stop me. "Hold up. I'm not trying to hurt you." He stood slowly. Why I didn't run away . . . I don't know. Maybe it was the melodious voice that told me he wouldn't harm me, maybe it was my subconscious wanting me to make sure he was OK, maybe it was the night air and the fact I'd never met a man in this type of situation. Anyway, I was rooted to the spot. "Girl, you pack a mean punch." I could see that at his full height, he was around six foot two inches and lanky as a basketball player.

You know how you get that tingling when you meet someone? That was me at that moment. My hair flattened, my toes hummed, and I wrinkled my toes in anticipation.

The man took a step forward, and all tingling ceased as my fight-or-flight instinct returned. I moved farther away, toward the safety of the patio doors.

He saw me. "Wait a minute. I'm not going to eat you." The timbred voice stopped me, and I waited. "I see we've gotten off to a bad start." White teeth shone in the moonlight, but I couldn't see his face. "I'm Tommy, and you are?"

All right, at least he was pleasant. I took a hesitant step forward, eyes searching in the darkness for features, and stretched out my hand, reaching tentatively for his. "I'm Sonata."

"Glad to meet you, even though I scared you half to death," Tommy replied. His face moved out of shadows. I could see dark skin, a goatee, and those blinding teeth.

Not too bad. "Yeah," I replied, thinking the same thing.

He cleared his throat. "I've been noticing you for the past hour." I gave him a doubtful look. "Really. I'm here with some friends, hanging out for the night, and saw you over by the fireplace all alone." He laughed. "I wondered what in the world was wrong with these men in here! When I saw you leave, I thought I'd follow you out and introduce myself."

Uh-oh. Here we go. Wonder which category he's in? I held my breath for whatever was coming next. He must have read my face, because he held up his hands in surrender. "No, I'm not married, don't have a girlfriend, I rarely date, and I'm not gay or down low and in denial."

Well, he just answered all my questions. "Sure?" I teased, feeling like a weight had lifted.

"Positive. I'm free as a bird. Promise." Tommy crossed his arms across his chest in an act of sincerity.

This information made the bad start worth slugging through! I giggled as I thought of how I must have looked to him—crazy. "I'm in the same boat you're in then," I said, still giggling.

Tommy looked back at the doors. "This party is dead for me." Then he looked back at me. "Want to go somewhere for a drink and get better acquainted?"

My mama always told me never to go anywhere with strangers, but I was beginning to feel this man. I took a chance. "Sure. I know a nice bar not too far from here."

He nodded. "You driving?"

"Of course," I assured him. "You can follow me. I'm in the red Miata."

His lips parted in a teasing smile. "Gonna leave the top down?" he baited.

What's the point of owning a Miata unless the top is down? "Of course!" I threw back at him and strutted toward the door to leave.

We met in front of Lorenze's Bar and Grill not five minutes later. I was surprised to see his car was a Crown Victoria. The last man my age I'd seen in a Crown Vic was a cop. I definitely wondered if he was overly conservative; translation: dull as hell.

I kept my thoughts to myself as he opened the door for me. Chivalry is not dead! The bar's crowd was light so we grabbed two stools near the middle and quickly ordered. I was happy to see that unlike the norm, Tommy actually looked better in the light—Adonis versus Big Foot with a shave.

"So . . . what do you do?" I asked, making conversation.

The drinks arrived, and he paid for them before answering. "Now don't laugh, but . . . I'm a massage therapist."

A massage therapist riding in an old-ass Crown Vic? I couldn't help it . . . I laughed.

Tommy rolled his eyes and shook his head. "I knew you would laugh."

"So . . . sorry," I wheezed between breaths. "I was expecting you to say something totally different." Like mortician, postman, or minister. What? Plenty of ministers frequent Lorenze's. You know what they say, "Same crowd, church or the club."

"I know, teacher, banker, or something along those lines."

Not the lines I had in mind, but I kept it to myself. "Yeah, something like that."

"Hate to disappoint you, but I'm just a little massage therapist." He fisted his hands and patted his chest.

Suddenly my mind went on another tangent. "Hey, that's not code for a stripper, is it?" I interrogated, a frown on my face. The last thing I wanted in this day of AIDS was a stripper, aka a screw-anything-for-money man, as a boyfriend. Yeah, we weren't even there, but the potential was in the air!

He gave me an astonished look before he swiped the air and frowned. "No, indeed not! Do I look like a stripper?"

I gave him another once-over and decided he might be a little lean for the strippers I'd seen, but his body was buff, and if he was packing, he would fit the bill. I lifted an eyebrow. "You could. . . ."

"Girl, I am *not* a stripper! Now, think. Could you see me doing a table dance?"

That visual was something to write home to Mama about! I

could see him slowly pulling his shirt open, revealing—hope-fully—hairy nipples, and then gyrating and grinding those hips while he flexed his chest muscles, his tongue hanging out between those succulent lips—

"Hey, you still there?" Tommy was waving his hand in front of my face.

I was so caught up in the fantasy, I didn't respond until he snapped his fingers under my nose. "Yeah. I'm still here."

"You looked like you'd gone into outer space or something. I was beginning to wonder—"

I cut him off. "I'm here. Wonder no more."

Tommy looked at his watch. "Wow, it's already two A.M."

This made me suspicious. "You got a curfew?" I asked, wait-ing to hear him go back on the "I'm free as a bird" shit he'd said earlier.

"No. Just have an early appointment."

OK . . . I guessed he must not be a stripper, because he couldn't hang all night. "What time?" I inquired.

"The first one is ten A.M. After that, I've got them every hour until four P.M."

I didn't even realize that many people got massages. "Do you go to their homes, or do you work in a shop?"

The smile was back. "I'm a mobile masseuse. My slogan is, 'I'll rub you down wherever, whenever.' "

"That's some slogan. You could read anything you wanted into it." I winked.

He backed up, hands back in the air. "Oh, no. I'm strictly business. No 'extras.' "

I laughed at that. "I'll bet they're asking."

He laughed along with me before replying, "Not too many, but some do ask."

"I know why," I mumbled before I took a sip of my drink.

"What?" Tommy asked.

"Nothing." I smiled to assure him, and then I pulled his wrist to mine and looked at his watch. "Time's moving on. Since you have an early appointment, I'll get out of your hair."

His eyes became hooded. "If there was ever anything I wanted entangled in my hair, it's you," Tommy said, his low, liquored breath flitting across my face.

I couldn't help it. My estrogen surged, clit jumped, uterus contracted, and my nipples stood up and saluted. Tommy saw the nipples and licked his lips. I squirmed in my seat, felt the juices welling at the entrance. Tommy noticed. He traced along my cheek and down my neck to the throat. His knuckles grazed my pulse. My clit pulsed in sync with my heartbeat.

Tommy leaned in. I saw his lips part, felt his hand along the back of my neck, pulling me closer. Could have cried as his other hand found my waist and squeezed lightly. His lips made contact with mine. At first, I was hesitant, but as his tongue parted my teeth and flipped my tongue every which way but loose, I found my hands reaching up to palm his ass, squeezing. His muscles contracted under my fingers; my clit engorged farther.

He slanted my head and deepened the kiss. I opened my eyes to see him watching me, desire glazing his corneas. My tongue was thrusting and twisting, intertwined and entangled. He kept pace, pulled me tighter. Shit! I felt the wetness seep from my coochie, felt my pelvis begin a slow grind in search of its counterpart. I'd begun to slide from the stool—

"Ahem." A voice dragged me back to reality. "Y'all need to get a room."

Oh, my goodness! I'd forgotten where I was . . . and the fact that I really didn't know this man. I snatched my mouth from Tommy, the red shame creeping up my neck.

Tommy looked over my head and smiled in the direction of the bartender. "My bad. Guess we got carried away."

"Yeah. Now you need to carry her away up out of here." I heard the peevishness in the voice and felt my face flame hotter.

"It's all good," Tommy replied with a chuckle before looking down at me. "You ready to go?"

I nodded. Tommy stepped back, and I slid off the stool and walked on shaky legs to the exit without waiting for him. How could I have been kissing a man in public like that? A man I'd met less than an hour ago? The embarrassment made me walk faster.

"Hey, you trying to get rid of me?" Tommy said as he stepped in front of me to open the door.

He didn't know how close to the truth he'd come. I kept my eyes averted as I answered, "No. I'm just ready to get home." I never broke stride once on the sidewalk.

Tommy put his hand over mine as I opened the Miata's door. "Wait a minute." I stood still, back to him. He turned me stiffly around. "Hey, this has got you all stressed, hasn't it?" He ran his hands up and down my arms as I stared into his chest. A finger lifted my chin, and I looked into eyes, which were full of concern. "I agree we got carried away, but it's not the end of the world. We're two adults who seem to dig each other. . . . We just happened to find out in the middle of a bar full of people," he finished. "Not against the law. Maybe poor judgment but not against the law."

His arm-rubbing, along with his positive spin on the situation, seemed to calm me. He was right. We may not have used the best judgment, but kissing in public *ain't* against the law except . . . I wanted to dick him down right there. Now that *would* have been against the law! I gave a shit-sorry grin and remained silent.

"Want me to follow you home?" he asked.

A part of me wanted him to do more than follow me home. I wanted him naked under me, on top of me, behind m—

"Earth to Sonata." Tommy was waving his hands in my face again.

I blinked at him. "What?"

"Your body was here but your mind over there." He pointed to the left.

Uh-uh. My body was way farther down the road than that. "Sorry."

"Apology accepted. So, do you want me to follow you home?"

"No. I'll be fine," I said.

Tommy pulled me close, kissed my hair, and then released me and opened the door. He had it halfway shut before he opened it again. I gave him a questioning look.

"Can I have your phone number?" he asked politely.

I know, halfway to bed and don't even know his phone number . . . or last name. My face flamed anew. "Sure," I muttered and rummaged around in my purse before finding a business card. I wrote my number on the back and handed it to him. He looked it over a minute before asking, "And can I take you out tomorrow?"

I wasn't expecting the question, so it made me pause. After a moment I concluded I hadn't been on a date in a minute, so I was game. "Where and what time?"

"Hmmm." Tommy looked into the air. "Since I don't know where you live, how about we meet here and go from there?"

"All right. Dressy or relaxed?"

Tommy leaned in close, voice low again. "I tell you what. You get dressed like you want to, and we'll let your dressing style dictate where we go."

That was a novel idea, and I liked it. "Got money to burn, huh?"

Tommy laughed. "Not really, but I can hold my own."

"We'll see. I can be high maintenance," I fenced, feeling him again.

"You're in luck. My last job was a maintenance man," he answered before closing the door tightly and winking.

My, my, my . . .

3

Manicures, pedicures, hairstyling, and clothes shopping took up most of the time before my date with Tommy. I couldn't get over how I was acting like a high school girl—anxious, hoping he'd like what I wore, praying my hair would stay beauty-shop ready. By the time I hopped in the tub just a little after five, my nerves were frayed and my self-confidence hanging on by a piece of lint.

Tommy called around five thirty and said he would be in front of Lorenze's at seven. I oiled, patted, and perfumed in anticipation. I discarded the clothes I'd bought just that day and decided instead on a spaghetti-strapped number that could be formal or casual, depending on how he was dressed. Manolo Blahnik stilettos completed the outfit.

I drove to Lorenze's at six forty-five and waited outside. Tommy pulled up not five minutes later in the Crown Vic. He parked and walked back to me, holding the door open as I exited the Miata. Before he spoke, a whistle split his lips.

"Girl, you looked good last night, but you outdid yourself today!"

I giggled at the appreciative look in his eyes. "Quit," I said, punching his arm lightly.

"I'm serious." He whistled again. "You look yummy enough to chow down on!"

His compliment went straight to my head, and I twirled to show myself off fully before I struck a pose—legs wide, hip thrust to the side, one hand on my waist.

I saw his khakis began to tent, and my smile widened. My fingers ran lightly across his poloed chest before landing on an erect nipple. Tommy's eyes glazed over. He shook his head. "Let's get out of here before we end up making out on the street this time." He held out his hand.

"You think?" I asked innocently.

"Not think, I *know*," he emphasized.

The air crackled with energy. I grabbed his hand and strutted past him, pulling him along. I wiggled my hips like Mama taught me and was rewarded with a, "Yes, indeed. I must be living right." I didn't know about all that but was elated at the attention nevertheless.

He seated me in his car before sliding into the driver's seat and turning toward me. "I had one place in mind, but looking at you in that dress, I'm thinking somewhere totally different." His eyes searched my face.

"Is that right?" I vacillated between hoping he meant his apartment—where I knew he'd get me to do anything he wanted—and taking it slow.

"What's your fantasy?"

That question hit me from outfield. Usually a man asked me that when we were in the act or just about to sex each other down, not during the preliminary talk of our first date. Something about the earnest look on his face made me want to tell him the truth: I wanted a ménage à trois with two men.

Yes, two hot bodies rubbing against mine, two mouths suckling my tight nipples as I held and stroked two cocks. Forget that two-woman shit, I wanted a man pumping into my cunt while one loved my ass at the same time. My clit lurched at the thought alone. God, I wanted to feel two sets of balls slapping into my ass, taste two cocks in my mouth . . . but I couldn't bring myself to mouth the words, so I stared, silent.

He must have taken this as a too-strong come-on because he said, "Hey, just forget it. We'll go where I'd planned in the first place."

I deflated. I don't know why, because he *did* ask, and I'm the one who didn't answer him. I guess I wanted him to press the issue, find out the *real* truth about me. Instead, I gave another sorry smile and looked out the window.

The rest of our conversation was safe. No more revealing questions were asked by him, and I followed suit. Soon Tommy slowed and drove into the parking lot of Tahoe, a new dinner place I'd heard about but hadn't gotten around to discovering myself.

The place had a nautical theme—rope with anchors tied into it, fish netting on the wall, and oceanic prints everywhere. The maître d' found our reservation and seated us in moments. I ordered an apple martini and chilled shrimp as my appetizer. He asked for the salmon canapé.

"So, tell me again why a woman as delicious-looking as you is single?" Tommy asked after the waiter left.

I thought of the trite answers: I'm waiting for Mr. Right; men are dogs; I want love and a commitment. Lies . . . but I didn't believe he could handle the truth. So instead I said, "Oh, I guess I'm . . ." I waved my hand, searching for an appropriate word. When none came to mind, I settled on, ". . . different."

"Different. How?" Tommy quirked an eyebrow.

How do you tell someone interested in you that you don't want to share a man but . . . you want to be shared by two men? I've tried and tried the monogamous relationships, but, truth be told, they get stale after a while. If I were honest, I'd admit that I've gotten to the point where two people having straight sex was boring as hell. I *craved* more, something rare, unique.

I ran my tongue over my lips, buying time. Shoot, the way he was looking at me, I ought to tell him I'm gay or . . . a man. I changed my mind when I remembered the reactions of people when they found out something like that. "I don't seem to . . . go with the norm." There.

"You mean you don't like to do stuff like other women?"

Most women I knew would love my idea, but he wouldn't understand, so I said, "Something like that."

Tommy nodded. "Doesn't sound like you're too different. My sisters hate to shop, hate to sit around beauty shops all day and gossip, and hate to cook."

"Sounds like me, all right."

The waiter returned with our appetizers.

Suddenly I decided I was tired of the usual get-to-know-you dinner. I wanted something different. Spicier. "So where did you *really* want to take me?" I asked before I bit into my shrimp.

Tommy placed the canapé halfway to his mouth and then back on the plate. A smile played across his lips. He cleared his throat. "It's a place called Video."

"Never heard of it."

"It's exclusive, so unless you're a member, you wouldn't."

"Where is this club?"

"Club? It's not a club . . . per se."

This piqued my curiosity. "What does 'not a club, per se' mean?"

"It's . . . *difficult* to explain. I'll just say the entertainment is something you probably have never seen before and may never see again."

I liked that idea. "Unique" was my middle name. "We still got time to go?"

"You sure?" Tommy took my hand. "This may change your . . . opinion about me."

"What opinion? I just met you yesterday, remember?"

"All right. Let's go."

Tommy signaled for the waiter, paid the check, and buckled me into my seatbelt. Before he pulled out into traffic, he said, "Get ready for a mind-blowing experience."

I didn't know what was in store, but my self-confidence had climbed back to maximum capacity, and I refused to miss out on another thing that interested me, good or bad. "I already am."

4

We zipped along the downtown area. I wanted to ask more questions, but I followed his lead and kept quiet, waited to see for myself. The street we pulled onto had brownstones lining it from one end to the other. I could see no building that would house a club . . . *per se*. Tommy found an empty space halfway down the block. No people were outside, and I was thinking he had made a detour to his house before we continued on. I changed that thought when he stepped outside, walked over to my side, and opened the door.

"We're here?" I asked.

"Yes. Guess you were expecting something else, huh?"

"Yeah," I replied as I looked up and down the residential area. "I would never have expected a club called Video to be here, that's for sure."

"You'd be surprised at what goes on on a nice, quiet street like this," Tommy said, mouth just above my ear.

His breath made my clit jump, and I zoned out for a moment. I came back when he pulled me beside him and began walking down the street. We stopped in front of a nondescript door two houses down. Tommy pushed the buzzer, and I was surprised to see a small window slide open and a voice ask, "Password?"

"Hedonist," Tommy replied with a smile.

This was getting interesting as all get out! I waited expectantly as the door swung open and a blond man wearing sunglasses ushered us in. He stepped outside and looked both ways before stepping back inside and closing the door.

Hmmm. I clutched my purse tighter.

"My man," the man said and embraced Tommy.

"What's up, Sims?"

"The same old stuff." Sims turned to me. "And who do we have here?"

"Sonata, Sims. Sims, Sonata," Tommy answered.

I held out my hand, and Sims took it and brushed it with his lips. "Delicious."

Tommy grabbed my hand from him. "Enough of that."

Sims laughed and winked before looking at Tommy. "I understand. What will be your pleasure tonight?"

"Straight," Tommy replied.

"Straight two, three, or anything goes?"

My mind was churning from the code play. What did "straight two, three, or anything goes" mean? I didn't get much time to ponder as Tommy stared at me a moment and then answered, "Let's start with straight two."

Sims popped his fist with Tommy's before he said, "I feel ya. Need the set up, huh?"

"No, but don't want to overload Sonata too soon."

With what? I wanted to scream.

"Soundstage Two ought to do the trick," Sims assured him. "Better hurry. The show is about to start."

"Good deal. "

Tommy took my hand and pulled me down a hallway. Doors were on both sides. I couldn't hear anything but the hiss of the central air. We stopped in front of a door with the number 2 painted on it. My anticipation level moved into the anxiety zone.

He opened the door, and I could see a well-lit room with rows of theater seating. A curtain hung in front of the first row, but I could see more light through the cracks. Television screens were suspended on each side of the curtain. A few couples were already seated and paid us no mind.

A play! He'd brought me to see a play. I wondered what all the fuss was about. A play wasn't that unusual for me, so I couldn't understand all the subterfuge. We settled on a row a third of the way down and in the middle seats. The lights began to dim just as we leaned back in our seats.

"Which play is this?" I leaned over and asked.

"What?" Tommy frowned.

"Which play are we seeing?" I clarified. I knew there were some playing in town, but it wasn't out of the norm to have a local artist put on something I hadn't heard about. Get local input and all.

Tommy chuckled and patted my hand. "Girl, I'll just say, you haven't heard of this one before."

Definitely a local artist.

I settled in my seat and waited for the curtain to open. I didn't have to wait long. In moments the red velvet slid open to reveal an apartment setting with a large bed in the middle. *Great, another relationship drama.* I held my tongue as canned music began playing, and a blond woman wearing hot pants and a halter walked into the room. Men holding cameras zoomed in from the sides. The televisions clicked on, and close-ups of the action on the stage began playing.

"What kind of play has cameras?" I whispered.

"This kind. Just watch and wait," Tommy whispered back.

The woman puttered around the bed, shifting pillows and pulling at the comforter, before sitting on the edge and removing her shoes. I gasped as she began removing her clothing next. Her breasts were large, and the nipples a dusty gold-brown and pointed. Her bush was shaped into a triangle, and her fingers spread her lips until her clit was visible. I gripped the seat, entranced and appalled. Tommy saw my reaction, smiled, and then winked.

A man emerged from a side door wearing only a bathrobe. He didn't speak but walked up slowly behind the woman and grabbed her around the waist. She turned in his arms and opened her mouth wide as he pressed his mouth on top of hers. The man's hands roamed and then cupped her ample behind. The woman pressed in closer, and her hands disappeared beneath the bathrobe.

My mouth felt dry as a lightbulb went off in my head. This wasn't a play. It was a porno video shoot!

My idea was confirmed as the man shrugged off the bathrobe, revealing an erect cock wrapped in the woman's hands. As the cameras shot a close-up, I saw that his cock was long—nine or ten inches—and fat. She pulled her mouth from his and kneeled. Her tongue licked up one side and down the other before she pressed her lips around the swollen red head. Another close-up showed her engulfing it an inch at a time. The man grabbed her tresses and pulled himself deeper. She bobbed her head slowly; a moan escaped from her throat. I almost moaned with her as my clit engorged, and pussy juice leaked past my lips. I shifted in my seat and crossed my legs against the sensations, my eyes held hostage by the images.

The woman now sucked in earnest. The man held on to her hair, set his feet, and pumped into her waiting mouth. I could see the imprint of him in her throat.

Shit!

"That's it, baby. Suck it all," the man encouraged.

My tongue inadvertently licked my lips. I wanted, no, *felt* like I'd changed places, and his fat cock was down my throat. Tommy placed his hand over mine and began massaging it slowly. His touch made my pussy juice multiply exponentially.

I wanted to leave . . . and I wanted to stay. *You wanted excitement, so you've got it,* my mind chided me. I glanced around the room and saw people in various states of sex play—tongues down throats, hands down blouses, and one head where there'd previously been two.

The man pushed the woman onto the bed. He spread her legs wide before licking the insides of her thighs and moving upward. He parted her lips, and a zoom shot of her stiff pink clit made my womb clench. He dipped his head and latched on to it. His tongue roamed over her clit before he sucked the tip. The woman's hips lifted off the bed at his touch.

Damn! This shit is good!

His head swirled, bobbed, figure-eighted as his tongue vibrated on the clit. A finger slipped inside her. The woman bucked against his face, grabbed his head, and pressed him closer.

I leaned forward, nipples sensitized as hell, as I watched the screen. Tommy massaged my back. I inconspicuously slipped my hand beneath my dress and tweaked my own clit.

The man slid lower, his tongue now pushing inside her labial lips. His head and fingers thrust in concert. I knew the woman was about to come as she cupped and sucked her own breasts. In seconds she screamed, her juices spewing out.

I could barely sit; my hips gyrated on their own now. I was held rapt as the man smeared his hands in her honey and massaged it over his cock. He then removed some clamps held by a chain from a nightstand and clipped them on to her nipples.

The woman just moaned. He turned her over and pulled her to her knees, the chain held in his hands. He positioned himself behind her and then surged inside her with one great thrust. The woman arched her back and yelled, "Deeper, baby, I like it deeper," and pushed her ass higher into the air

The man gripped her ass and rode his mare. His huge balls swung in the air, smacked against her clit. The man slapped her ass hard. The woman gyrated. He slapped her ass again and again and again. Her ass was red, but still she gyrated like hell!

I never realized my dress straps had been lowered until I felt fingers pulling on my nipples. I wish I could say I jumped up, slapped Tommy, and ran out of there.

Instead . . .

I turned and pulled his head down to my breasts. My mind cautioned me to go slow; don't let things get out of control. But as his hands weighed and squeezed my heavy globes, I threw caution to the wind. Didn't care if FAST was stamped on my forehead as soft lips licked the turgid tips and then suctioned them deep. *Damn!*

Hormones zipped through my bloodstream, and my body trembled as his tongue slowly circled my stiff berries. I arched my back as the invisible string connecting my breasts and clit was drawn taut, so taut. Molten fire curled in my pussy, licked outward to burn my stroking fingers. I held on to the back of his head, kept those glorious lips melded to my aching buttons. My clit throbbed in pleasure; I stroked faster.

I couldn't stop my body's reactions, became a willing prisoner of pleasure. I shifted Tommy to the other nipple, felt his hands nestle in my curls, commandeering my clit. I opened my legs, gave him room to part my labial lips, find my fiery pussy.

I gasped as Tommy's fingers massaged my clit slowly, thoroughly. His thumb slid open my folds, dipped into my nectar, and then spread the slippery honey around the entrance. Other fingers joined the thumb, and muscles liquefied as he pushed one, two . . . more inside. A loud moan escaped from my mouth but was abruptly killed as he found my G-spot and the air stilled in my chest.

I tried to regain some semblance of sanity, tried to slow my traitorous body, but the combination of his mouth on my nipples, thumb on my clit, and fingers in my pussy drove me out of my mind! I writhed in ecstasy, my body moving innately to fulfill its need.

I grabbed Tommy's head, unlatching his lips from my nipples, and licked the succulent oral twins before I clamped them on mine. He stabbed, probed, and tied my tongue in knots, promised me Xanadu with his lightning sword. I swallowed, inhaled, twisted beneath his luxurious mouth; whimpered in pleasure as I tried valiantly to match his pace.

"Like that?" Tommy whispered against my lips.

I answered by bucking against his hand, felt his wood as I groped the front of his pants. My hands squeezed, roamed up and down the thick muscle, thumb stroking across his tip. He squirmed, pressed fingers deeper inside of me, letting me know I was on point. I moved lower, cupped the sac. He inhaled sharply, hands tangled in my hair, as his tongue shifted into high gear. I rubbed and stroked, needed to take him where he had taken me.

Oh, how I wanted to drag his dick into the open air, push his cock inside me, and ride as I felt my juices slide between my cheeks. Wanted to throw my legs across his shoulders, let him sip the nectar he'd manufactured, when—

The man on the screen screamed, pulled out, and sprayed himself across the woman's ass. My clit lurched. I tried to slow my hips, Tommy's fingers, but it was beyond my control. I bit Tommy's tongue as pinpricks leaped up my legs to my clit, where a geyser of juice covered his stroking hand. . . .

The curtain closed, and the lights stayed dim. I could hear the sounds of lovemaking going on around us. Tommy was biting my ear, blowing occasionally. My body still hummed, clit still strummed. We shared breath as our heartbeats slowed. Still, I could hardly move when he said, "Ready to go?"

I was . . . but where to?

5

The drive back to Lorenze's was quiet. I was still on my sexual high, trying to suppress the moans waiting to be heard as I replayed the night's scenes over and over. It might be whorish of me, but I'd be lying if I said I wished I'd never gone to Video. That kind of shit was just what the lover in me needed in order to wake things up! Tommy was right about one thing: my opinion about him did change. He had zoomed to the top of the attractiveness meter.

I was strung out, tight with sexual energy, as we pulled behind my Miata. I wanted more than his fingers. I wanted his dick licking the insides of my pussy, making my nectar flow like water from me. Tommy must have felt the energy. He stopped and said, "I don't want this night to end. I want to love you up and down. See you come on me. Me come in you."

My clit lurched again. I tried to suppress it, tried to act nonchalant, not too eager. My throat was dry; my voice faltered. "I . . . I want that, too."

A smile split his lips. "What a woman wants . . . I want also. Your place or mine?"

"Yours," I said, giving him a return smile.

* * *

I followed him to his apartment. I was happy to see it was an upscale complex; no need to worry about the Miata. He parked and rushed back to open my door. I grabbed my purse and took his outstretched hand.

As we rode the empty elevator to the seventh floor, hands brushed and lingered with promises. A kiss was placed behind an ear, a squeeze made on tight buttocks, a finger run across a tented front. By the time the elevator door opened, my legs closely resembled thick ropes of cooked spaghetti as I exited in front of him.

A key was inserted into the lock, and the door sprang open. I eyeballed the layout briefly before Tommy turned me into his arms, pushed me against the door, bruised my lips with the force of his kiss. I reciprocated fully. His fingers tap-danced down my neck to my breasts. Fingers grabbed and released, plucked tight nipples through silk. I sighed into his mouth before cupping the outline of his sex. The room whispered with the sounds of flesh meeting flesh, moans rumbling deep in throats, and fabric sliding on fabric.

With lips still melded together, a hand was placed beneath my knees, and I was lifted into the air. He strode down a hallway and through a door—to his bedroom. I could *smell* the masculinity in the room. He lay me down gingerly and then turned me over. I wondered what he would do next . . . but not for long. His fingers pulled at my zipper, slid it slowly down my back.

Tommy's breaths increased in frequency; I smiled in the moonlit darkness.

His hand lingered on my butt before spreading the silk and the straps from my shoulders. The dress moved down my body like well-oiled machinery—no hitches. I was left only in lacy white pantalets. He teased them from me slowly.

A drop of perspiration fell onto my back; my skin sucked the moisture in.

I heard the rustling of him removing his clothes. I didn't turn over to watch but waited for him to rejoin me. A knee dipped the bed. His fingers teased up my back to my neck. The brief contact made me grit my teeth in blissful agony. The fingers stiffened, began a circular rotation on my upper back. They kneaded, rubbed deliciously across my muscles. Oil was dripped down my spine and blown upon. It heated, created a mini inferno on my skin. My ass lifted, begged to be included. Tommy ignored it and massaged the oil into my back. He was *definitely* a masseuse!

His lips found my ear and blew into it; I pressed my clit into the bed. His tongue followed; I gripped the spread. He nipped my neck; I opened my mouth, gulped air. His hands slid beneath me and plucked my nipples; my hands massaged his arms. His tongue trailed down my back to my hips; my body clenched as he kissed the cheeks.

The oil returned. It dripped across my hips and then down the valley between. He straddled me. His cock lay against me. My legs opened slightly, allowed the cock to dip between them. His hand began massaging my hips, light and then firm.

His tongue was in the curve of my back. I trembled. "Well, well, well, what do we have here?" Tommy whispered against my hips. I trembled more.

I couldn't reply as his tongue slid down into my valley . . . and lower. My cheeks were spread. His wet tongue traced around and around before flicking across the entrance.

Oh, the sensations!

My trembling legs opened, gave him full access. His tongue flicked across a few more times before it pressed inside. I moaned, shot onto my elbows, lifted my ass. His tongue swirled, stabbed at the virgin tissue. My pussy snapped, gushed from his anal ministrations. His fingers filled that beseeching orifice. I bucked from the double onslaught.

More fingers pressed into me; more pussy lubricant resulted. His thumb found my clit; his tongue stabbed deeper. I wanted to cry, wanted to sing as his lips, his tongue, his fingers annihilated me. Left me breathless, strung tight as a bow.

The lips, tongue, and fingers were removed. My body cried for their return. I heard the crackle of plastic before the appendages resumed where they had left off.

My nerves hummed with anticipation . . . anxiety. I *needed* to be filled. Needed to be stroked, pumped, pistoned into. I gyrated my ass and was rewarded. Tommy lifted, grasped a thigh in each hand, and pulled backward, propelled me to my knees. His cock wasted no time filling my pussy. It wasn't as large as I craved, but it filled me up nicely.

Tommy pumped slowly at first. The pleasure-pain was excruciatingly delicious as he withdrew an inch at a time before pushing back into me inch by inch. My pussy groped, sucked, grabbed at his dick, bathed it in slippery lovers' juice.

I tried valiantly to match his strokes, let him set the pace, when my pussy's innate rhythm took me over. It forced my hips to clench and swirl, forced my legs and arms to thrust backward on the dick faster and faster. Forced Tommy to piston forward into me, match me pounding thrust for pounding thrust. My hips slapped against his belly; his balls slapped against my clit as we bumped, humped, grinded, and swerved toward the same goal. I reached between my legs and squeezed the juice-covered balls. Tommy kicked into high gear.

I was *so* into this shit now! I released his balls, arched my back, and bucked him. The sound of bodies slapping against each other reverberated around the room. When I Kegeled him, his breath faltered, body stiffened. In seconds, a roar of, "*God-*

damn! *God*damn! Goddamnnnnnnn!" split the air as he spasmed, hands melding my hips to his dick.

His reaction made the pinpricks zip from my feet to my nub. I detonated. My clit sprayed; my pussy squirted cum. We slumped onto the bed.

Spent.

6

I woke to lips on my earlobes and hands roaming up my belly before fingers tugged at my nipples. Tommy's breath drifted across my cheeks and down to my breasts. My hands reached behind me, roamed up and down his legs, his hips. His fingers moved from my nipples and flitted into my belly button before, tangling in my bush, where they stroked and massaged and then landed on my clit. I moaned and undulated on him. I felt his dick rising, poking into my hips.

Tommy's fingers rubbed and plucked at my clit. My hands squeezed his ass before nestling between our melded bodies and cupping his dick. My fingers slid lightly up his rod and encircled the head. I felt his pre-cum and lubed his long shaft. He grabbed my face, stuck his tongue down my throat, bathed my tonsils in his saliva.

I gasped as a finger entered me. Tommy left my mouth and attached his succulent lips to my breast. He suckled. The sensation felt like a hot wire was connected between my nipple and my clit. I moaned and coated his finger in juice.

Tommy shifted and laid me down on my back before he

lifted over me. His finger never left my pussy. Instead, more fingers joined the first. My legs splayed wider, my gut clutched, my pussy leaked like a half-opened faucet. Tommy kissed down my chest and my abdomen to my pubis. His teeth pulled lightly at my bush.

My body was overheated, on fire with desire. I rubbed his head, gyrated my hips, guided him toward my mother lode. Just as I thought he would lick my yearning clit, he lifted and rolled me onto my stomach. I felt shortchanged . . . but only for a moment. He spread me wide before letting his breath flutter across my ass. His tongue trailed across my cheeks and lower to my pussy. I felt his fingers spread at my opening. Then . . . his tongue surged into me. I yelled into the night as his long oral muscle overtook me, melted any resistance I might have had.

My body now hunched and rotated with abandon on his lapping tongue. I mewled like a kitten as he slurped my cum rum, stabbed and probed me with his mouth dick. Without a thought, I flipped onto my back and said, "You, on top. Now!" Tommy didn't hesitate but turned and positioned himself over me. I wasted no time pulling the fat love pop into my mouth. I held on to the head as I licked up one side and down the other. I felt the moan rumble through Tommy's body. I fisted the shaft before pulling it into my hot, wet mouth.

"Shit!" Tommy yelled.

I sucked his head methodically, tongue coating it sufficiently with my saliva, before I pulled him deeper. Then I began pumping on it slowly . . . excruciatingly slowly. The head swelled farther. I felt it plump out, fill my mouth more.

Tommy spread my legs wider, lifted my pussy into the air. He ground his mouth on my clit, slipped a finger into my wet snatch, and . . . in my ass. I growled around his dick and pumped with abandon against his hand and mouth. My actions made him hornier. He fucked my mouth, his dick sliding easily down my lubricated throat, kissing my tonsils. I gagged a little but held on to the pumping, pulsing dick. This action was worth a sore throat!

My fingers found his anus and stroked across the opening. Tommy's hips clenched; his pumping became erratic. He bit my clit, and my grinding went ballistic—herky-jerky, cum sliding back into my bush. We were both ready to explode!

I stuck a finger inside his ass. Tommy howled before he gave me three deep pumps, tensed up, and spurted his salty cum down my throat. This set me off! I pointed my pussy toward the ceiling and bounced his face off me as my nerve endings hummed, sizzled, and then popped! I screamed and squirted his face. He held on and lapped and lapped and lapped. . . .

As we came off our fuck high, he rolled off me and lay there, panting. I giggled as I saw his open mouth breathing and his juice-covered face. "What's funny?" he asked.

I smiled in the semidarkness. "Oh, just thinking about how little ole me . . . could make a grown man scream," I said.

Tommy lifted his head and eyed me a moment before he smiled, too. "Yeah, you did that. I hope I didn't sound like a girl."

"Babe, if a girl sounded like you, her name was Malcolm." We both cracked up at that.

7

It'd been five months, and Tommy Shapiro—yes, I learned his last name—and I had been dating on the regular. I couldn't have asked for a more attentive lover. He was thoughtful, creative, adventuresome, and, most importantly, he thought my pussy was the mother of all pussies! I loved how he didn't want to be up under me all the time. He understood that I needed breathing room and gave it to me whenever it was needed.

Honestly? I was starting to really dig this man here. Really. He had me rethinking all the negatives I'd previously had about relationships. Maybe I *was* still into the "couples" thing. Maybe the ménage à trois fantasy I'd had was just borne of being with the wrong men who didn't take my mind and body . . . *there.* I don't know. I just knew I was feeling Tommy more than I'd felt a man in a long-ass time.

In fact, my parents were coming to town to spend Thanksgiving Day with me, and I asked him to meet them. That was a huge step for me. My parents hadn't met any men I'd dated since college. I'd learned the hard way you just don't trot out the men you are sleeping with unless the relationship is going somewhere. Too many questions asked later I didn't want to answer.

I vacuumed the living room before I loaded the dishwasher. I checked on the turkey and then glanced at the clock. I had two hours before my folks showed up. The bird should be coming out of the oven just as they arrived. I then headed for the shower. Tommy would be here any minute. He had two calls—what lonely fuck gets a massage on Thanksgiving?—and I might have to "stroke" out some work tension or something. I wanted to be prepared, just in case.

I showered, lotioned, spritzed, and styled my hair, while watching the minutes tick by . . . with no Tommy in sight. I dialed his cell phone, and his voice mail picked up immediately. I left a message anyway. I waited and waited and waited. *Where the hell was Tommy?* With only thirty minutes until my parents' arrival, I finally put on my clothes. Wasn't gonna be no sex right now.

As I checked the turkey one last time, the doorbell rang. I was hoping Tommy had finally made his arrival. I opened the door eagerly, a smile plastered on my face . . . and saw my parents. My disappointment must have been clearly evident because my mother said, "Sonata, what's wrong?"

I bounced back quickly and replaced the smile on my face. "You're early. I was just surprised. That's all."

"Oh." They both looked at me oddly.

"Really! Come on in. Let me have your coats." We hugged, and I bustled around, trying to make up for the faux pas I'd just committed.

After I got them settled and checked on the food, I walked back in and saw my mother running her hands across the fireplace mantel. "You've done some redecorating, I see," she said, nodding slowly and glancing around the room.

That was an understatement, because the last time she had been here, I was moving in and had only a couch and a bedroom set. The apartment was now completely furnished to my eclectic taste . . . which was a definite clash with their conservative, traditional one. What was new? "Just a little of this and a little of that," I responded. "You like?" I asked, knowing she already hated it, but I wanted to hear her "politically correct" answer.

"It's . . . it's . . ." She waved her hands in the air but had difficulty finding the correct adjective. "It's . . ."

"Wonderful," my father answered. "You've come a long way, baby. If you like it, I love it," he finished, eyes twinkling. "Now, where is this young man of yours?"

Question of the night. I smiled brightly before replying, "He'll be here shortly. He had to work today, so I guess he's just running late."

"Let's hope he gets here soon. I'd hate for us to start without him, but the dinner must go on. We've got a train to catch at eight o'clock," my father said with his off-brand kind of humor.

I didn't see anything humorous about it. I excused myself and ducked into the bedroom and dialed his cell-phone number again. Voice mail. I tried his apartment. Answering machine. I left a message both places and then returned to my parents.

After an hour of chatting about home and people I barely remembered, my father cleared his throat. "Honey, I don't know where your friend is, but let's get this dinner started, and he can just get a plate when he comes in."

My face reddened, but I knew he was right. We couldn't just sit around waiting for Tommy, hoping he'd show up. Besides, I couldn't stand it if he *didn't* come and they left without eating at all. I sat the dishes on the table, praying all the while that Tommy would ring the doorbell.

Didn't happen. We ate, talked, and I finally saw them out at seven with no Tommy in sight. Thankfully my parents never asked another question about him. After they left, I stomped around the apartment, cussing and fussing with myself. My emotions swung from halfway worried that something bad had happened to being pissed at his whole no-show act. I tried the cell phone and apartment phone repeatedly with the same results: no answer. By midnight, I had settled on one emotion—rage.

I paced around the apartment in my sexy-just-for-my-damn-self underwear, since I'd long ago stripped out of my clothing. I found a pack of cigarettes left from some party or another and began smoking them in multiples—one in each hand—and opened a bottle of zinfandel I'd stashed for a special occasion. I gagged, coughed, and wheezed but continued to smoke until none were left and the bottle was drained. After I passed the hall mirror and realized that the spike-haired, crazed-looking woman was me, I went to bed.

Tommy called me early the next morning. My head was pounding as the phone shrilled beside me. I groggily reached for it.

"Hello?"

"Hey, baby. I thought you would be awake by now," Tommy said, no apology in his voice.

My pissed state came back in full force. "Tommy, where have you been?" I asked nastily.

"Whoa! What's all this?"

"Did you forget about yesterday?" I couldn't wait to hear his explanation.

"No. I just got held up, that's all," he responded calmly.

"Got held up? All night?" I retorted.

I heard him take a deep breath. "A client of mine had some . . . trouble, and the situation was intense. I stuck around to see it through."

"And you couldn't call to tell me you couldn't make it? I called you half the night, worried out of my mind!" I shouted.

"I wanted to call, but, like I said, the situation was intense, and I didn't have the chance." He still spoke calmly.

Now, I don't know about anybody else, but I've got a man-bullshit radar that is rarely wrong, and right then it was telling me Tommy was lying his ass off. I'd called until midnight. Unless the client was threatening suicide, I couldn't imagine what could be so "intense" . . . unless it was sex. This thought made me see red. "Listen, I'll talk to you later," I said through clenched teeth.

"Wait a minute. Let's get together today. I don't have a client scheduled, so let's just make up for yesterday today," he offered.

Oh, now he had time for me. "Yeah, well I've got something planned today. We'll just have to see each other some other time." That'll show him!

Tommy was quiet for a moment; then he said, "Fine. Talk with you later."

I hung up, jubilant that I'd stood up for myself . . . but mad because I really wanted to see him.

Shit.

8

The phone was ringing off the hook! Morning, noon, and night, *ring, ring, ring*. My brushing Tommy off must have made him realize I wouldn't put up with foolishness for some dick. Hell, a woman can get dick any time she wants. He needed to recognize I could give away more than he could ever get!

I ignored him the first week, and the calls still kept coming. My answering machine was full of hang-ups and sweet, pleading messages. The anguished words tugged at my heartstrings, but I held my ground. I would never again be an afterthought! Another week went by before I decided he had learned his lesson. I answered his next call.

"Sonata?" he asked tentatively.

"Yeah," I replied in a bored tone.

"Umm . . . how have you been?"

"Not too bad," I assured him. "And yourself?"

"I definitely can't say the same," Tommy responded. He took a deep breath. "Sonata . . . I'm sorry for what happened on Thanksgiving."

Me, too. "Uh-huh," I answered in an offhanded manner.

"Why don't we start over, see if we can recapture that magic we had. . . ." Tommy left the sentence open.

"Why?" I asked, not ready to give in so easily. I was worth working for!

"Because . . . I care for you. I can't sleep, can't eat, thinking you are feeling hurt from my actions. I swear, I didn't mean to not call, but—"

"I know, the situation was . . . *intense*," I finished for him.

"Yeah, it was. But I was thinking that if we go back to say, Video, we could find *us* again," he finished in a whisper.

Just saying the name "Video" made my pussy leak. We'd never returned, much as I'd wanted to. Somehow he'd never mentioned it again . . . and I'd punked out and never asked. But I wanted, no, *loved* seeing another person fucking or getting fucked. Wanted to see the expressions of desire . . . wanted to be the voyeur I'd never known I was. I now had another chance. This made me say, "What time?"

"Y—you'll go?" he asked, surprise evident in his voice.

"I said I would. What time?" I repeated. I *craved* the Video experience again.

"Four o'clock. Is that good for you?"

I didn't have anything planned but washing my hair, so I was game. "Four o'clock, it is. And, Tommy . . . don't be late."

"Believe me, I won't be," he finished.

Tommy arrived at three forty-five on the dot, a shit-sorry, limp smile in place. His eyes drank me in, and I posed, allowing him to view my entire being. It had been a while since he'd seen me, so I'd dressed in something sexy, let him know what he was missing. The sweater was low-cut and the pants tight, outlining my plump ass. Tommy gulped as I turned to grab my coat. I leaned seductively over the chair, giving him a bird's-eye view of my rear curvature. His pants were bulging when I turned around, and he was licking his lips. I ignored his reaction and said, "Ready?"

I saw the lusty thoughts zip through his mind. I smiled and held out my hand for his. He took it in silence and followed me out.

We rode to Video in my Miata. I felt too . . . free to ride in the stuffy Crown Vic. Tommy must have been feeling free also, because his natural *savoir faire* seemed to return in the car. Neither of us began a conversation. Instead, our hands spoke for us as one roamed across my exposed chest and I reciprocated with a crotch squeeze. My clit jumped and pussy weeped as fingers stroked my clit through tight pants. Bad as I hated to admit it, this man had me turned out!

Finally Video was in sight. I sprang from the Miata, not waiting for him to open my door. It was evident he was just as anxious as I was. We nearly trotted to the entrance, our hands brushing as we both pushed the buzzer. The peephole slid open, and a familiar voice asked, "Password?"

Tommy replied, "Sexaholic," this time.

The same guy, Sims, opened the door and ushered us in. Once again he checked up and down the sidewalk before he turned and bowed before me and then brushed my hand across his lips. I giggled.

"Well, well, well, back again," Sims said, staring at me over his sunglasses.

"Yes, we are," Tommy answered, pulling me from Sims's grasp.

Our eyes held a moment before he shifted his to Tommy. "What will be your pleasure this time?"

Tommy eyed me a moment. "I don't know. . . ."

Sims trained his eyes back on me. "We have some . . . unique stuff, too—same, retro, fetish, twisted . . . or a combination of the above." His eyes bored into mine.

The code talk made my head swim. I had some idea, but then again, I really didn't. All I did know was I wanted to see somebody fucking someone sometime soon!

"Let's try retro . . . fetish," Tommy finally answered.

I knew what a fetish was, but the retro threw me. I gave Tommy a questioning look. He shrugged. Sims slapped him on the back and said, "Hmph. Good choice. That one is interactive, too. Soundstage Seven. Enjoy."

We traveled back down the same hallway until we stood in front of a door with a 7 painted on it. Warm air whooshed out as my eager hand opened the door. The layout was identical to the previous room we had visited. Not many couples were inside, just a few men and a lone woman. From the bald skull and gray hairs, I wondered if maybe Tommy had chosen wrong, if we could switch rooms if this one was a dud.

Tommy read my face and said, "Let's just see. I've never been in here either."

I kept silent as the lights dimmed and the curtain rolled apart. The setting was a bare stage with a bench set in the middle of it. The bench was unique in that it had bars rising from the seat and a tray in front of it. I wondered if this was some baby playacting shit. Not that I'm against playacting . . . I just didn't like the idea of somebody wanting to be a baby and having sex. Just didn't seem . . . normal. But, then again, Video wasn't a normal place.

A robed figure walked from the side, the spotlight catching them halfway across. I saw it was a middle-aged brunette. The woman walked to the bench, straddled it, and sat down. I looked around, expecting a man to walk from the side and join her, but no one came. She removed the robe, and *humongous* breasts were revealed. Somebody gasped; a few men sat up straighter and scooted to the edges of their seats. I leaned forward for a better look myself.

The cameras panned to her extensive chest. The pendulous breasts puddled at her waist, stretch marks evident, nipples like saucers. One thing was for sure, no one had used the adjective "perky" on them in some time.

I glanced at Tommy, a request to change rooms on the tip of my tongue. It was obvious that "retro" meant older and the fetish was either huge breasts or older women. Neither of them did a thing for me . . . so I thought.

The woman licked her fingertips before massaging the wetness into the huge nipples. Surprisingly my pussy began to leak as those huge nipples contracted and then elongated until they were three-inch, pointed darts that begged to be licked, nibbled, sucked.

Tommy's hand slid into the top of my sweater, plucked at my own nipples. My skin flushed, aureoles tightened, stretched as his fingers massaged them. A firecracker exploded in my cunt as he pinched the sensitized tips. I flinched as sparks showered from my clit; I felt the saliva collect in my mouth as the woman then lifted her heavy breasts and placed them on the tray. With a smile on her face, she turned toward us and said, "Anybody wanna suck?"

A moan escaped from my throat, not because I wanted to suck her titties—maybe I did; I didn't have time to figure it out—but because of the way she said it. Her voice was deep, rough—fuckable.

The lone woman beat the men to the stage.

I rolled in my seat, felt the juice pouring from my lips, soaking my panties as I watched the woman shed her clothing, her breasts bouncing in the air. Tommy wasted no time unrolling his dick from his pants, pulling my hand over it. I tangled my fingers in his bush, stroked base to tip as I watched the action, was rewarded when pre-cum leaked onto my nimble fingers. I coated my fingers in the expected moisture before I vised his shaft and rubbed upward. Tommy lurched, his hand covering mine, choreographing my movements—squeeze the base, pull, stroke the tip. I followed his lead and smiled as he grunted and pre-cum flowed copiously over our doubled hands.

Tommy was ensnared as I slowly navigated my lips with my tongue. I saw his chest still as I dipped my head to his love stick. I lapped at the pre-cum before I engulfed the head, sucking slightly. Tommy wheezed, wrapped his hand in my hair as I slid my lips lower onto his cock. I sucked inward, drawing my tongue up the side as I moved upward. Then reversed . . . slowly.

"Baby, what are you trying to do to me?" Tommy uttered in a low voice.

My clit was on fire, nipples throbbed as I swirled and sucked his cock. My hands trailed my hot lips; I felt him swelling, pulsing beneath me. I began pumping rapidly.

"Shit!"

Tommy slid down my zipper, yanked pants from hips, buried fingers inside my folds. My body clenched as he twiddled my clit. I felt my lips open, rain honey onto his magical fingers. I sucked with relish, felt fingers plunge inside my folds in response.

Tommy pulled me from his cock and spread my legs wide before dipping his head into my bush. His goatee scratched my inner thighs, and I opened wider, allowed him ample area as he seated his mouth on my clit. Oh, the feel of his tongue, his mouth as they lapped and sucked. His fingers pumped inside me, filling that hole. I bit my lips, clamped down on a scream as the sensations swirled all over my body. My legs involuntarily closed, locked Tommy's head in place as he lapped and sucked. He shifted, moved lower still.

I lifted from my seat as he rubbed his goatee into my cheeks before he circled my lower hole with his tongue. My body felt as though it was about to burst as he created a fiery path with his tongue, dragged it back and forth between the two holes.

My legs trembled, body shook uncontrollably as a finger slowly pressed into this flesh. I grasped the digit, pushed it within . . . deep. Home.

Tommy lifted, turned me over . . . pulled me onto his pulsing dick. I jumped and bucked. He bucked me back. I was slung over the row of seats as he stood on tiptoe, hit my center. I grinded and rotated, rammed backward onto his cock. My sweater was yanked down, breasts released, bobbing into the air. I grasped the armrests to steady myself; uttered unknown words as the sound of front thighs slapping back thighs rang in the air and my tits bounced erratically. Tommy's hands were everywhere—breasts, clit, ears, ass—as he love-pounded me. My pussy clenched, grasped, sucked with relish.

My entire body tensed, clenched with the need for release. I couldn't help myself. Tommy and I both screamed as my body stiffened and his cock head mushroomed; we both exploded in ecstasy.

9

We were definitely back on track. With both of us being busy people, a conscious effort was made to spend our weekends together, and we made the most of them. Video was a frequent destination. I was hooked on our bimonthly trips there, and we always chose a new ... variation whenever we went. I will admit that our last trip made my old hopes of a ménage à trois resurface.

Tommy had chosen "same ... anything goes." You may have guessed that *same* is "same sex" and *anything goes* means what it says: people doing anything you willingly let them do to you. Of course, because Tommy chose, *same* meant a lesbian feast. Tommy was open to many things, but gay male sex wasn't one of them. And that was good because I'm sure my opinion of him would have shot into the shady zone. Honestly I wasn't feeling his choice, because no dick was involved, but I went along with it and kept an open mind.

I tell you, after watching that video shoot, Tommy's dick was hard enough to cut diamonds. He fucked me raw! I can't say I minded, 'cause the sex was off the hook! I swear I saw

stars and heard a band playing and cannons booming as we climaxed together. Then he asked me the question: Would you
have a ménage à trois? He said it so innocently, like we were
talking about the weather. My response?

"We talking another woman or another man?" I asked.

Tommy's eyebrow quirked. "What do you think? Another
woman, of course. I'm not having no man touch me! I'm not
down with no gay shit!" he huffed.

He was thinking the other person was going to be touching
both of us, so he thought it was perfectly fine for another
woman to touch me, but not another man touch him. I see. His
skewed thinking pissed me off. "What's wrong with another
man? Besides, he won't be there to touch you, he'll be there to
fuck me," I retorted.

He backed up. "Girl, have you lost your mind? There is no
way I plan to watch another man putting his dick up in your
snatch."

I took a step forward, crowded his space. "But it's a great
idea to watch you put your dick in another woman's snatch."

The puzzled look on his face told me he had no clue as to
why I had a problem with that. "Unlike your crazy man idea,
the woman will be there to fuck both of us. Just like the girls at
Video," he asserted.

I knew his reaction was one to be expected, but it grated on
my psyche anyway. I took a breath before I offered a compro-
mise. "I'll tell you what. I do yours, and you do mine."

He frowned. "What does that mean, 'I do yours and you do
mine'?"

I refused to back down. "It means I'll do your female ménage à trois if you do my male ménage à trois." There. I'd said
it.

His nostrils flared. "Girl, you are crazy as hell. That shit is
abnormal."

I couldn't believe we'd spent all that time in numerous

rooms watching sexual variations, deviations, and perversions, yet he was still close-minded when it came to a woman getting hers like she *really* wanted it. I stared at him a moment before stating, "We will have to table this . . . adventure because we can't come to an agreement."

Disappointment bloomed on his face, but the way I saw it, if he couldn't do it for me, I couldn't do it for him. We never spoke about it again.

I know I said that things had gotten back on track, but Tommy's actions over the Christmas/New Year's holiday let me know that wasn't true at all. Because Christmas fell on a Saturday—our normal hook-up day—I expected to see him as usual. Besides, he hadn't told me anything different, and we'd talked the Thursday before. Usual week.

I'd window shopped for weeks before I found the perfect gift for him. I'd had it wrapped and couldn't wait to give it to him. It had been a long time since I'd shopped for a man, and I found that I'd missed the experience.

On Christmas Day, I dressed my sexiest best, waiting for him to come over. I'd cooked the holiday favorites—chicken and dressing, candied yams, chocolate cake, yeast rolls—and decorated from top to bottom. A small platinum tree was adorned with red bows, the room smelled of pine needles, and Christmas favorites played on the stereo. Everything was just right. I waited expectantly.

As three o'clock approached, I decided to find out what was taking him so long. There was no answer at his apartment or on his cell phone. I left messages both places; a frisson of unease passed down my spine. Déjà vu.

I ate dinner by myself at six, still hoping the dread I was now feeling would be erased by Tommy's arrival. I called again at eight o'clock. No answer either place. I searched my mind to figure out if he'd said he was spending the day with his family.

But try as I could to convince myself otherwise, I knew he'd not told me that.

Tommy finally called at ten o'clock. I was irritated, and it showed in my voice.

"Hey, Sonata. Merry Christmas. How has your day been?" he asked easily.

"You'd know if you were over here," I snapped.

"You sound . . . funny, like something is wrong."

Plenty was wrong, and its name was T-O-M-M-Y. But if he wanted to act like he didn't know, I felt it wasn't my job to enlighten him. "Nothing's wrong. I'm fine."

"O . . . K," he answered, unconvinced. We both were silent after that. Me, waiting for him to tell me he was coming over. Him, probably hoping I wouldn't ask.

Tommy finally broke the silence by saying, "I was trying to make a decision, but I see that you're in a mood, so I'll let you go. Talk to you later. Bye," and hung up the phone!

I sat in stunned muteness . . . but the curses flowed in my head.

The day after Christmas, he called "to see if I was out of my mood." I wasn't. I was pouting like a schoolgirl. He'd never even *offered* an explanation of where he was at Christmas—a special day in any country—but he was available as hell the day after the holiday. It smacked of a consolation prize any way I looked at it, and believe me, I viewed and reviewed it from every imaginable angle. I passed on his offer but told him to call me later in the week. He informed me that he had a full schedule, but perhaps we could get together on New Year's Day. That made me feel a smidgen better, and I said I'd try to keep my calendar open.

10

On New Year's Eve I decided to party like there was no to-morrow. Shindigs were being held all over the city, and the last thing I'd planned to do was bring in the New Year pouting be-cause my man had to work. *Ain't that much work in the world, girl*, my mind chided me. I pushed it away, excused his actions as part of his job.

I'd chosen to party at my favorite place, Lorenze's, and dressed in a festive red for the occasion. The place was packed with bodies of all shapes, sizes, and colors. The music was thumping and the air thick with smoke. I'd just navigated to the bar when the deejay announced an amateur stripper contest. The prize was one thousand dollars . . . and you could bare it all if you wanted to!

I thought that would trip the folks up, but scores of women, many already in various stages of undress, swarmed the stage. They filled out the info cards rapidly, eager to show their tits and ass to the world. A huge gong was rolled out, and the dee-jay announced the rules: thirty seconds to strip your ass off, and if the crowd booed, you got gonged.

I perched on a vacated bar stool, interested in what the women would do. I tried not to laugh as the first contestant—a young woman well into her cups—grinded the air off-rhythm and then stumbled and fell as she tried to pull her shirt over her head. The gong rang loudly. The second and third were no better. The second looked like she'd hooked one year too long—garish makeup, drooping breasts—and the third was definitely somebody's grandmother. . . . You get the picture.

Now, the fourth contestant had it going on. She strutted to the edge of the stage and shimmied her ass to the floor while unzipping her dress. A male patron pushed to the edge of the stage and held out dollar bills. This energized the woman, and she rolled and ground her hips just for him. The man flailed the bills in the air now. But when the dress dropped to the floor, there was a telltale bulge at the front of her panties because *she* was a . . . *he!* Boos rang across the room at that one. The gong was banged and banged. I wondered if it was truly because it was a male or because they'd been hoodwinked.

I'd become bored as others took to the stage without much skill or success, when my ears perked as I overheard a loud conversation from a group of men at the end of the bar.

"Man, I'll bet you five hundred dollars you don't have the balls to go up there!" a spike-haired man said to a well-buffed hunk.

Interesting, indeed. The tall golden hunk held my attention by his chest span alone. He was definitely a gym patron. When he smiled, showing off strong white teeth, I was further enthralled.

"You mean to tell me you would waste your daddy's hard-earned money just to see me shake my ass onstage? You want to see my dick that bad, man?" Golden Hunk asked. The rest of the group hooted and hollered.

"Puh-lease. My dick has been bigger than yours since birth!"

Spike Hair retorted. The group oohed at the low blow. "You talk a lot of shit, but let's see if you can back up some of that. Cassa*ho*va ain't scared, is he?" Spike Hair challenged.

"Hell, naw! I'm all they say and more!" Golden Hunk assured him.

"Prove it," Spike Hair urged, waving the hundred-dollar bills under his nose.

Golden Hunk sat his drink down and said, "Watch this shit."

He strode to the stage and filled out a card. He then stood behind the last of the few remaining women, waiting for his turn. The deejay had something else in mind.

"Ladies, we have a treat for you! It seems we have a *real* male who wants to strut his stuff! Let's welcome Felix to the stage!" The women whooped and clapped loudly. The gay patrons stood on tables and gave catcalls.

Felix began a slow grind from his position at the back of the line when Prince's "Insatiable" blasted from the speakers. He gyrated as he glided to center stage, hips making promises all us women hoped he could keep. Felix unbuttoned his shirt teasingly slowly before he licked his fingers and rubbed them on his hairy nipples. I had to moan at that. I heard others moan with me.

He turned, his body liquid sex, and pulled the shirt from his pants. My mouth went dry as his well-toned, muscular back was revealed. He dropped the shirt to the floor. There was a minor ruckus as women fought for the material. I saw Felix smile at the women, and then his hands were on his zipper.

I held my breath as he undid the button at the top and slid his pants open. The gay parade went ballistic. They were standing, clapping, and yelling for him to "Take it off! Pull it out!" Felix squatted, leaned backward—one arm on the ground—and pumped the air with his pelvis. All the women were whistling and screaming now. I didn't know about them, but I definitely hoped he wanted to bare all! The jealous men booed. The women screamed louder. It was wild in here!

When the standing people blocked my view, I stood on the rung of my bar stool to see the action. Felix had rolled onto the floor and was humping it rhythmically. My pussy wept, sent out a pheromonic message old as time as I watched his butt rise into the air and his chest muscles clench. Felix then stood and kicked off his shoes. His hands were at his waistband, and I fervently hoped his dick would be standing at attention when he dropped his pants.

The pants were slipped down thick thighs a centimeter at a time. My nipples tightened shamelessly; my tongue wanted to lick those bulging thighs. I couldn't help myself as I screamed, "Work it out, baby! Work it out!" The men around me laughed, but I didn't give a damn. None of them could hold a candle to this hunk of masculinity on the stage.

Felix removed his hands from the pants, and his pants pooled at this feet. The boxers he wore were white and fit like a glove. He wasn't erect like I'd hoped, but it was obvious he was carrying heavy artillery . . . and I most *definitely* wished to be his target.

He tugged at the waistband of his boxers, showed us a glimpse of tight ass. This set the women—and men—off! A flaming gay patron rushed the stage only to be tripped up by the women. It was on, then! The man was fighting furiously, and the women ganged up on him. Others in the gay parade joined, and eventually the ruckus spread as toes were stepped upon, drinks spilled accidentally, and unseen hands touched the wrong people. The bouncers tossed people right and left, trying to restore order.

Exit, stage left!

I shoved on the backs of the slow-ass people in my need to get outside. They moved slowly—some bottlenecking, others hoping order would be restored and Felix's strip would resume—but picked up speed as a glass flew over our heads and shattered behind us.

Eventually we were on the sidewalk. I chuckled in the cold air. We didn't make it to midnight, but the year was coming in with a bang anyway. I strolled toward my car, eyes ever watchful around me. Just as I clicked the remote lock, I heard, "Pssst. Pssst." I jumped a foot as a deep voice said, "Hey, over here."

Common sense dictated that I enter the car as rapidly as I could . . . and I did. But just as I cranked the ignition, someone tapped on my window. I screamed. Then I realized it was the Felix guy that had just been stripping onstage. I let the window down a few inches and asked, "Yes?"

"I've lost my friends, so could you give me a ride?" His eyes pleaded with mine. I glanced downward, saw he was clad only in his boxers. He saw the direction of my eyes and without me asking said, "They got all my clothes. Left me in only this." His face wrinkled in distaste as he pointed to the well-filled-out boxers.

I had to chuckle at him. Freezing cold outside, and he was clad only in skimpy boxers. No telling what would happen to him if I didn't come to his rescue. I clicked the lock open, and he dashed across the front of the car and hopped inside. He rubbed his hands together briskly. "Thank you so much!" he said with much enthusiasm.

"You're welcome," I replied.

He gave a few more rubs before he held out his hand and said, "I'm Felix—"

"I know," I said, cutting him off.

He gave a faint smile. "Caught my striptease, huh?"

And that big dick of yours, too. "Yeah," I answered, shaking his hand. "I'm Sonata. First time at Lorenze's?"

He nodded. "Yes. First time, and I leave almost buck naked as a baby." We both cracked up at that.

After the laughter died down, I asked, "Where to?"

"I'm over on Bryant. It's pretty quick if you take I-26 and exit—"

"I know where it is. It's on my way to work," I interrupted. "Cool."

We continued to make conversation as I pulled into the heavy traffic. I had to brake hard a few times to avoid the drunken revelers, but eventually we were on I-26. Felix kept up a steady stream of information.

"I'm a lab technician at County Memorial Hospital," he informed me.

"Really. I'm the senior veterinarian at Dogs Inc."

I saw his eyebrow quirk in the semidarkness. "The big outfit by the Press Mall?" he asked.

"The same," I acquiesced.

"Wow. I don't think I've met a woman veterinarian before."

"Guess that means you don't have any pets."

He shook his head. "Naw. Not a pet person, myself."

I chuckled. "Everyone says that until they own one." I took the Bryant exit and turned to him for further directions.

"Take a right at the light, and then go two blocks down." He pointed. I followed his directions and soon parked in front of a brick ranch. "Sonata, I truly appreciate this. Want to come in for a nightcap?"

"You sure?" I asked. The ranch screamed "I'm settled," and my mind yelled "married with children."

"Yeah. What? You think I'm married or something?" He held out his hand, and no ring or telltale sign of recent-ring-wearing was present. "See? No ring."

I smiled at this information, but I pressed him further. "Just because you're not wearing doesn't mean you aren't married. You could be faking it while the wife and kids are out of town or something."

Felix's sincere eyes stared into mine. "If I were married, there is no way I would disrespect my wife by not wearing my ring. I'd want her to wear hers to tell the world she was no longer available, and I'd do the same. That's the kind of man I am."

I fairly melted. A man who believed in marriage for real? Not just fronting about it while trying to get as much pussy on the side as he could? I *definitely* needed to get to know this dude better. "I see."

He showed his pearly whites again and then glanced at my car clock. "Hey, it's almost midnight. We've still got five minutes to get a toast ready . . . bring in the New Year right," he whispered, eyes burning, face yearning.

Looking into his eyes, I knew I wanted that and more. Yeah, I didn't know him at all, but I *felt* like I could trust him. Then . . . Tommy's face swam into my mind. *Damn.* I wrinkled my nose and said regretfully, "I'm seeing someone right now."

"Serious?"

I swear, I couldn't answer that. Tommy and I were on one day and off the next, but I still had . . . hope. "We're working on that," I answered lamely.

He nodded reluctantly. "Tell you what. How about I give you my number, and if things change, you'll give me a call?"

Nothing wrong with that. I fished a piece of paper from my purse and clicked on the inside light as he wrote down his number. Our hands brushed, and electricity shot through me as he passed back the paper. We held each other's eyes for a few moments before I broke the contact. "Will you be able to get inside?" I asked, eyes trained on the house.

He was quiet for a few seconds and then replied, "Of course. I always leave myself . . . options." With that he gave me a salute and exited the car. I watched as he walked behind the house, and, in seconds, an inside light came on. I backed out to the street and headed home as the radio announced the New Year. Felix was all over my mind.

11

New Year's morning, I awoke with a song on my lips. I was jubilant as I recited my new resolutions. Not even the gray skies could dampen my spirits.

Just as on Christmas, I'd cooked a large festive meal—complete with black-eyed peas—to celebrate. I was hoping Tommy would make his arrival just after lunch. I'd thought about calling him to find out but decided to wait and not show how eager I was to see him.

I napped through the Rose Bowl parade and yawned watching the ball games afterward. Late afternoon—and still waiting for Tommy to show—I dressed and cracked open a new novel I'd just picked up, Sydney Molare's *Small Packages.* This book was hot! In fact, I was so engrossed in the storyline I was shocked when I glanced at the clock and saw it was after eight . . . and no Tommy.

My blood simmered as the unwanted but now familiar feelings washed over me. I snatched the phone and punched in his number. He answered on the second ring, sleepiness evident in his voice.

"Hello," Tommy whispered.

"Hey, it's Sonata," I answered.

"Happy New Year, Sonata." He yawned and then cleared his throat.

"Same to you." I cut to the chase. "So . . . what's the deal?"

"Huh?" I heard the confusion in his voice.

I inhaled deeply. "It's Saturday night, New Year's night, and we were supposed to hook up," I explained as calmly as I could.

"Oh, yeah. I forgot."

He forgot? Forgot he was supposed to spend New Year's Day with his sweetheart? My pressure spiked. "You forgot," I repeated.

"Yeah, it's been a long week, and I guess I was more tired than I realized. After I saw my folks earlier, I came home and zonked out."

Let me get this straight. He had such a tiring week he wanted me to believe that he couldn't come over and hadn't even *thought* of calling me to let me know, yet he *did* have time to spend with his family? My man-bullshit radar shrieked at sonic-boom level. "I see. I'll talk to you later," I huffed and slammed the phone back into its cradle. Besides, what could he say? It was obvious that the only one in a relationship was me.

The phone rang seconds after I'd hung up. Probably Tommy. I ignored it, fished in my purse for the scrap of paper with Felix's phone number on it. No reason to sit pouting when there was another interested party available. The phone continued to shrill, and I lifted the headset and hung up without answering. After a few seconds, I dialed Felix's number.

"Yo! Yo! Yo! Happy New Year's!" his voice boomed through the phone in greeting. I heard music in the background and hoped I hadn't caught him in the middle of entertaining.

"Felix?" I asked in a low voice.

"Yeah?"

"Ah . . . this is Sonata. I met you last night?" The phone beeped, but I ignored it.

"Hey, girl! This is such a surprise! I was hoping you wouldn't throw a man's number in the trash." His exuberance was refreshing, to say the least!

I giggled. "Nope. Didn't ditch the number," I confirmed.

"Glad you didn't. So, what's up?"

Suddenly I felt shy as a schoolgirl. I swallowed before saying, "I was wondering if you wanted to maybe . . . do something tonight."

"Sure. How about . . ." His voice faded as my phone beeped again.

"What did you say?"

"I said how about within the hour? I know a great place that has a karaoke night that is off the chain. If you feel like laughing your head off and hanging out—no strings attached—I'd like to take you."

Now this is what I was talking about—quick and easy, no subterfuge or fumbling around. "What time? I'm already dressed."

"Give me the directions to your house, and I'm on my way."

I did so with a smile.

Felix arrived thirty minutes later. I was glad to see he was dressed semicasually in khakis and a black sweater. I'd left on my low-slung jeans and a sweater so we matched perfectly. Felix held out a bouquet of yellow roses, and I smiled. Tommy had been good, but he never remembered the little things like flowers and candy.

"You shouldn't have," I gushed.

"Now, I couldn't just show up without something to give to a beautiful woman like you," he replied.

"Thank you," I responded sincerely. I held out my arms, and he walked into them. I smelled the spicy cologne as I brushed my lips along his cheek in a friendly peck, and we hugged. Felix squeezed me longer than was appropriate for the occasion, but I didn't push away. Finally he said in a tight voice, "We'd better get going."

"Yeah." I placed the flowers in a vase, and we exited.

As we rode down the elevator, I wondered what he drove. I was hoping it wasn't a huge Cadillac or a souped-up, hydraulically challenged jalopy. I was floored when I saw the Alfa Romeo Spyder, and I whistled appreciatively.

"Guess you weren't expecting that from a suburb-dwelling lab tech, huh?"

"Definitely not," I said, eyes still roaming over the gleaming black metal.

"Well, keep your mind open 'cause I'm *not* your average man," he assured me.

I couldn't wait for him to show me!

12

Sienna's Bar and Grill was located in a small strip mall. If you didn't know where to look, you would miss it completely. Obviously others did know where to look, because the parking lot was full. I was glad to see there weren't the usual loiterers outside, and because the cars were upscale and expensive, I expected the crowd to be short on the younger patrons.

Felix paid the cover, and we entered a large room with tables spaced over most of the floor. People were dancing, and laughter tinkled in the air. We found an empty table near the far wall. A waitress strode over, and we ordered drinks.

"This is nice," I said, still looking around the room.

Felix nodded. "It's pretty cool. I happened to stumble upon it a year or so ago. The music is mixed, the food is smoking, and the karaoke will have you screaming."

"My kind of place, all right. Do you ever karaoke?" I asked, interested in learning more about him.

"Naw. My pops told me a long time ago to get my education because singing was *not* my forte."

"I hate to admit it, but I got a similar speech from my mother when I was eight." I giggled.

"Shoot, personally I think he is wrong because when I'm in the shower, I nearly bring the house down . . . literally."

I laughed aloud as a visual popped in my mind. Then I remembered something from last night. "Hey, did you get your money?"

He frowned. "What?"

"Did your friend pay off on his bet?"

Felix grinned. "You overheard us?" I nodded. "I sure did. I had to threaten to put his scrawny ass in a choke hold, but he paid up."

I grinned with him. "Guess Lorenze's didn't pay, though."

He chuckled. "I called, but he said with all the damage to his place, he just couldn't see himself paying the person who'd started it. So, no, I didn't get the thousand dollars."

"Poor baby."

"But at least it's a story I can tell my grandchildren."

"Yeah, I can see you now, saying 'I was the shit back in the day. In fact, one time I showed my body, and the women tore the place up! I had them on fire!'"

"It ain't even like that!" Felix said but laughed anyway.

Oh, but it is. Baby, it is.

We talked and laughed as the waitress returned with our drinks, and Felix ordered some hot wings. The deejay then announced the beginning of Karaoke Night. I'd seen it on television but never actually attended one myself.

I was excited as a nervous-looking woman with hair to her butt began a rousing rendition of Tina Turner's "A Fool in Love." The crowd sang with her as she strutted to the edge of the stage and copied Tina's trademark shimmy perfectly. The hoots and catcalls she received were worthy of her efforts. I clapped along with the rest of the crowd as she finished and bowed.

A pimply, stiff-looking, blond man stepped up to the mic next. I expected something along the lines of Lawrence Welk or Willie Nelson, but when he came with a believable cover of Shaggy's "Bombastic," the crowd went wild. Felix grabbed my hand and pulled me onto the floor. I wiggled and undulated like an island girl as his hands skimmed my waist and he matched my movements from behind. His pelvis touched and then backed away teasingly. I felt life down there but resisted its pull. The song ended with us spooned together, rocking in sync.

We were on our way back to our seats when the deejay announced a house regular—Criss-Crossed. Felix halted me and said, "Hold up. This is something you've got to see."

We threaded our way back through the crowd to get a good spot. Two men and one woman strode onto the stage. The men wore baggy suits, and the woman had on a sequined short set. Each one's hair was slicked back, and mascara rimmed their eyes. *Interesting.* The music that blasted from the speakers was familiar: Donna Summer's "Bad Girls." My hips moved instinctively because this song was a favorite from my childhood.

The trio's choreographed movements were on point. A strobe light was switched on, and the dance floor jammed. I was surprised at the low tenor of the woman's voice, but she was singing her ass off! The backup singers had high falsettos, but they blended with hers perfectly. I clapped in glee as they playfully slapped the woman's butt during the chorus. But when they reached the "Toot! Toot! Beep! Beep!" part, my mouth hung open as the suits were stripped away to reveal females, and the wig came off the woman, exposing the spike-haired man from Lorenze's. . . . Felix's friend!

The crowd gave off a roar of appreciation. I gave Felix questioning looks, and he grinned back at me. We were dancing heatedly now. Hips grinded, pelvises touched and backed away, fingers roamed . . . wherever.

The singers switched places, and the women brought it home and the place down! I had to admit that that switcheroo thing had just the right spice to make them stand out from the usual. They finished the song to much adulation from the crowd. We returned to our table, and the questions poured from my lips.

"That was your friend from last night, right?" I asked.

"Yep. His name is Freddy Mac." Felix had a teasing smile on his lips. "Guess you're wondering if I'm gay or bisexual now."

I tried to deny it, but finally I said, "Yeah."

"I'm not. Freddy isn't either. He just likes to be . . . shocking."

"That he was!"

Felix laughed. "He's been like that since we were kids. And please don't dare him." He rolled his eyes.

"He's one of those people who won't back down from a challenge?" I assumed.

"You've got him pegged correctly. He'll do anything he thinks won't get him killed or jailed and sometimes some stuff that will. Just his personality."

"Did you know it was him up there on the stage?"

"Yeah. He's had his group, Criss-Crossed, for years. Normally he dresses like a man, so he must have wanted to change things up with the drag thing tonight."

"It was most definitely different," I assured him.

"Yeah, it was. I'm a little surprised, but, then again, he has those women's noses opened wide, so I shouldn't be."

"What do you mean?"

Felix gazed at me a moment before answering, "Both of the singers are his lovers."

"What!" My eyes were like saucers.

"Yeah, he sleeps with both of them," Felix confirmed for me.

"They don't mind?"

"Doesn't look like it, does it?"

I had to admit that there was no obvious tension there when the group performed. But thinking about this made thoughts of a two-male ménage à trois flit back into the forefront of my mind. Freddy had his . . . so why couldn't I get mine? "Nope, it sure doesn't."

"I can't figure out what his scrawny behind told those two gorgeous women to make them do his bidding. I mean, whatever Freddy says is gold." Felix shook his head again. "I'm wondering if he's sprinkling cocaine on his pole or something, the way he has them hooked."

"You think?" I asked playfully.

"It's something—"

"Hey, man! I thought that was you!" a voice interrupted us.

I turned and saw Mr. Spike Hair himself, Freddy Mac. Felix man-hugged him a second and then growled, "Two times in one day is just too many times to see your ugly mug."

"Puh-lease. I wouldn't have seen you earlier if you hadn't threatened me with bodily harm," Freddy responded good-naturedly. Then he looked at me. "I know he must have kidnapped you because nobody goes anywhere with Felix willingly. Want me to call the police?"

I tried to hide my smile as Felix elbowed him. "Man, keep gabbing your mouth and Shirl and Donatella will wake up in my bed tomorrow morning."

"In your dreams, chump, in your dreams," Freddy said, elbowing him back.

"No, in theirs," he shot back.

They laughed at each other, and then Freddy resumed talking to me. "I'm Freddy Mac, since this Neanderthal didn't introduce us."

"My bad. Sonata, Freddy. Freddy, Sonata," Felix announced.

We exchanged greetings, and then Freddy asked, "Did you enjoy our show, Sonata?"

"Immensely. It was definitely one of a kind."

"That's me, all right—one of a kind." Freddy winked and then said, "I'll get out of your way and let you guys enjoy yourself. Great meeting you, Sonata. Hope to see you again soon."

We ate hot wings and talked some more before we decided to call it a night.

I didn't feel anxious as we rode home. No flutters in my stomach, no anticipation of sexual romping. I just felt . . . peaceful. Good.

Felix rode the elevator upstairs and walked me to my door. I turned and asked the same question he'd asked me, "Want to come in for a nightcap?"

He smiled and said, "Yeah . . . but you're not ready for what I really want."

My heart thumped, and anxiety did stir within me then. "You think?" I shocked myself by replying.

"Yep." Felix's eyes grew soft; fingers stroked my cheek. "I'm not looking for a . . . casual fling with you. I know we just met, but I sense something . . . unique . . . here, and I'd like to explore it further before we get off into the sex thing."

I appreciated that. "I like that idea."

"So, if you aren't doing anything tomorrow, I'd like to hook up—go hang out or something."

"Sounds like a good plan." I held his eyes, conveyed my real thoughts to him.

Felix's fingers roamed, and he stared into my eyes another moment before saying, "Get inside. I won't be responsible for my actions if you keep looking at me like that."

I slipped my key in the door, opened it, and closed it slowly behind me.

13

The knock startled me. I was surprised to see Felix still standing there. I opened the door and stared at him.

His face was serious as he spoke. "I . . . I know what I said,
but I just can't let you go." My breath caught as he reached for
me, pressed his sexy lips onto mine. I didn't protest as his velvet
tongue swirled within my mouth. My hands climbed his chest,
wrapped around his thick neck, fused him to me.

I nibbled and sucked his ear; Felix licked the hollow of my
throat, nipped my chin. I exhaled deeply as tentative hands
moved down my back, massaging slowly. I closed my eyes,
breathed deeply as they moved lower, cupped my hips.

"Girl, I don't know what it is. . . . I'm just digging the hell
out of you," he whispered in my ear.

My hands curled upward, encased his head as I found his
mouth again. I poured all my insecurities, my disappointments
with Tommy, into that kiss. I let Felix know the sensual creature I was capable of being.

We parted and stared at each other. My heart pounded with

anticipation as I watched him, emotions playing across his face. No words were spoken as Felix slowly rolled my sweater up my chest and over my head.

A smile played on his lips as he stared at my bra-covered chest. "You're more beautiful than I imagined."

Talk about saying the right thing. I stroked his chin before I reciprocated, revealing that glorious chest again. I couldn't stop my fingers from running across his pecs, stroking his nipples, which hardened under my touch. Feeling bold, I leaned in and sucked a nipple into my mouth, rolled around the stiffening button on my tongue.

"Girl, that feels so good," Felix muttered before he reclaimed my mouth.

Hands released my bra clasps and dragged the material from my breasts before cupping and claiming my orbs. Felix pressed my flesh together, sucked both nipples into his soft, hot mouth. I leaned back on the wall, moaned as I felt his suckling down to my clit. My hands slid up and down his back and squeezed his ass as he alternated between nipples.

I opened my jeans, unzipped them in an unmistakable invitation. Felix accepted as he kneeled, pulled them slowly from my hips. He stared at my vee. I pulled the material taut, outlined my lips fully.

"Damn."

Felix leaned in and inhaled my female scent. He parted my legs, was dipping his head—

The ringing of my bedside phone intruded, forced my eyes open. I was disoriented as I stared at the ceiling. Then I yanked the phone from the cradle.

"Hello?"

"Sonata, it's Tommy."

What's new? "Hey, Tommy." I felt a headache beginning in my temple.

"I tried to call you back last night, but I guess you weren't in the mood or something," he said peevishly.

"Or something" is right, and its name was Felix. "Yeah," I answered noncommittally.

"I'm sorry I forgot about New Year's." *Here we go!* "I want to make it up to you."

"Don't worry about it," I replied nonchalantly.

He ignored it. "Really. I'm not busy today and wondered if we could hook up."

Since I'd already given Felix the OK for today, that wasn't possible, so I said, "I've already got something planned for today. Maybe another time."

Tommy was silent. "What's going on with you, Sonata?"

Going on with me? He was the problem, not me! "What do you mean?" I asked through clenched teeth.

"You always used to be available, and the last couple of times I've called, you've brushed me off."

I couldn't believe he wanted to play this high school game! Trying to swing the blame to me, when in reality it was his fault. I refused to take the bait. "I'm available when I say I will be. You're the one that doesn't show up. So why should I continue to hope you'll fit me into your busy schedule?"

Anger inflected his voice. "It's not like that. Things are always crazy this time of year. People want massages and give them as gifts, so I'm always overbooked around the holidays." But he had time to see other people . . . just not me.

"I understand. Hey, let's plan something for later in the week . . . that is, if you're not *too* busy," I suggested, sarcasm dripping from my voice.

He switched back to a conciliatory tone. "I'll make time. When is good for you?"

"Tuesday?" My mind ran over my schedule to be sure. "I work late Mondays and Wednesdays, but Tuesday I'm off early."

"Want to go back to Video?" he offered.

My pussy sputtered to life. He had his faults, but he knew how to get back in my good graces. "Sure."

"Tuesday, it is. Six good for you?"

That was cutting it close to when I left work, but I agreed to it anyway. I'd just leave early and rush home to dress in time. "I'll be ready."

"See you then. Bye."

I clicked off with a smile on my face. Tommy was still feeling me, no matter what his actions said.

Felix arrived just after lunch. Another bouquet of flowers was clasped in his hands. Peonies this time. I smiled as I took them from him, and our lips brushed before I placed them in a vase beside the first ones.

I turned to him. "Where are we going?"

"Just hop in the car, and let's see," he said mysteriously.

I took his hand as we rode down the elevator and walked out to his car. The Spyder had been gorgeous last night, but in the daylight it was just breathtaking. He'd put the top down, and I liked it even more.

"I should have asked if you wanted to grab a scarf for your hair, but I forgot."

I ran my hands through my mane and said, "Don't worry about it. I can always brush it out later."

He opened the door and helped me inside. We zoomed away with my laughter floating behind us.

Felix parked on the banks of the river. The dark waters of the mighty Mississippi rushed by and soothed me as water always did. "You know, I love being on water."

"Really? Did you grow up by the ocean or something?" His eyes sparkled with interest.

I shook my head. "No. But I've always been drawn to large

bodies of water. It calms my soul just watching the water swirl and gush around."

"I can take it or leave it," he admitted.

"I'll take it. There is something about coming home from work, walking out, and seeing water that I believe would make all the badness go away. When I buy a house, it will most definitely be on the water."

"Unless you move, you'll pay dearly for the location."

I turned determined eyes toward him. "When it's something you truly want, you find a way to pay the price."

"Truer words were never spoken," he said, another meaning in his eyes.

We sat for another hour in the dimming daylight before he backed out and exited onto the highway. "Where to now?" I asked.

"Got a little surprise for you." He winked.

I'd found that I loved surprises, so I hushed and waited expectantly. We took the Bryant exit and retraced the route to his house. I said nothing as he stopped in front of his ranch and cut the engine. I took the proffered hand and followed him inside his door. I was elated to see the elegant furnishings—polished wood floors, leather couches, ethnic carved tables—that decorated the place. It was what I'd envisioned in my own home.

Felix took my jacket and eased me onto the sofa. He clicked on his CD player, and Hall & Oates' "Sara Smile" wafted from his speakers. He then walked into his large kitchen, and I watched as he poured two glasses of wine. As he held one out to me, he asked, "Want to see some more water?"

I was confused but said, "Yes."

He took my hand and guided me to the French doors. He swung them open to reveal an enclosed swimming pool with a whirlpool spa off to the side. "This is beautiful!" I exclaimed. The mosaic tile at the bottom gave the pool a Moroccan flair, and the chandeliers hanging around the pool made the yard seem like a ballroom . . . that just happened to have a pool in the middle of the floor. I saw a wooden structure off to the side. "What's that?" I asked as we walked toward it.

"A sauna. I had one installed to help me . . . relax."

I was loving this setup more and more. Felix felt my vibe and said, "Want to try it out?"

Did I? I clapped and jumped. "Yeah. Tell me what to do."

Felix chuckled again. "Go into the cabana, take off all your clothes," he wiggled his eyebrows, "and put on a robe. Then come back out. I'll have it set, and we'll go from there."

I didn't even hesitate. I trotted over to the cabana and shut the door. Towels and robes lined one wall. A bathroom completed the room. I disrobed and then tied the oversize garment over me and walked outside. Felix was reclining beside the sauna. He grinned when he saw me. "Didn't have your size, huh?" he joked.

"Nope, but it'll do in a pinch," I parried back.

"Great. Just go inside, take off the robe, and pull a towel over your hips. You pour water over the coals in the middle to create the steam."

"You aren't coming in?"

"You . . . want me to?" he sputtered.

"Yeah. What am I supposed to do in there by myself?" I quirked my eyebrows.

"Meditate. Relax. . . . None of which you will be doing if I come in there."

"I know. We'll just talk our heads off, get to know each other better." I smiled, offered him a no-strings friendship.

He smiled back. "OK. You go get settled, and I'll join you in just a few."

I opened the door and eased my way inside the sauna. There were three benches set around an open pit with coals in the middle. I couldn't figure out how Felix got things heated up so quickly, but I imagined that the coals were fake and burned on gas because burning charcoal in a confined space would give you carbon-monoxide poisoning.

I shucked off the robe, lay down across a bench, and pulled a towel across my hips. I wish I could say I felt self-conscious, but, honestly, I felt divine. The door opened, and Felix joined me minutes later, two wineglasses in his hand.

"You like?" he asked as he handed me a glass and then sat on the bench across from me. I'd hoped he would disrobe and I'd see the mother lode, but he just cocked a leg up and pulled the robe close, making sure he was fully covered.

"Very much," I assured him while taking a sip of the cool liquid, trying not to allow my spilling breasts to become more visible.

He took a sip and then looked over my body appreciatively. "Sonata, you are a very beautiful woman."

"Thank you," I replied graciously.

"I knew you were . . . different when we met. It's only been confirmed today."

He'd read me well. "Because I helped a duke in distress?"

He grabbed a towel, covered his lap, and then opened the robe and fanned it before responding. "That and . . . you aren't fake. I believe that you bring the *real* you to every encounter. Not the you I want to see or that society says I should expect."

"Glad you like my flavor," I whispered seductively as I stared at the outline of his sex. The sweat rolled into the hollow of my back and pooled.

"I do. I truly do." He locked eyes with mine. The air sizzled with expectancy. To my amazement, as I stared, the towel began tenting, slowly, like one of those charmed snakes. I felt moisture collecting between my legs. I refused to meet Felix's eyes as I willed his dick to grow; I refused to shift my legs closed as the pussy juice pushed at the outer lips. Felix didn't try to cover himself, didn't try to act like he wasn't getting an erection. My nipples were on high alert. I felt the tips pushing between the slats in the bench.

Felix's dick pushed up, up, up . . . until the red tip was winking at me. It was larger than I'd daydreamed it would be. An unbidden moan escaped my lips. My palms itched with the need to wrap them around his shaft, to roam up and down body real estate I'd never known. Felix must have sensed this. He casually pulled off the towel and lay on his back. My tongue hung from my mouth as I gawked at his stiff pole.

He surprised me when he held out his glass. "To new . . . friendships."

My hands trembled as I toasted him back and then attempted another sip. The angle was oh-so-wrong, but I couldn't very well raise up without exposing my bullet nipples. Instead I stretched my neck upward. Bad move. The liquid coursed down my chin, ran a race to cross the finish line at my chest. In my effort to stop the cold trail, I lifted from the bench, my breasts now on open display.

"Want a towel?" Felix purred, dick aimed at me now.

"Sure," I said, face flaming . . . body following suit.

Felix shocked me when he pulled the towel from my hips and slid a tantalizing path up my back, over my shoulders. My pussy began a slow burn. I moaned as he stopped in front of me, and I got an awesome up-close-and-personal view of his cock.

Felix kneeled and pushed the material between my breasts. My breath caught, arms tingled. He stroked at the insignificant amount of liquid slowly, hands grazing my skin. My pussy juice pushed past engorged lips, dripped steadily to the floor. He removed the glass from my unsteady hands and set it on a shelf. His hands threaded through my hair, massaged my scalp.

"If I make love to you now, it won't be a booty call. I'm just feeling you and believe . . . you are feeling me, too," he said, voice low and sincere. "If you think I'm moving too fast . . . we'll wait."

I didn't want to take time to unravel whether it was lust or the beginnings of something more. I just knew I wanted this man. Tonight. Here. Now. Carpe diem.

I reached my hand out, traced it across his eyes, his nose, his cheeks. He kissed my palm, tongue licking the center as it passed over his succulent lips, strummed across his chin. He grasped my hand and pulled it back to his mouth. He sucked the tip of my index finger before pulling it into his hot orifice. My womb clenched and pelvis ground into the bench as he moved to other digits.

His lips released the fingers; his tongue left a saliva trail as he nipped up my wrist to the crook of my elbow, my shoulder. He claimed my mouth, ravished it in his need. My hot hands brushed across his hard chest, lightly pinched his berry nipples. I sighed in his mouth as he reciprocated.

Felix stood, lifted me to my knees, and clasped me to his body. His dick pushed into my stomach; his heart thumped in my ear as I ran my fingers over his taut ass. The pussy juice snaked down my legs.

"You are driving me out of my mind!" he growled low into my hair.

I rubbed my distended nipples across his chest in response. My hands closed around his thick head, felt the pre-cum leaking. Felix shuddered as I squeezed, released, squeezed, released. I flicked across the tip with my thumb, was rewarded with a pump forward. His fingers dove into my pubic hair, searched for my clit. It was my turn to shudder.

His glorious fingers captured my nub between two digits and fiddled. I undulated from the sensation, stroked his shaft in return. I grasped his sac, rolled his balls in my palm.

"Sh . . . shit, baby," Felix stuttered.

His fingers slipped inside my leaking pussy, pulsed and

pumped. I blew air out of my mouth, began deeply stroking his cock. I rolled and swirled, Kegeled and undulated on his fingers. He melded his lips to mine, sucked the moisture from my mouth as we tongue tangoed.

He pumped with gusto now. His hips clenched, fingers pistoned. I shifted to my feet, squatted to give him more access. He kept his lips fused to mine as he stroked, thrust, flitted in me, over me. I smeared his moisture in my palm and stroked deeper. Our teeth bit, nipped, tongues licked, lips sucked overheated skin. I put my back into it and slammed against his stiff fingers. He bucked beneath my hand.

Felix mashed my clit, and the needles zipped from my feet and up my legs to my clit, where the sensations radiated throughout my body. I yowled and howled as I bucked erratically on his fingers. I unconsciously clenched his cock and set off his climax. He bit my shoulder hard as his cum spurted and spurted and spurted over my hand. . . .

14

Felix didn't speak as he cradled me in his arms and strode toward the house. He laid me on a fluffy rug and then left me and entered the kitchen. In moments he returned with a basket of fruit.

"Thought you might be hungry."

I was . . . but it wasn't for fruit.

I selected a banana. We held eyes, and I winked before I looked down at his dick and nodded. I licked up one side of the banana and down the other. I laved it with my saliva and kissed its length.

Felix coughed.

My teeth nibbled at the stem before I clenched it with my teeth and broke the skin. I pulled the folds down slowly, revealing the fruit within.

Felix's dick began rising.

I opened my mouth, placed the fruit between my lips. I sucked the banana slowly in. I twisted it this way and that as it disappeared an inch at a time, and then . . . I pulled it out and repeated.

Felix's stick pulsed.

I licked the tip again and then forced it halfway back into my mouth and bit it off. After I'd swallowed, I finished the other half.

Felix breathed deeply in the quiet room. He then selected a trio of cherries. He placed all of them inside his mouth and sucked. He then pulled them back out except one . . . which he plucked from its stem with his bared teeth.

The blood suffused my face.

His tongue vibrated across the bottom of the remaining two cherries before he swirled them with his tongue. The cherries glistened.

My nipples grew tight.

He sucked both cherries into his mouth and pushed them back out repeatedly, tongue thrusting between lips.

My pussy cried viscous tears.

With one swift movement, he snatched both of the cherries off the stem . . . and then licked his lips seductively.

We lunged toward each other. Our bodies rolled, rubbed in our desire. He pulled me on top of him and slid me forward until my nipples were at his mouth. He licked around the sensitized tips and then covered one and sucked.

I lay with the head of his cock pressing against my clit. I gyrated against the head and felt it blossom even more. The pressure of his lips was good, but I needed more. "Bite," I whispered in his ear. His teeth clamped onto the tingling flesh, and I rocked my clit on his dick head.

Felix's lips burned down my chest. I pushed my heavy breast around his head. He tugged at the nipples.

My pelvis slid against the hard dick, fit it securely between my legs. Felix moaned and rolled me onto my back. "We're about to get carried away." He lifted from the floor and strode down a hallway to my left. He returned in seconds, a silver packet in his hands. He held it out to me.

"Not yet." I dropped the packet on the floor beside us. I grasped his cock and, with no warning, pulled him into my wet mouth.

"Ump" was all he could utter as I licked, nibbled, and sucked as I'd done the banana. His body stiffened as my tongue wet his balls and I pumped him with my hand. My cheeks bulged as I stuffed his cock between my lips and mouth-fucked him rapidly.

Felix grasped my head, his face scrunched. "Baby, you gonna make me come," he eked out between tight jaws.

"I know," I admitted and pushed my mouth back on his love stick, trying to resume my sucking. He stopped me.

"I want to be inside your hot, wet pussy when I do," he explained.

I grabbed the condom from the floor and tore open the packet. I placed the latex in my mouth and then rolled it onto his dick with my tongue.

Felix kneeled and pressed his lips to mine. "Girl, what am I gonna do with you?"

I didn't hesitate. "Fuck me blind."

He lay on his back. "Ride this dick."

And I did. I climbed on top and slid slowly down his big-ass cock. When I'd fitted as much as possible in me, I leaned forward and rocked. He filled every inch of my pussy! I squeezed on the outward stroke and relaxed on the inward. Tissues strained, muscles ached as I mashed, humped, and circled on his mighty mountain.

I needed more. I turned around and sat back on his root, felt it going deeper. I'd swear his dick was in my stomach! But *damn!* It felt good! I leaned elbows on the floor as I fucked that dick like I owned it!

Pop! Felix spanked my ass, and I moaned and pumped. He

lifted his knees and pump-jerked me back. My ass bounced into the air.

But when his finger wormed its way into my chocolate love hole, I sprayed, humped, and jerked into oblivion as he pounded into me without mercy. He spasmed and spurted seconds later.

15

Tuesday couldn't come fast enough! My escapade with Felix had unleashed the sex beast within, and Video was just what I needed to quench some of the fire in my pussy.

Tommy arrived all smiles . . . until he noticed the flowers. I refused to divulge any information. His nostrils flared, nose twitched as I defied all his investigative attempts. He needed to understand that I had options, too. I didn't plan to waste away, hoping he'd get around to me.

He insisted on driving the Crown Vic, but I refused to let it dampen my spirits. We rode in silence. Him, wondering what was going on with me and whomever; me, hoping he understood that if he wouldn't, somebody else sure would.

I jumped in my seat as the brownstone housing Video came in sight. I didn't look at him as I walked briskly to the door and rang the buzzer. When the voice asked, "Password," Tommy remained silent; he stared at me. I arched a meaning-filled eyebrow at him.

Sims repeated, "Password."

Tommy's visage was granite as he glared at me. He finally responded, "Fellatio."

It was definitely time for me to get my own membership!

Sims followed his normal routine and then turned back, smile in place. He sensed the tension between us. He pulled down his requisite sunglasses and stared at us over the top. He then asked pointedly, "Honeymoon over already?"

We remained silent.

He sighed. "Guess that answers my question. What is your pleasure tonight?"

I kept quiet, waited for Tommy to answer like he always did. Instead he remained silent, eyes glittering in the light.

Sims stepped up to the plate. "Let me suggest something to help get your fires burning again: mono . . . anything goes. Soundstage Four." He winked at me and then walked back to the door as it buzzed.

Once again, I didn't have a clue as to what was to come. But from my past experiences, I was positive I could work with it no matter what.

Soundstage Four was completely deserted. I wondered if maybe Sims had misinformed us, but Tommy closed the door behind us and propelled us to seats in the front row. In moments the lights dimmed and the curtain parted.

The spotlight clicked on, revealing a bronzed woman, dressed in a sarong, sitting Indian style on a large rug. Celine Dion's "Have You Ever Been In Love?" began playing. My curiosity was piqued.

The woman scratched a match on a box, and the match sputtered to life. She took her time as she lit the candles surrounding the rug. Then she looked directly at us as her fingers began slowly coursing over her body. She stroked her fabric-covered thighs like a lover would, squeezed and pressed her flat belly, and then cupped her breasts. The material peaked as her thumbs pulled at their center. Her hands continued to travel upward past her neck, ending at her hair. The severe chignon was released, and a river of hair floated down, reached the floor.

Tommy shifted in his seat and sat straighter.

I watched as she stood, pulled at the binding behind her neck. When it was released, the material pooled at her feet.

The woman was magnificent. Her round breasts rode high, and her nipples were black as night—a stark contrast to her golden skin. Her waist indented before wide hips, and slender thighs completed the package. She had me beat hands down.

Tommy leaned forward in his seat.

The woman held Tommy's eyes as she palmed her breast, brought the stiff tip to her open mouth. Her lips tugged, teeth pulled as she suckled herself.

Tommy squirmed in his seat. I could tell he wanted to suck on her tits himself.

Her body snaked as she ran her hands up and down her naked flesh into her hair. A bottle was grabbed from the floor. Oil squirted onto her skin. My clit lurched as she leaned over and massaged it into her firm ass while still snaking her body to the rhythm of the music.

Tommy reached for me then. He pulled me onto his lap, cupped my breasts from behind. I felt his stiff dick pushing into my ass, and I ground on it.

The woman turned and smiled at us now. She squatted, legs open wide. The camera panned her shaven pubis. Her pussy "winked," forcing a drop of honey to the edge of her orifice.

Tommy unbuttoned my blouse and pulled my titties over the top of my bra. His fingers played with the nipples before he pinched them. He turned me to the side and sucked one into his burning mouth, eyes still trained on the woman.

A box at her side was opened and a long blue dildo removed.

The woman licked up one side and down the other, leaving a saliva trail.

Scenes of the banana . . . and Felix played in my mind. I shoved my breast farther into Tommy's mouth. My pussy sniffled.

She sucked the tip before pushing two inches . . . four inches . . . eight inches into her mouth.

Tommy released my breast, shifted me, and unzipped his pants. My hands closed around the thick girth; I squeezed.

The dildo was now on her clit. She turned it on, the vibrations barely heard over the music. Her pelvis rocketed forward as it touched her clit. She gasped and then moaned.

Tommy lifted my skirt; fingers found my clit. I vigorously stroked his dick.

The tip was at her pussy. She spread the lips and pushed it inside. Deep. Both hands grasped the dildo as she fucked herself. She gyrated as she pumped, juice spurting out occasionally.

My pussy was sopping wet as Tommy finger-fucked me. His hips fucked my hands with relish.

She rolled onto her back, lifted her hips into the air, and continued pushing the latex dick rapidly in and out. In and out.

Tommy stood, turned me so that I was leaning on the stage—six feet from the woman—and spread my legs wide. He kneeled, his tongue fused to my pussy. I clenched my ass and moaned in ecstasy. Felix's face flashed into my head again. I moaned louder.

The woman was on her knees now, fucking herself furiously. She saw us, crawled over to us, still fucking herself with the dildo. I didn't know what to do . . . but didn't care either. She stopped inches from me, eyes glazed in lust, mouth open.

"Sit up here," she croaked.

I pushed at Tommy's head. He resisted. I pushed again. "What?" he said, eyes confused. I pointed to the woman. She crooked a finger at him. Tommy beat me onstage.

She pushed me onto my back. Tommy's dick throbbed as he watched the sex play. I wasn't sure what she'd planned, and, in truth, I'd never been turned on by women before. But I was horny as hell right now. The woman leaned over me and pressed her lips lightly to mine before her tongue parted my teeth. I melted as her lightning tongue commandeered my mouth.

She moved from my mouth to my breast. Her fingers plucked the stiff buttons before her lips surrounded one. Tommy's fingers slipped inside me and stroked. My body arched, clit engorged from this twin assault.

I stuffed her long nipple into my mouth, was surprised at the texture, tanginess. We licked, sucked, bit each other's burning tips.

Tommy sucked my pussy. His tongue ran rapidly up and down from clit to pussy. I couldn't control myself as I ground on his face. He pushed my legs up and spread them wide. I mouth-fucked the nipple as his tongue laved around my anus. He vibrated his tongue on my clit, undulated in my pussy, stabbed my ass.

"Shit!" I screamed as my body strained toward release.

The woman crawled away from me and toward Tommy. I leaned up on my elbows, watched as he wrote his name in my humping pussy with his tongue. The woman rolled onto her back again, slid beside Tommy. She pulled a thigh across her head. Tommy dipped his hips toward her waiting mouth.

My pussy clenched as she engulfed his big-ass dick three inches. Tommy growled as she pulled him deeper. I leaked cum as she passed the six-inch mark. Cunt sobbed when his entire nine inches disappeared down her throat. Tommy fucked her mouth like it was a pussy. The woman pressed the dildo back into her wet snatch and bucked on it. I pinched my nipples, rubbed Tommy's head, rubbed her thighs.

Tommy suddenly made a fuck face. His hips undulated in

the air rapidly. His eyes rolled in his head. The woman flung her legs wide, pushed the dildo deep into her pussy. Humped the air. Tommy grabbed hold of my nipples, and I erupted, convulsed. My legs held him in a headlock as I sprayed his face, his chin.

Bliss.

16

You would think at this point that I had the best of both worlds—my cake and was eating it, too. Not so. My sex drive was in overdrive, and I was sexless in the city!

Tommy continued his disappearing acts—Valentine's Day and my birthday—and Felix worked the night shift, so our schedules rarely collided. I made the decision to find someone who had the time and energy to train all his attention on me. Neither Tommy nor Felix had stepped up his game, no matter how much hinting I'd done, so it was time for some new players.

I called Tommy first. No answer, so I left a message. He called me back an hour later.

"Hey, Sonata. What's up?"

"Glad you called me back. I need to talk to you."

"Talk."

Guess he didn't think I had something that needed to be said face-to-face. That was fine. "Well, we've been seeing each other off and on for the past year. . . ." My voice trailed off as I collected my thoughts.

"Yeah. And?"

I took a breath, decided to get to the point. "Tommy, I like you, but I'm not going to see you again."

He exploded. "What's this shit about? We're doing fine."

He thought seeing me once or twice a month was fine. I definitely knew where I stood with him. "I just feel that, after a year, we should have . . . progressed."

"Progressed? I'm a busy man. I see you when I can." Which wasn't too much.

"I realize that. It's just not . . . enough."

"Not enough."

"No. Not enough for me."

"So you're telling me you want to stop seeing me altogether even though we don't see each other . . . *enough* . . . for you right now," he spat.

My logic sounded warped coming from his lips, but I stuck to my guns. "Yes."

"This is *bull*shit. Just *bull*shit," he snarled. "I can't believe you'd come at me like this."

His attitude pissed me off. "Well, I am. I don't see you enough, you don't try to make more time for me, and I need more than what we have. Have a good day." I hung up. It rang seconds later. I refused to answer. That's when my cell phone began singing . . . and singing and singing.

I called Felix an hour later. He had been sleeping, but his voice brightened when he heard mine.

"Sonata, good to hear from you."

"Maybe," I began truthfully.

"You sound different. What's going on?" he asked.

"Felix . . . I've enjoyed the time we've spent together."

"Me, too."

"But . . ." I hesitated, not wanting to continue but knowing he was too nice of a guy to string along, "but the fact is . . . I'm not going to see you again."

"What happened?" he asked, surprised.

"You just don't have the time to spend with me that I'd like."

He was quiet before he said, "I know. I've been trying for months to get on the day shift, but we're low on staff, and I haven't been successful."

I was quiet.

"Sonata, please don't give up on us because of my work schedule."

"It's not just yours, it's mine also," I replied, frustrated at life.

"We can do better. Tell me what to do."

"I have," I reminded him. I'd asked him to surprise me when he got off. Spend the night on the spur of the moment. So far it hadn't happened. All our dates had been planned, orchestrated affairs.

I heard him sniff, but he didn't speak.

"So, I wanted to let you know. Not act funny and leave you in the dark."

His voice broke as he said, low, "Ca—can I call you back a little later? This has thrown me for a loop."

"No need. I think we've said all we need to."

"But—"

I hung up the phone with him still talking.

My cell phone rang all day. As I saw patients, I heard the ringing. As I did surgery, I heard the ringing. When the staff remarked on the ringing, I put it on vibrate. All this wasn't working, and it continued to ring.

Finally the day ended and I drove to Lorenze's to cool my heels. The ringing had given me a headache, made me short with clients, rough with patients—an all-around bad person to be near today.

I pushed the bar door open with something akin to relief. . . .

17

Present day, continued

They both stepped back, and each offered me their hand. My skin tingled as I watched them stare at me. Make-up sex was definitely in the air . . . but which one?

Suddenly my fantasy of two men popped into the forefront of my mind. I imagined twin lips, hips, thighs intertwined with mine. Two sets of hands stoking my fires, two sets of cocks stroking me deep . . . but, no, that was a fantasy, not reality.

Or could it be?

When *else* would I have two men I really dug, who knew about each other, ready to give me sex? My body trilled with excitement, fear. I knew it was now or never.

"Well, guys, you want to continue this?" I asked, feeling like the dominant one for once.

They never looked at each other, only me, when each replied, "Yes."

Well, guess we're *all* back together! I took each one's hand

and started for the door. Make-up sex . . . times two . . . has got
to be the bomb!

We left Lorenze's and drove to my apartment in our respective cars. My heart was thumping and my mind jumping all
over the place. I'd never had two men sex me down at one time.
Yeah, it'd always been my fantasy, but the reality was something I hadn't planned because I never believed I could find two
men *I* enjoyed that would be willing participants. Sharing
pussy wasn't one of their strong suits.

My hands were sweaty as I unlocked the door.

Felix and Tommy never said a word. In fact, they never even
looked at each other. Each time I peeped at them, they were
staring only at me. I ushered them in with little fanfare.

Showtime!

I took a deep breath and then cleared my throat. "Why don't
I freshen up and we go from there?" I suggested.

"Cool" was Felix's reply. Tommy answered moments later
with, "Fine."

I strode into the bedroom on shaky legs. I stripped out of
my clothes and let the massage jets steam up the bathroom before I entered the shower. I washed myself slowly, trying to
plot my strategy.

Both at once, or one at a time?

One at a time would be business as usual. Shoot, since I didn't
know when I'd even get another shot at some double-dick action like this, I decided to go for the gusto—both in me at the
same time, in whatever fashion we wished . . . Video style.

Suddenly the shower curtain was drawn back. Felix's golden
body stood on the other side, naked and aroused. His cock was
throbbing, and a drop of pre-cum was present on the tip. He
stepped inside, pulled me close. My breasts mashed into his
massive chest as his tongue raped and pillaged mine. *He's never*

kissed like this before! I thought as he swirled and twirled with abandon.

His hands grabbed my cheeks and spread them, allowing the pulsating massage jets to tickle my anus. It was unique and pleasurable. My pussy juice multiplied rapidly. He pressed me against the wall, began sucking my nipples. The sensation was felt from my clit to where his lips clamped on my breasts. I sighed.

The curtain was pulled back again. I opened my eyes to see Tommy's dark body step into the tub. Felix never stopped his suckling as Tommy shifted behind me. Tommy's lips sucked along my earlobe, my neck, my back, while his hands plunged into my bush, stroking, pulling, pushing inside of me, forcing me to respond. I couldn't stop if I wanted to. I was on fire!

Felix moved lower, stopping momentarily to lick my belly button, until he was eye level with my clit. Tommy splayed me open wide for Felix. Felix's tongue caressed my outer lips, inner lips, and then pierced my love hole. I moaned as his thick mouth dick lapped at my juices. Tommy stroked my pelvis, pulled my nipples taut as Felix fed on my lubricant. I undulated against the hard dick at my ass and mouth at my pussy.

Tommy's dick slid between my ass cheeks and throbbed. He blew in my ear, whispered, "I plan to fuck you like nobody's business tonight." I moaned and wiggled harder. He humped my ass; balls brushed my cheeks. I writhed in ecstasy, dislodged Felix's head from my pussy. When Tommy inserted a finger into my anus, I screamed as the needle pinpricks flowed upward and exploded at my clit. . . .

I felt them drying me gently before one of them picked me up and laid me on the bed. I don't know who did what, because I was still on my "high," and my eyes were tightly closed. Kisses rained on my face, my eyes, my neck, my back. I heard the tear-ing of the condom packet and mentally prepared myself for this love assault of my body.

I didn't have to wait long.

I opened my eyes as Felix pulled me on top of him. His dick pulsed in my stomach as he grabbed a handful of my hair and pulled me higher. He bit my lips and chin, and I reciprocated because I loved being bitten. Tommy pulled my butt into the air while Felix and I plundered each other.

Tommy's tongue swirled and lapped around the anus. I arched my back involuntarily, wanted more of what he offered. He spread my cheeks; his tongue pushed inside me. My belly clenched; I opened my legs wider. Tommy took his time working his anal magic. His fingers tag-teamed with his tongue to hold me open as he tongue-fucked me deeper. I was thrusting backward on his face now, pussy juice dripping onto Felix.

Felix mashed my breasts together before fitting his large dick in the groove. As he pushed upward, I flicked the tip and sucked briefly before he slid downward. This tease play mildly irritated me. I wanted more, damnit! I added additional suction and, soon, Felix was surging into my mouth, my breasts forgotten as he tried to fit all of his dick inside my hot orifice.

The oil was warm as I felt it dribble down my cleft. Tommy skillfully massaged it around and inside of me, preparing me for him. He lightly tapped his dick's head on my cheeks. Goose bumps broke out along my skin as I felt his dick pushing at the sphincter. I gasped around Felix's cock as Tommy entered me. Tommy took his time stretching me and then waiting for me to adjust. There were some sharp pains initially, but I relaxed my body and accommodated him. As he pushed deeper, something overtook me. I pumped back on that hard dick like it was in my pussy. My nipples were rock hard, clit stiff as a pen as I pistoned back on him.

"Yes!" I screamed as Tommy pumped forward and I pumped back. "Yes!"

My fingers found my clit and began mashing, pulling on it.

"Oh, baby, this shit is good!" Tommy said as he kissed my back.

I didn't say a word, just kept pace with him.

"I want some of this," Felix said. He held my face. "Let us both love you . . . together. OK?"

Yep, that's what I wanted, all right!

I nodded, and he slid lower. Tommy stopped as Felix "suited up" and positioned his dick at my pussy's door. He pumped into me slowly. I could feel the tissues expanding: pleasure-pain. Felix stopped and gasped, "I don't think I can get any farther without us stroking it in."

I couldn't answer with my voice, so instead I undulated my body to help things along. Tommy pushed from the back while Felix alternated from the front. In five strokes, he was snuggled inside me. The sound of slapping flesh was . . . so, *so* delicious.

The dicks slid and slipped over and around each other, separated only by a thin membrane of tissue. I rocked and undulated with everything I had, increased the tempo.

Gawd, the sensations!

Tommy grabbed my hair. Felix squeezed my breasts and pinched the nipples. I twisted, moaned and fucked, with every muscle in my body straining for fulfillment. I inserted my hand beneath my legs and began massaging two sets of balls. Both of them yelped.

Felix pistoned upward as Tommy pistoned downward. I brushed my clit and, suddenly, the needle pinpoints were zinging up my legs and thighs to my clit. I stroked deeper than I ever had before then . . . my entire body locked. Tommy moaned loudly; he smacked his pelvis forcefully into mine. Felix's fuck face betrayed him. His eyes rolled back into his head as he mumbled incoherent words before lifting me high off the bed with his final stroke. . . .

I now stand corrected. Make-up sex . . . times two . . . *is* the bomb!

Pure Pleasure

Fiona Zedde

1

Ian woke up still dreaming. The last vestiges of a woman, slim hipped with a pretty bottom and a viciously tight pussy, made him call out in his half sleep. The hoarse, preorgasmic shout woke Ian fully from his dream. But he wanted to stay. He pushed his hips into the bed, fighting to keep the sensation of the woman's sweetness around him. Ian pumped against the bed, his dick caught in the silken cotton that, for a few necessary moments, was like the slick, clasping inside of his siren, the woman who often claimed him in sleep. The muscles of his ass bunched and shuddered as he came, gasping, into the pillow.

Ian's wife, Zoë, had been dead for almost five years now. Some days it seemed like five minutes since he got the news of her car accident. Other days it seemed like fifty years. Today was one of those in-between days when he had a good perspective on things and the blame he shouldered for her accident— an argument that pushed her screaming out into traffic and the path of a drunk driver—weighed him down only a little. He could usually tell right away what kind of day it would be, even before he left his bed. This morning the sign was his explosive orgasm and the almost sound of his dream lover's name on his lips.

Ian never had any illusions that this woman was Zoë. She was too voracious in her appetite for sex, and her body was too slight for her to be his dead wife. Ian pushed away from the bed and its sticky sheets, stretching each muscle in his long body as he headed for the bathroom. After a quick brush of teeth, his morning push-ups, and a few rounds with the punching bag, he went for the shower.

Under the spray, water sluiced down his sculpted toffee-brown physique, tracing the muscled arms, chest, and belly. His dick was soft, but with one touch it began to awaken. The unbidden memory of the dream woman slowly brought it to full hardness, and he stroked himself.

But he didn't have time for this. One more come and he was going to be late for class. It wasn't even like he had the excuse of a real woman to be late for. There hadn't been a real woman in his bed for a long time. Almost two weeks now. The constant round of disposable bodies had worn him out. The women in California were so beautiful and available that, even with the shadow of Zoë's loss hanging over him, Ian had initially gobbled up the most tempting pieces; but there had been no substance to them. Now it all seemed like a waste of energy. Ian rediscovered that he preferred spice and challenge in his women. He hadn't found that in California yet.

After a full breakfast of wheat pancakes, eggs, and a protein shake, he quickly left his house and drove down the winding, sun-splashed streets to the university. Six years after moving to California, he still wasn't used to it. The campus was a buffet of all things the Golden State had to offer: tall, short, bronzed, brown, and pale sex goddesses, all in their prime with juicy breasts, tiny waists, and lush asses on display. It was a smorgasbord of sexual plenty that Ian had often tempted himself to try to taste. But his appetite was never up to it. His mama told him never to shit where he ate.

"Good morning, Mr. Tate," one of his students greeted as she walked toward him in the hallway, gravity-defying breasts bouncing in her white tube top.

"Good morning, Loren."

If her jeans rode any lower, she'd be giving the whole campus a guided tour of her Pandora's box. Her belly-button jewel winked at him as she passed, but Ian only spared her a single glance before stepping into his first class of the day.

2

———————————

Earlier in the semester, Ian had realized that most of his students were more interested in fucking him than learning about the Harlem Renaissance. He paced once more in front of the class, today's lesson falling from his lips like memorized lines. Some of the students were actually paying attention. Jasmine Hannah sat right in front, with her pen moving steadily across her paper, taking down every pertinent word. There were others, too. Vincent Mueller and Craig Johnson were model students, but only because neither wanted to repeat the class again. Ian's gaze swept over the class, acknowledging the bored, dreamy-eyed, sleepy, interested, and variously pained expressions on the faces of his students. He shrugged inwardly and continued with the lesson.

After class, Maddie Lang came up to his desk all pouty and flirtatious in her head-to-toe Gucci. She and her three girls approached his desk like they were going to war, with all their feminine weapons at the ready.

"Did you read my essay, Mr. Tate?" she asked, knowing full well that her essay wasn't so much a commentary on the role of white patronage in the growth of the Harlem Renaissance but a tour of the pornographic fantasies of a very imaginative young lady. Complete with museum-quality illustrations.

Ian gave her his most charming smile. "The artistic part of the assignment was well done, Maddie. But, if you notice, this class is Literature and Life During the Harlem Renaissance, not Art 101." He pushed her paper across the desk toward her. "I gave you a D. If you'd like to redo the essay on the topic we discussed, then I will consider giving you a higher grade."

All four girls gave him a blank look, as if he'd been the one to fail the assignment. Apparently that seduction technique of hers had worked before. What did she expect him to say, "See you after class when we can discuss your essay at length," and then bend her over his desk and fuck her the way they both knew she wanted? Maddie Lang wasn't worth it.

Her lips tightened. "Thanks, Mr. Tate." She took up her essay and pivoted, her girls falling into place like the waving tail feathers of a peacock, and walked out of the classroom. Ian watched them walk away, switching their cute little behinds for all they were worth. A teasing sight, but for all that, they barely made his balls twitch. He went back to his paperwork.

The other faculty thought he was gay. They didn't come out and say so, of course, but after the first few refusals of blind dates and his obvious lack of lust for the sun-toasted California coeds, they thought he was a pussy, not that he wanted to fuck one.

Ian knew he wasn't the usual kind of straight man. He got focused. Sometimes it was on getting laid, sometimes it wasn't. After he'd gotten with Zoë, there was no one else for him. He met her in a capoeira class his first year of college, and that was that. He had been seeing a few girls at the time, some glamour-girl sorority types who'd been drawn to his clean, upper-middle-class look—polo shirt and khakis, cargo shorts and slogan tees even in the middle of winter—and his lean, sleekly muscled swimmer's body. His ready smile and *GQ* features only added to the attractive package that most girls were eager to unwrap.

Ian had to work to get Zoë. In class she was the one who excelled far above everyone else. She was tricky in her game, her kicks hurt, and her bottom always looked good in those loose dancer's pants. Flashes of her belly and sweat-soaked sports bra when she turned effortless somersaults in the air had him instantly hard. For months everyone in the class thought he was shy and never wanted to play. The truth was that he wanted to play only with her. He wanted a close-up view of the sweat dripping down her face and neck that collected in the shirt clinging to her thick breasts and nipples. He watched all the other boys, and some of the girls, get turned down by Zoë time and time again. She played with them, and the rest of the class got to watch, every single player hiding hard-ons or uncomfortably wet panties. Ian didn't think he stood any more of a chance than most with her, and that excited him.

One cold and blustery day, they both came early to class. Ian asked her to play with him, just a warm-up. For once he wasn't thinking about fucking. He was just frozen and wanted to raise his body temperature. To his surprise she said yes, smiling into his eyes before sweeping off her oversize sweatshirt and dropping it to the side next to her bag. She had on another shirt, tighter and smaller, that was the same burnished copper as her skin. If he looked too fast he could fool himself into thinking that she was topless. Her long, curly hair, which he later found out was her single source of pride, she doubled up and gathered in a club at the back of her neck. Zoë put on the music.

"Ready?"

He wasn't, but he stepped to her anyway. Their play was rough. She bested him several times, reeling up from the floor with powerful kicks and spins when he thought he had her cornered. It was even better than he thought.

At the end of it, Ian was breathing hard, his breath coming

in harsh puffs against the now comfortably cool air of the studio. He felt the sweat coating his naked back and chest, and the heat of his workout glowing under his loose sweatpants. Zoë watched him. She wiped the sweat from her face with the back of her hand and licked her lips. Her chest rose and fell in a quick tempo that pulled Ian's eyes to her breasts and the hard points of her nipples.

"Fuck." He didn't realize he'd said the word out loud until she looked up at him with something naked and raw in her face. Want. For him.

"I'm going . . ." She gestured behind her toward something, but he didn't understand her. "Bathroom," she finally got out and backed away.

Ian didn't know why, but he followed her. Down the hall, past the other two studios that had classes in session, past the men's showers and bathrooms. The women's showers smelled like shampoo and perfume. Zoë slipped through the doors, and he followed still, like a hypnotized cobra, as she backed into an empty shower, a private one with a real door. Her back was to the cool tile wall, and she licked her lips again. That was all the invitation he needed.

Zoë tasted of sweat and sweet, an aphrodisiac blend that burned from her hotly spiced mouth. Her hands roved over his chest, pressing him and pinching his flat nipples. He pushed her bra up and out of the way to find what he needed—the feel of her skin, sweat-slick and salty wet under his tongue, and the black-cherry nipples he'd only fantasized about, hard and ready in his mouth.

"Fuck me," she hissed in his ear.

Zoë pushed her pants and panties down and off for him to push his dick—oh, sweet heaven!—inside her soaked pussy. She grabbed his ass to pull him deeper. Her deep, urgent noises spurred him on, swelled his dick until he was panting as loudly as she was, slamming into her and then pulling almost all the way out before diving back into her pussy. Her ass slapped rhythmic and wet against the tile; she grabbed his shoulders, his back, clawing at him with her ankles locked together below his ass.

"Fuck me! Fuck me! Fuck me!" she chanted as he pounded into her. Their sweat and sex smells rose up, surrounding him until he was swimming in his desire, hot and rushing, his muscles burning to get them across the finish line of orgasm.

Her arms reached up to grab the industrial-strength shower rod as her hips pistoned against him, fucking him as much as he was fucking her, her lips skinned back and feral, the "Fuck me!" chant still pouring out of her. He squeezed the breasts popping coyly from beneath the rolled-up edge of her bra, pinching the nipples between his fingers in time to the push-pull of his dick. She was starting to come. He felt her pussy clench around his dick, one tight squeeze and release after another; each time she pushed her back in a more extreme angle off the shower wall, arching into him.

"Goddamnit!" She came in a hoarse shout, pitching him over the edge with her as she milked his dick of everything it had.

They shuddered against the tiled wall and each other, sweating and breathing rapidly. Her skin was hot. Ian pulled back, and she made a small sound, a low grunt when his dick slid wetly out of her. They both looked at each other as they had the same thought. *Shit! No rubber.*

But everything worked out. They both got tested, a little too late but better than not at all, and started to fuck every day, sometimes three or four times, depending on if they had class or not. He stopped seeing the other girls. A year later they were married and making plans to leave Atlanta for New York or some other big city in which they could both do well in their respective professions. Four years later, Zoë was dead.

3

"So, everyone knows what they have to do to get ready for this trip?"

All six of the students in the meeting, four women and two young men, nodded or made some noise of agreement. Ian sat on top of his desk, feeling relaxed at his last campus commitment of the day. He looked at Jasmine.

"I know you have that engineering conference coming up next week, so don't worry too much about the Ojai writers' conference. Just get what you need out of it, and then turn in your assigned story in two weeks."

Jasmine smiled. "I'm not worried, Mr. Tate. I'm just grateful for the chance to go along with the rest the group. Even though I'm not a Creative Writing major, I still appreciate you making room for me."

"I'll take that as a 'yet,' Jasmine. You're a great writer, but I understand about the engineering thing. You've got to eat, after all."

"Not all of us are gonna be starving writers, Mr. Tate." Olivier Richey, who had aspirations of being the next Stephen

King, waggled his pencil at Ian. "I plan on making as many connections at this conference as possible."

"Good for you, Olivier," said Natalie, one of the more obviously gorgeous women in the class, and an MFA candidate. "Just don't mow down any of us on your path to fame and riches."

Ian chuckled. "And I think that does it for our last organizational meeting before the conference." He looked at his watch. "It's a little after six. I imagine you all have places to be?"

"There you go again, always trying to get rid of us. If I didn't know any better, I'd swear you didn't like being adviser to our little writing club."

"And you do know better." Ian said, smiling at Samantha Ng. He picked up his briefcase and the folder with his papers to grade for the week. "So, everyone, to recap: we're meeting in front of the Humanities offices on Friday afternoon at three. The van will be parked near my car and unlocked if you want to put some of your things in it. We leave at three thirty."

"Got it, Mr. Tate." Jasmine gathered her things and, after a quick glance at her own watch, dashed out the door while wishing everyone a good evening.

"She must have a hot date or something," Olivier said with a casual leer. "What I wouldn't give to be a fly on the wall for that hot piece of business."

"Why do men always turn into pigs by the idea of two women together?" Samantha groaned.

"Because it's hot," Natalie said as she too headed out the door. "See you, Mr. Tate."

Samantha looked at Ian and rolled her eyes. "Can you believe her?"

"No comment." Ian chuckled again and waved good-bye to his students.

"Come on, Sam. You need a drink." The other club members jostled her out of the classroom, teasing as they went.

As Ian went to turn off the lights, a bright orange folder caught his eye. A quick glance through it told him that the folder was Jasmine's. In it was an essay and notes on some complicated engineering something or other. After a moment's hesitation, he put it in his briefcase. She might need it for her presentation at the conference that was less than a week away. He decided to be a good samaritan and drop the folder off at her house on his way home from the basketball court later on.

Ian rang the doorbell to the small Spanish-style bungalow that was supposed to be Jasmine's house. As he waited for someone to come to the door, Ian noticed a couple walking their dog on the sidewalk bordering the house. They held hands as they walked together through the quiet neighborhood. The dog, a ghost-gray Weimaraner puppy, leaped and played behind them, sniffing at every bush and rock it passed.

"Can I help you?" A girl, not Jasmine, stood in the doorway. She nibbled at a crustless peanut butter and jelly sandwich as she waited for Ian to speak.

"Oh, yes." He smiled at the pretty, gamine girl. "Sorry. My name is Ian Tate, and I teach at the university—"

"*The* Mr. Tate?" She laughed and paused with the sandwich halfway to her mouth. "You're the one who's chaperoning Mina and the other girls to Ojai?"

He didn't know why she seemed so surprised. Who was this girl anyway? "I am. Is there a problem?"

She laughed again. "We'll see." The girl looked back over her shoulder and yelled out, "Mina! There's someone here to see you. And he didn't call first."

The girl turned back to him, and Ian was struck again by how lovely she was, with her short, natural hair; odd, pointy ears; and the wide, dark eyes staring unblinkingly up at him. She looked away as a sweatpants-and-T-shirt-clad Jasmine bounded up behind her. His student seemed distracted.

"Hey, Mr. Tate. What's going on?"

"Sorry, but for some reason it never occurred to me to call." He produced her folder from his briefcase. "You left this in the meeting earlier tonight."

Her expression cleared. "Thank God! I've been looking all over for that." She hugged it to her chest, smiling. "Thank you! I wanted to look over those notes tonight, and I was going crazy when I couldn't find the folder."

The other girl retreated from the door. Ian watched her slim back, left bare by a psychedelic-print halter top, disappear as she slipped into the candlelit recesses of the house. Something about her seemed vaguely familiar.

"No problem, Jasmine. Your house isn't very far from mine. Anyway, I'll let you get back to your studying." He stepped back from the doorway. "Good luck with that presentation."

"Thanks." She started to close the door.

"Oh, by the way." Ian turned back to the house. "Who was that girl who answered the door? I didn't know you had a sister."

"Oh." Jasmine giggled, sounding a little like the girl who answered the door. "That's my mom. She can be a little rude sometimes. Sorry about that."

Her mother? "No, it's OK. She wasn't rude. I was just curious." He gave her his professor's smile. "I'll see you on Friday afternoon."

"OK." She smiled back and closed the door.

As he walked back down the path past their garage, he felt eyes on him. Ian looked around and then up. It was Jasmine's mother. She sat at the upstairs window, perched on the window seat like a cat, watching him. When she noticed that he saw her, she didn't look away. If anything, her look intensified. Then she smiled.

Ian got into his car and drove off, feeling her eyes on him the entire time. At home he couldn't shake her look. Or the feeling that he'd seen her before. He graded some papers, planned an itinerary for himself during the Ojai trip, and then took himself off to bed.

She was draped in candlelight. In a scene straight from a soft-core porn, she sat in a high velvet-covered bed, naked with just the light playing over her silken flesh, flickering over her ankles, thighs, the subtle curve of her hips, her sweeping back, and the welcoming smile turned coyly over her shoulder. He felt his own nakedness in the slight breeze that came from an open window. Her gaze caressed his body like her soft hands soon would, skimming over his chest, his flat belly that contracted at the look of her, and his slowly hardening cock.

"Come," she said. And he went to her. She turned slowly, and his breath escaped him. How could someone so lovely and innocent-looking be so bold? She kissed him, brushing her breasts against him, teasing with her hands. She cupped his balls and whispered hotly in his ear.

"I need to taste you."

Her hands pushed him gently onto the bed. The velvet enfolded him as she moved down between his widening thighs. She smiled again. And covered him with her mouth. His neck arched. His body sizzled. She retreated to lick the head of his dick slowly while keeping her eyes on him, watching the agonized pleasure in his face. Her mouth opened, and she swallowed him, taking him deep into the back of her throat, sucking in a slow, building rhythm until his hips moved with her head and his hand drifted over her hair, cupping her vulnerable scalp as she watched him with her big eyes. Her cheeks hollowed as she took more of him into her mouth, feeding his pleasure, trailing fire down his belly and into his balls. As though she sensed their sudden heaviness, his sudden need to come, she cupped him and hummed something. He exploded in her mouth. Her smile was angelic and hungry, and she climbed up his body, opening up her gorgeous pussy above his mouth.

"Your turn."

Ian opened his mouth, anticipating the soft wetness on his tongue and that low gasp of hers when he gave it to her just as she liked. Instead he got the sound of his alarm clock.

"No." He rolled over in the bed and swept his arm to where he knew the alarm clock was. "I'm not working today," he muttered to the merciless alarm clock that had taken away his dream. Her slick pussy had been right there, its pink insides tender as a conch, just waiting for him to slide his tongue inside.

Ian groaned and sat up. "Fuck."

His sheets were wet from when he had come in her mouth. He hated to let her go. In his dreams she was perfect, always ready to please him. In his waking life all he had of her were cryptic looks from a high window and sticky fingers holding on to a peanut butter and jelly sandwich. Ian froze. And that was it. Just that simply, he knew where he had seen Jasmine's mother before. In his bed. In his dreams.

4

Ojai was a nice town. Ian hadn't been there in a long time, not since he'd first come to California and thought about becoming an artist. What kind of artist, he hadn't really been sure. All he knew was that he wasn't in the mood to deal with the school bureaucracy and bullshit anymore. Then he'd ended up in Irvine. He fell in love with teaching again, and that was the end of his artistic aspirations.

"All right, ladies and gentlemen. We're here."

He pulled the van up to the hotel. It was a small two-story guesthouse an alum had rented to him and his students for practically nothing. His students peered outside the van, looking around the small art town like they had been traveling for hours and had finally arrived on Mars.

"Thank the goddess," Natalie said. She slung her backpack over her shoulder and jumped out of the van. "One more freaking round of Faulkner trivia and I was gonna put my head through the glass."

"You're just pissed because you didn't get any of the answers right." Samantha picked up her pink duffel bag and starting walking toward the small adobe-style hotel to check in.

Jasmine bumped Natalie's shoulder and laughed. "She's right. Don't be such a sore loser." She grabbed her friend's hand and pulled her toward the hotel.

Kendra McNeal and Archie Kennedy quietly emerged from the back of the van. Though physically mismatched, the pair had been inseparable since they met in the group at the beginning of last year. Plain and studious Kendra, with her thick hair more often than not held back in two afro puffs, and Archie Kennedy, gorgeous academic wonder boy and soccer star. The two had spent the entire ride snuggling and talking quietly in the back corner seat of the large van.

"The ride was fine, Mr. Tate. Didn't feel a single bump in the road." Archie grinned, and Kendra smiled up at him adoringly before nodding back at Ian.

"We're going up to the room, now," she said, her voice strong and mature despite her petite frame. "How much time do we have until we meet you back here?"

Ian looked at his watch. "About two hours. After that it's three hours at the conference for registration and the first opening sessions, and then we all come back here."

"No problem. Thank you," Kendra said; then the couple started off toward their room.

"You're welcome."

In his downstairs room with a balcony overlooking a sloping valley tossed with wildflowers, Ian put his body through a round of deep stretches and silent capoeira moves before taking a quick shower. He'd been restless all week. Dreams of this woman—he didn't even know her name—came to him even more frequently now. It didn't matter if he was in the classroom or in the pool swimming laps until his lungs burned. His body was hard with the awareness of her.

Last night, standing up from the pool with the water running the length of his body, Ian had been even more aware of its potential as an instrument of sex. The muscles in his arms and shoulders, the curving flesh of his ass, the plains of his belly with its hard ridges and smooth skin, all seemed made for her. Meant for pleasing her. He hadn't felt this aroused or obsessed by a woman since Zoë. Even in their most heated moments, with the sweat blinding their eyes, their bodies straining against each other, and his dick buried deep inside Zoë's pussy, none of that matched the intensity of what he wanted with his dream woman. And he hadn't even fucked her yet.

The time at the conference flew by quickly. After a full day of meeting new people, fending off advances from the attractive but unremarkable women, and making contacts for the university's writing program, Ian gathered his students and went back to the hotel.

"Is that place just one big pickup joint?" Samantha asked as they left the van.

"Pretty much," Archie said. "Did you see how everybody was eyeing us when we walked in? It was definitely about the tits and ass and dick, not about any sort of writing. And did you see that sleazy old guy who tried to get into Natalie's pants? That was some funny shit when she shot him down." He mimicked shooting off a gun and laughed.

"Most of the writers are acting like they're rock stars, and we're just here for them to fuck," Natalie said. "I'm not into that groupie shit."

"It wasn't that bad," Kendra said. She'd apparently been to a good intro session about writing and making connections of the nonsexual kind.

Olivier looked a little disappointed. "Hey, like some schmuck said not too long ago, 'Tomorrow's another day.' I'm holding out for a good hookup this weekend, as long as the chick can tell me who I can send my manuscript to while she's riding my dick." He looked at Ian. "Sorry, Mr. Tate."

"Forget Mr. Tate, what about the rest of us?" Jasmine wrinkled her nose and leaned away from her classmate. "That was disgusting, even for you."

Olivier smirked. "Thank you."

"I've heard worse," Ian said. "Just don't forget to use rubbers if you end up in the saddle."

"Definitely; I can always cop a few off Archie. I know he's got a couple hundred in his bag." Olivier chuckled. "He and Kendra fuck like goddamn rabbits."

Luckily the amorous couple was far behind them, walking slowly side by side as they watched the sunset wash the landscape around them in pink and amber flame.

The others snickered.

"What about you, Mr. Tate?" Jasmine asked. "We saw that hot chick with the tattoos giving you the eye."

Ian smiled at the unexpected question. "She was definitely attractive but not my type. I'm working on something else right now. Something better."

"Damn, someone more fine that that?" Natalie shook her head. "Still, I'd take up tattoo chick on her offer on principle. She's hot."

"Whatever, Natalie," Samantha said. "I'm sure Mr. Tate isn't going to have sex with some woman while he's our chaperone. No matter how hot she is."

"Chaperoning doesn't mean you have to cut off your dick and check it at the door." Olivier apologized again. "I'm sure if he really wanted it, Mr. Tate could arrange something after all you kiddies were off to bed. Right, Mr. Tate?"

Ian chuckled. "You're right. Because I certainly did not check my . . . um, package at the door."

His students laughed.

Back in his room, Ian showered and changed into loose pants that sat low on his hips and showed off the vee of muscle and the nodding weight of his dick. He poured himself a glass of Scotch and bypassed the comforts of his room for the terrace outside.

The sun was already gone, leaving behind on the horizon only a trace of its gorgeous color. Ian leaned back in the chair, savoring the quiet of his evening. His friends all thought it was strange that he took so much pleasure in being alone. He enjoyed company, but there was just something fulfilling about spending time by himself and enjoying the minute passing of time.

There were times he got lonely, but it wasn't very often. During those times he thought of Zoë and how she used to treasure her quiet time, too. They had had separate spaces in the house in which neither could come unless invited. It was a nice arrangement, one that had been her idea but Ian didn't object to. It was certainly more fun when she got tired of being by herself and came looking for him. He'd turn to see her at his door, asking with a smile to be let in. He never once said no, especially not when she came with sex on her mind.

She'd never liked her big breasts, thought them too much of a bother when she was doing capoeira or going about the business of her life. But she loved them when they were having sex. She loved to have them touched and stroked, and he'd obliged her, washing them with his tongue, sucking the hard nipples until she begged for him to slip inside her. Zoë had loved foreplay but quickly realized she'd met her match in Ian. He could go for hours, holding on to his orgasm like a miser with his gold until just the right time. He loved that ache in his balls, that tightening in his belly. Ian loved to savor that particular kind of pain. When he came, it was fantastic. Better than the rushed nut that a quick fuck could give. And he also loved to play with his woman's pussy until it purred and salivated for him. Until his dick or tongue or fingers were all she wanted in that moment. Nothing else. No one else.

When he heard a moan, Ian thought that it was his dream Zoë. Her moans were often rough and urgent, ones that got his dick even harder as they fucked. The moans he heard from his balcony were soft, reluctantly teased out of the woman. But sometimes Zoë gave him those, too, when he was working on her fourth or fifth orgasm, and she thought her body was too tired to go on.

She often came to him smelling of want and patchouli. He couldn't resist her and didn't want to. In his sunlit study, she stood near his chair, the one he knew she loved to fuck in. He watched her as his dick came to full hardness under his pants. She just stood there, gorgeous and undeniable with her heavy breasts, slim athlete's body, and neatly trimmed bush. He could almost see her pussy swell and get wet, its walls thickening to receive him.

A moan came again, and this time Ian knew it wasn't his memory of Zoë. It came from one of the upstairs rooms, a woman's urgent sounds, and then a man's, a rough counterpoint to her melodic vocal slide. Ian relaxed deeper into the terrace chair. His pants tented, and his head fell back. Between the twin stimulations of his memories of Zoë and the moans raining down on him, he was ready. He sipped his Scotch and savored the heathery burn of the drink on his tongue and down his throat. Unbidden, his hips moved against the chair, his ass grinding against the air as arousal washed over him. The woman's moans came louder; then words, soft and indecipherable, fell between them. Ian pushed his pants down below his hips and took his cock in his hands. It pulsed hot and hard against his palm. Pre-cum already made him slick. He spread the moisture down and around his dick with a smooth up-and-down motion, imagining it was Zoë's pussy that made his dick so wet, that made his balls leaden and ache.

In his study, Zoë slowly lowered herself onto his thick erection. His head fell back, and he grasped the arms of the chair tighter. Her thick breasts waved close, bringing her scent of sweat and perfume more strongly to him. He moved his head snakelike toward them, capturing a thick nipple in his mouth and sucking softly, a gentle buildup of intensity he knew she liked. He squeezed the other breast, teasing its nipple with his thumb. Her pussy swallowed all of him then, and she tightened her internal muscles on him, squeezing his dick once and then twice. Ian groaned. Her breast fell from his mouth with a soft pop, and it hovered in his field of vision, moist from his tongue, before his eyes fell shut and swept away the delicious image.

She rode him slowly, moving her hips, squeezing him until his body was a hard, wonderful ache. He grabbed her ass, urging her faster. Zoë wanted it fast. She was trying to do it slowly for him, building up to the crescendo he liked. But he could have his time after. He'd give her this come, shoot inside her pussy now, so he could play with her flush-softened body later, lay her out on the rug and fuck her long and deep until they were both sore. But now. Her breasts hopped in front of his face as she sped her movements. The sweat limned her face, collecting on her upper lip above her fiercely snarling mouth. Ian massaged her breasts, squeezed her nipples until she grunted, riding his dick hard and fast, panting and urging him on. She came with a minor roar, jerking on his dick until he was close and then closer. His eyes clasped shut, and his hands held tightly to her hips as she grunted and gasped, her pussy squeezing and gliding around him. Ian opened his eyes and saw another face, one mischievous and laughing, with a mouth sticky from grape jelly and peanut butter.

He came all over his hand and stomach, the cum splashing up on his tightened stomach muscles and down on this pants. Ian gasped softly and then sighed. This would have been a good time to have a towel handy. But he was just too drained to get up and go to the room for one. Ian chuckled. He hadn't jerked off this much since high school. And even back then he was getting enough pussy to make it more of a hobby than a necessity.

He licked his lips and drained his glass of Scotch dry. Upstairs the amorous couple was quiet. There was the occasional giggle, an answering laugh, but they seemed to be done fucking for the night. Ian looked up at the stars. Maybe it was time he found himself a woman. At the rate he was going at it with his own dick, he'd get carpal tunnel *and* go blind. Ian chuckled ruefully again. Yeah, it was time.

5

They made it back to Irvine with no casualties or STDs. If possible, Kendra and Archie seemed even closer, while Samantha found an unexpected hookup of her own with a townie who lived only a few minutes away from her.

Ian dropped off his students Sunday afternoon but was back on campus Monday morning. He had a test planned for his Harlem Renaissance class on Tuesday and wanted to be sure he was just as ready as the kids were supposed to be. At a few minutes past one, Ian finished up his work and, after a brief internal debate, decided to leave early.

"See you tomorrow, Ian." Ella, the secretary for the Humanities division, smiled at him as he walked by her, crouched at the filing cabinet.

He heard her soft hum of appreciation as his jeans-clad backside passed by. Ella was fourteen years happily married, but, as she'd commented to him several times, "It doesn't hurt to appreciate the beauty around here, does it? Especially not if it gives me a little more bounce in the bedroom later on in the day with my husband."

"Good afternoon, Ella!" he called back. "Don't give that husband of yours a heart attack this evening, you hear?"

He closed the door on her delighted laughter. It was yet another gorgeous California spring day. Ian put some distance between him and the sun with his shades and gripped his briefcase more tightly in his hand. He felt like going out tonight. His first class wasn't until eleven in the morning, so he would have plenty of time to recover if he decided to stay out past his usual bedtime. Ian was still pondering going to the club, when he heard someone call his name.

"Hey, Jasmine," he answered when he recognized his student.

The young girl stood near an electric-blue Mini Cooper convertible idling quietly by the curb. When she straightened up from lifting her backpack out of the rear passenger seat, Ian saw that the person behind the wheel was her mother. He nodded in greeting to the older woman. "Good to see you again." He turned to Jasmine. "I thought you were away in Berkeley for the conference this week."

"It's this coming weekend, Mr. Tate. That's why I'm taking your midterm early, remember?"

"That's right." He nodded, clearing the cobwebs from his brain. "And speaking of the midterm, just go to the Lit Club office tomorrow at three, and it'll be all set up for you."

"No problem. Thanks again for being so understanding."

"Any time. It's not every day I can play a part in helping a genius accomplish her life goals."

Jasmine smiled. "See, Mama? Isn't he the nicest man?"

Her mother smiled benignly from the car. "Of course he is, darling."

The young girl rolled her eyes and then leaned down to kiss her mother. "See you later, Ma. I can get a ride from Kenyatta, so you won't need to pick me up. Bye, Mr. Tate. See you in class."

"See you."

They both watched her walk off toward the classrooms, her small body held in a graceful scythe that cut through all the superficial beauty around her. She was a lot like her mother. He looked away from Jasmine only to collide his gaze with the older woman's.

Ian cleared his throat. "It was good to see you again, Mrs. Hannah," he said, starting to walk away to his own car.

"It's Miss." The woman looked him over again, very much like she had the first time she saw him in her doorway. "That is, if you must use my last name. You can call me Tam, though. Or Tamarind. Either way is much less formal, don't you think?"

"Absolutely. Then please call me Ian."

She looked up at him from the driver's seat of the tiny car in a way that made it seem like he was the one looking up at her. Before he could say anything, she reached over to the passenger side and opened the door. "Why don't you come for a drive with me, Ian?" It wasn't so much of a question as it was a demand.

Why not? Ian tossed his briefcase in the backseat and got into the car. She pulled carefully away from the curb. But once they were outside the campus, she took off for the highway, opening up the nimble little car and slipping quickly over into the far left lane. The wind and open convertible top allowed for little conversation, so Ian just used the time to watch her and appreciate her pixielike beauty. And to compare the reality of her to the insatiable creature of his wet dreams. How could this woman have a nineteen-year-old child?

Ian looked back at the road as he felt the car slow. Tam slipped quickly from the left lane to the right and then off the highway.

"You like what you see?"

He glanced at her, guilty, until he noticed the teasing look in her eyes.

"Yes, I do."

"Good."

The car now glided along one of Orange County's many scenic side roads. To the left of the car, mountains rose up, solid and sun dappled. The earth fell away on Ian's side in a gorgeous, slow descent of glittering rocks, clinging vines, and sand to the beach with its ribbons of waves and the seagulls swooping above the glittering blue Pacific.

"You're not trying to take advantage of my daughter, are you?"

Ian looked at her in surprise. "Does it seem like I am?"

"That's what I'm trying to figure out. Jasmine likes you." Tam shifted to second and guided the car down a narrow road leading toward the water. "She thinks you're a really good person, and I don't want that goodness and niceness rising off you to be your way into her affections and her panties. She is secure about her lesbian sexuality, but she's also naive about the world, especially about men."

"Little girls aren't my thing," he said, watching the last of fellow car-bound travelers fade in the rearview mirror.

"So what exactly is your thing?"

Tam shifted into third, and they picked up speed, flying down the narrow road with wispy sea grass brushing against the car as they went. The wind stirred the folds of her dress, and the white cotton fluttered up, revealing her knee and a smooth length of thigh. Ian laughed.

Until that moment, he wasn't sure what had been going on. Was Tam interrogating him? Was she trying to make him feel small for finding her, his student's mother, attractive? Or did she just have the sudden urge for a stranger's company in her sporty little car? But now he knew exactly where they were heading. She must have smelled the lust on him.

"My *thing*," he emphasized the last word with another soft laugh, "is intriguing women. Like you."

"Flatterer."

The car slowed as it reached the beach. Sunlight made the stretch of beach even more beautiful, gilding the waving sea grass and the ocean that rippled iridescently under its bright rays. Except for a lone house nestled higher up in the rocks, the beach was deserted.

"You're very beautiful, Ian," she said and brought the car to a stop. "But I'm sure you've heard that before."

"I have."

Tam laughed. She dropped the car keys in the cup holder and got out. The hem of her long white dress brushed against her bare ankles and feet as she stepped on the sand. Ian had no choice but to follow.

"This is where I come to paint sometimes." She gestured around them with a bangled hand. "A friend who lives in LA owns it. He doesn't come out here very often, and he doesn't mind me using it." Then Tam turned to him as if he was more interesting scenery than the one she had just been looking at. "Along with other things." She tilted her head to look at him, mischievous charm in the full curve of her mouth and her warm eyes.

"Ian." She sighed his name and smoothed a small hand over his buttoned-down shirt. She trailed the fingers of the other hand over his and then up his muscled forearm, over the folded cuffs of his shirt, up to squeeze his biceps and then his shoulders. Tam parted the first two buttons on his shirt, and Ian watched, intrigued, and wondering just how far she would go. She went all the way. He stood while she undid every button, leaving the subtly striped cotton to frame the bare, hairless plain of his chest, the gilled muscles along his ribs, and his flat, chiseled belly.

Tam walked backward, inviting him to follow with the gentle tug of her fingers until her ass gently connected with the tail of the car.

"Have you ever had an older woman before?"

He shook his head, mind still unable to work out that he *was* going to have this older woman, this woman who looked more like one of his students than anybody he'd ever thought of fucking. His mind was a little slow on the uptake, but his body was already there. The full almost pain of his arousal pushed against the stiff material of his jeans. Then she reached for him and undid the zipper, allowing his dick to jut, full and hard, into the warm air. She wrapped her hands around him, and he had to steady himself against the car. Her fingers felt so good, so right on him.

"I want to fuck you, Ian," she said, moving her hand slowly from base to crown of his dick in an exquisite motion that threatened to buckle his knees. "This has nothing to do with my daughter. Or your school or anything else." Her thumb stroked the head of his cock and he jerked, beyond shame, in her hand. "You're beautiful. I want you inside me."

Although he was never planning on getting laid at this very moment, Ian was prepared. He fumbled in his back pocket for one of the condoms he'd put in his wallet the week before. Once he had it out, Tam took the condom and ripped the packet with her teeth before smoothing the rubber over his sensitized shaft. She watched the emotions play across his face.

"I'm really going to enjoy you."

"Believe me," he said with a low groan, his body flushed hot from her nearness, "it'll be mutual."

Ian lifted her. He swept her skirt up and out of his way, and she helped him, moving aside her flimsy panties so he could slide deeply, finally, inside her melting hot pussy.

"Jes—! Oh, fuck. . . ."

He'd never had a woman before. That was how it felt to be inside the weeping heat of her that surrounded him, clasped him, and invited him deeper. Nothing in his life had ever felt this good, not breath, not life—God help him, not even Zoë.

Her eyes stared wide into his, steadily keeping him captive as he moved inside her. Tam blinked and licked her lips. Ian lifted her against him, moving her slight body in time with his thrusts. Her breath caressed his face, brushed him with the scent of anise as she rose against and then above him. The sweet glide and squeeze of her pussy on his dick, the burn in his thighs and arms as he held her up, her heated breath on his face, all moved him in a slow, magnificent ascent toward his peak.

"Ian." Her heels locked behind his back, and he trembled. She moved harder against him but still slow, grinding her clit against him with each pass. Her eyelashes fluttered, but she still held him with her stare. "Ian."

She hooked him with that stare, grabbed his balls, his dick, his desire in an unbreakable grip and, with a measured, deliberate torture, began to squeeze.

He gasped her name and staggered under the weight of their combined lust; she fell back against the car, and he followed, thrusting deep inside her, keeping that slow rhythm that made them shudder against each other, made his breath go deep and hard, made her latch on to his shoulders in desperate pleasure.

"Shit!" He bucked against her, lifting her up against the car, driving her into the small machine with each measured motion of his hips. So good. She felt so good. Tam gasped, a quick catch in the back of her throat, and threw her head back. She came around him like magic. Her cunt conjured his orgasm, threw him into a brilliant scatter of thoughts and sensations—his muscles hard and arching, pleasure bursting in his groin, in his head, the exotically spiced scent of their sex around him, milking another twitch from him, another groan, another shudder.

"Thank you." Her wide eyes looked at him, wet with pleasure and amusement. "That was even better than I expected."

Ian assumed that was his hint to get off her and her car. He eased up, groaning involuntarily at the singing ache in his thighs. Damn, it felt good. With another groan he slipped off

218 / Fiona Zedde

the condom and tossed it aside. His body felt good and tired, overcome with the deep lassitude that came after an intense, satisfying fuck. He hadn't felt that in a long time, and, watching Tam, he realized how badly he wanted to feel it again. Her eyes smiled at him as if she knew exactly what he was thinking.

She brushed down her skirt and moved toward the driver's side of the car. "You ready?"

6

"Can you believe I'm banging that ass?"

Ian looked up from his paper. Simon Taylor sat down at the table next to him, holding a photograph. Michael Spencer, the university's philosophy professor, walked over with the coffee-pot in hand, curious about whatever Simon had to show. The university's posh interpretation of a faculty lounge was mostly quiet this time of day. Those who could go home did. Only instructors with later classes or with nothing else better to do sat around in the comfortably furnished but cold lounge. Ian had class in less than an hour.

He'd tried focusing on the upcoming lesson, but thoughts of Tam kept intruding. He remembered how she'd felt two days ago as she came around him, squeezing him, rubbing her clothed breasts against his chest. Even thoughts of their ambivalent parting in the school parking lot afterward, her distracted, almost puzzled smile as she'd left him alone to find his ride home, plagued him.

Simon passed the photo to Ian. It was of a cute girl in a bikini. Or, at least, half of a bikini. The bottoms sat low on her curvaceous hips while the top was held tightly in her hands as she lunged toward the person holding the camera. The child was nothing remarkable, simply young and firm everywhere that sagging men like Simon liked to touch. Most of their colleagues knew that Simon used his intro poetry classes as his personal dating pool, not hesitating to take advantage of his young pupils' naïveté and romantic notions.

"Don't you wish you had a piece of this, Tate?"

Michael smirked. "Maybe he's not into that kind of ass."

"You're right," Ian said, barely giving the older man a glance. "I like my women out of training pants."

"There's nothing wrong with enjoying the fruits of the university, Ian." Heinrich, a biracial German with a thick accent and a bulldog's face, said as he returned Simon's photo. "You know better than any man here how far these girls go to get their instructors into bed." Heinrich was happily married eight years now to another professor at the university. They had a notoriously open relationship and often had wild sex parties at their house not too far from campus.

"I agree, Rick. But the fruit here is not to my taste," Ian said. "Too young. Too simple."

"For shit's sake, you're going to fuck them not hire them to be your TA." Simon tucked the picture back in his wallet.

"You could do both, now."

Heinrich laughed at Michael's exaggerated piggishness. "True, true."

"I like a firm ass as much as the next man," Ian said. "But the idea of fucking someone on this campus actually makes me feel a little queasy."

"You must have a weak stomach then." Heinrich turned back to his laptop. "Most of your colleagues don't have that problem."

Ian reluctantly chuckled. "Obviously."

He walked into his classroom forty-five minutes later, ready to give out the exam. He wrote the instructions on the board and put test booklets on each desk before sitting down at his own. Then he waited for his students to come in and find their seats. They gradually filed in, already familiar with the routine. Most were quiet, already taking out presharpened pencils and ink-filled pens, knowing the intensity of his essay exams. At one minute after the hour, he closed the classroom door and told them to begin. For a moment he watched their heads bow over their test papers and listened to the frantic scratch of pencil and pen across paper, nervously cleared throats, and the occasional and unexpected curse word.

Then he looked down at his book and thought about her. There was nothing else for him to do. He would have liked to go about his day as if he got the best sex of his life on the tail of a Mini Cooper every day, but he couldn't. Now the siren had crossed over from the realm of dreams to reality. He knew what she tasted like. He knew how she felt. He knew the hint of sound she made when she came. In his dreams she had been a screamer, loud and passionate in her praise of him and their sex. The reality of her was better. Hotter. He looked forward to making her scream his name.

Later that evening he left school with no particular destination in mind but wasn't surprised when he ended up on Tam's doorstep. Ian hesitated about ringing the doorbell. He couldn't use Jasmine as an excuse to stop by; she was out of town at her conference. Which, truth be told, was why he was here in the first place.

"Sorry I didn't call first," he said when she opened the door.

Tam didn't seem surprised to see him; in fact, she opened the door wider, a cat's creamed smile on her face.

"This is a nice surprise, Ian," she said. She closed the door behind him and turned to walk back into the house. Like a puppet, he followed.

Ian swore he could smell everything about her, the salty wet in her panties, the fragrance of mingled herbs that lay between her breasts, the anise on her breath.

"Would you like something to eat?"

"Yes."

She wore a skirt today, a white, knee-length, linen thing draped over her perky bottom and a small tank top that showed off the small muscles in her arms and her wealth of soft skin. Tofu simmered in a pot on the stove. The sauce smelled of peanuts and coconut milk. Tam turned down the fire and walked to the kitchen's center island where she had been slicing vegetables before Ian rang her bell. She reached into the drawers of the island and took out two plates and a couple of glasses.

"How old are you?" she asked suddenly.

"Twenty-eight, and you?"

"Thirty-nine as of two weeks ago." She looked at him for a moment and then went to the sink to rinse out the plates and glasses.

"Oh, excuse me," Ian said, backing out of her way as she almost bumped into him on her way back to the island.

They moved around the room in an awkward dance, with Tam flickering strange looks at him until Ian wondered what exactly he was doing at this woman's house. So what if they'd had a great time against the back of her car? That didn't mean she wanted to date. Ian cleared his throat.

"I came over to get your number," he said. "I thought about calling but then realized I had no idea what your number was."

"Are you sure that's not just an excuse? I can't imagine you not having access to Jasmine's phone number." She finished slicing her carrots and swept them from the cutting board into a silver bowl already lined with freshly washed lettuce and pieces of broccoli. "Which, by the way, is also mine."

"Cut me some slack, I'm trying not to seem like a stalker here."

"Oh, I see." She smiled at him as she put away the cutting board and knives before wiping clean the checkered marble countertop.

Ian leaned back against the cupboards and watched her. She seemed so confident here, so sure of herself. Was he the only one caught unawares in this awkward moment? Then he noticed the slight tremor in her hands as she turned off the stove.

"I've been thinking about you," he said. What an understatement that was. Obsessed. Priapic. Under her damn spell. Those were better words to describe what he was feeling.

"And?" She finally stopped her movement around the kitchen. Her eyes bored into his.

"I think you should take some of the blame for that. If you hadn't invited me into your car . . ." or answered the door that night over a week ago or even existed, "then I'd be safe on my side of town and you'd be free to eat your tofu alone."

She bit into a baby carrot and chewed slowly. "Who says I want to eat my tofu alone?"

Ian watched her for any sign that she was playing with him. He stood up from his prop against the cupboard and felt the ground steady under his feet. Tam stayed where she was, chewing her carrot, watching.

Her skin *was* soft. He thought he had dreamed that, too. Velvet under his hand, buttery on the tongue. Ian sucked her finger into his mouth, tasting the hints of carrot, broccoli, and dish soap that clung to her skin. She fell into a deeper slouch against the island, and her lips parted as she watched him taste her. He kissed the back of her hand, the inside of her wrist, her elbow, and then her shoulder. Tam's arm draped on his hip bone, and her hand fell forward to rest against his ass.

"Beautiful boy," she murmured, exploring the contours of his round ass with her fingers.

He wanted to tell her that he was a man not a boy, but her skin entranced him, and all he could do was slide his palms up her back, and that motion became a lift onto the kitchen island, and then he was tugging off her panties and burrowing under her skirts to find the source of the smell that had been torturing him since he'd walked into the house.

She shaved. He hadn't properly noticed it before when they were fucking on the beach, but now his tongue glided over her smooth flesh without resistance. He sighed and then groaned. She smelled so fucking good. He teased her with his tongue, lightly touching the soft bud of her clitoris as he bathed the sensitive flesh with his breath. Her pussy eagerly opened up for him, and he went, gently, inside. She tasted like rain, fresh and abundant. Tam sighed and fell deeper onto the marble surface. Her legs floated up to his shoulders, and Ian caressed them as his tongue savored the delicate flavor of her pussy. This was what he came here to eat. Fuck the tofu. She gasped as his tongue pushed firmly inside her. His nose nudged her clit, and she gasped again. Her hand settled on top of his head.

"That's . . . perfect." Tam moved against his mouth, murmuring soft nonsense words as he ate his fill of her.

Ian freed his aching cock from the prison of his trousers, passed his hand briefly over it to put on a condom, and then he returned his attentions back where they belonged. His mouth was wet with her, his nose full of her smell, his arms full of her softness. He groaned against her clit, and she jerked. Her hand fluttered down to his neck. His mouth opened wider as he used the flat of his tongue on her clit, lavishing it with deep strokes and sucks until her breath was nothing but hisses and her nails bit painfully into his skin. Her hips cycloned on the countertop, thrusting harder and harder against his face.

"Oh!" The sound was reluctant, an escapee from her tightened lips. She bucked against him; then her cunt fluttered and flexed as she came. He stood up swiftly and buried himself inside her. The last flutterings of her pussy tugged him instantly deeper, hurling him toward his own orgasm. Too fast, but he'd take what he could get. He pushed his dick inside her to the hilt before withdrawing, then again and again. He was so close. She clung to him, scented, pussy wet, and warm. He could feel her building again, and he forced himself to slow down. He wanted her so much. His body sang with desire, heated like he'd just come from the sauna, breath out of control and loud in her kitchen.

Tam's hips flew into motion again, and he heaved, panting over her, trying to ram them both into the marble countertop. Her hands flew back, reaching for something, anything that wasn't him. A glass fell to the floor with a harsh crash. She slid across the counter, and he followed, grunting and ravenous. The sweat poured down her face and neck, staining the white linen of her blouse. Her nipples strained through the tank top, begging for his mouth, his tongue. He wanted to see them. He wanted to taste them. But—shit!

They came, panting, together and collapsed in a sprawl across the sweat-slickened surface of the kitchen island. After a moment she pushed at his shoulders. He was heavy. A groan escaped Ian as he slipped from her and then from the countertop. His thighs and arms still ached from their session on the beach two days before. Without bothering to hide himself, he stripped off the condom and dropped it in her kitchen trash. Then, noticing the broken glass, he carefully swept it up with a nearby broom and dustpan and tossed it in with the used rubber.

"That was a little presumptuous of you, don't you think?"

"What?" Ian looked up from tucking his shirt back into his trousers. His knees felt weak. What was this woman doing to him?

"To come here with a rubber in your pocket."

"It's not just you," he said. "I'm always prepared."

Tam lay back, propped up on her elbows, watching him. She was always watching. The wet flower of her pussy, framed by the white skirt and the sprawl of her thighs, made him stop, slow down, and almost reverse the direction of his zipper. Ian cleared his throat and backed away.

"Can I see you again?" He made a show of examining the salad bowl, ignoring the heavy drum of his heart. He wanted this. In the worst way. He had no idea what it was about this woman that had him by the balls, but she had him. "I'd like to do it in a bed sometime."

She threw her head back and laughed. "You *are* a presumptuous little fuck."

"Little?" He raised an eyebrow, and she laughed even harder.

Ian shook his head. She still hadn't given him an answer. But he knew she would say yes. The hum of her pussy around his dick was her yes. She just didn't know it yet.

Ian left the salad bowl alone. "Come on. Be nice to me, and show me around your house. Afterward we can have some dinner."

She watched him, speculation bright in her eyes. Then she hopped off the kitchen island and brushed down her skirt. "Why not?"

The house was made for comfort, clean smelling and cool, with plants scattered on every available light-filtered surface and an adventure of color— olive green, maroon, shell pink— on each wall. It was a feminine, cozy house, with canvas after canvas of beautiful art on the walls—large fantastical nature scenes, painstakingly realistic in their detail, down to the whisker on a bunny's nose, the dusty blue of a butterfly's wing, but with a hint of something otherworldly hovering in the background. The artist's use of light and shadow was beautifully effective.

"Your place is nice." Ian said. "I especially like the art."

"Thank you. It's mine."

"Really?" Ian nodded, impressed. "It's very good."

"I know. It pays the bills."

So she was a working artist. He looked around the house again. *Very* nice.

"You have a beautiful home." They ended the tour in her bedroom. "Very beautiful."

The room was like her, lush and overwhelming with its color. Red walls, a vivid blue rug on the hardwoods, a queen-size bed covered with a bright red Mexican blanket and six solid colored pillows. The only calm spot in the room were the bare canvasses on the walls, stretched and framed bits of white space scattered like light around the room.

"Thank you."

He felt his body reacting to her again. It didn't seem fair, when she seemed so unaffected. Ian wanted her to react to him. "Have you ever had a man in here?"

"Not with my child in the house."

"That makes sense." He looked at her again, considering. "Will you have me in here?" He pulled his shirt out of his pants and started to unbutton it. "She's not home."

Her hesitation didn't stop him. Ian stripped for her, tempting her with his tight, flexing body. One pair of pants, socks, shoes, and boxers later, he stood naked at her bed while she stared from the bedroom door. In the mirrored closet door he saw a reflection of them, Tam with her mouth bitten red and her nipples hard against her shirt as she leaned back against the closed door. Ian's body was hard and flawless, a visual feast of muscled calves, thick runner's thighs, hardening penis, washboard belly, and hard, hairless chest. His face was open to her, showing her how much he wanted to touch and be touched, how very much he'd like to fuck her on that holiday miracle bed of hers and knock all those damn pillows to the floor.

"You know, you can," he said. "Have me, that is."

"What makes you think I want you?"

It was his turn to laugh. "I know your pussy is wet for me

now." His eyes flickered over her body as if he could see beneath her clothes to the thickening cunt lips and the moisture gathering there. "You want me to go down on you again, or do you just want to fuck? The bed is right here." He decided to change his tone. "Making love in it would be so sweet."

"I don't believe in making love." She said the last two words with a scornful curl of her lip. "Only in fucking."

He shrugged. "I'm always down for that, too."

Ian didn't go to her. He waited for her to come to him, and she did.

"Did you bring only one rubber?"

"I'm sure you have some here." He prayed she did. The last thing he wanted to do was put his clothes back on and trudge down to the damn corner store for some condoms.

"You're right." Tam smiled. "I do."

She traced the muscles of his chest with her fingers as though she couldn't help herself. Her thumb flicked one nipple. Then the other. Ian drew in a quick breath. This woman was playing with him. Every touch of her hand, every smell of her turned his brain to shit. And she knew it.

Her hands roamed over his chest, tracing its contours and curves. She touched his throat, squeezing it for a moment, and then stroked his jaw, his cheeks, and the beginnings of his stubble.

"You're so fucking hot, you know that?"

It was a rhetorical question. One he apparently wasn't even supposed to pay attention to because she pressed close to him, crushing his hard, aching dick between his stomach and hers. Tam licked his mouth, tracing his closed lips with her tongue, begging for entrance with the quiet undulation of her belly against his dick, until he opened his mouth and let her in. She tasted like carrots. Her tongue slipped between his teeth, dancing against his tongue while his dick hardened even more and throbbed against her. He pulled briefly away from her to strip off her skirt and blouse.

Tam didn't wear a bra. She didn't need to. Her breasts stood up perky and firm in the cool air of the bedroom, inviting his fingers and mouth. He didn't bother complimenting her. She had to know how breathtaking she was. Now that the fever of lust was gone, he could take the time to savor her intoxicating beauty like fine wine. His hands shaped her body, traced the long-limbed smoothness of her, the softly sighing, pleasing length of her that made him feel a little mad, a little drunk, and a far way down the road to infatuation.

Ian pressed her backward on the bed, bending her lithe body until they fell onto the surprisingly soft blanket. He grunted softly. Their kissing was slow and teasing, a biting of lips and sucking of tongues, and then deep, sweeping tastes of each other's mouths that felt so damn good they almost didn't need to have sex for Ian to get off. The press of her skin against his was electric. Her tongue in his mouth, her hands on his ass, over his back, in his hair, all were driving him slowly insane with pleasure.

She rolled his balls in her palm while her tongue moved, sweet and slick, in his mouth. It felt like she was licking his balls, turning the flesh over on her tongue like candy. Tam moaned deep in her throat, but it was Ian who reared up, suddenly very eager to be inside her. He felt, ridiculously, like a fourteen-year-old boy again with his first woman, although he could swear that back then he had more self-control than now.

The bed sighed as he eased her onto her back and slowly parted her thighs. He was teaching himself control, too. It didn't make sense that he wanted her so badly, not when they'd just had a really amazing fuck in her kitchen. He'd always prided himself on his self-control where women and sex were concerned. Pleasure was Ian's way of keeping the women he wanted captive. Make them love the dick, love his tongue on their pussy, so they wouldn't think twice about leaving. Them dying wasn't something he could control.

She swallowed him without hesitation. The slick walls of her pussy welcomed him, sheathed him in liquid pleasure. Ian arched his neck back, a long, luxurious groan easing its way out of his throat. No pussy had ever felt this good. None. In a bed it was even better. Her legs slid up the backs of his calves and thighs, and she sighed.

He moved deeper inside her, slowly, hitting her clit on the downstroke. Their breaths came slowly, deeply as they watched each other, their combined efforts breaking out the sweat on both their bodies. Ian sank deeply again and then sped up his rhythm, alternating the deep, heavy fuck with the shallow, clit-skimming one that made her lips part in surprised pleasure. His body felt rich with desire for her, his dick, his balls, his muscles aching to please her even as her molten wetness dragged him near the brink. The red blanket exhaled the scent of lemons and rosemary as he propped himself up on his hands and fucked her harder. He felt the sweat gather in the deep muscles of his back, flowing down into the crack of his ass. Tam grabbed his biceps and gasped as her orgasm took her by surprise.

"Ian!" She reared up in the bed, rising up against him, but he held her, slowing his strokes but still diving against her clit to prolong her orgasm. He kept on going, and she chuckled through her sighs of pleasure.

"Are you on a mission?"

"Something like that," he grunted.

He could fuck her all night. Her fingers skimmed up his chest, sliding over the muscles slick with sweat. It didn't matter that she saw him as young and cocky, only that under him she sighed and moaned and clung, her legs winding around him like ropes as the bedsprings creaked and the lamplight flooded over them, highlighting her pleasure-streaked face and the eyes that grew wider and wider with surprise the longer he lasted and the more she came. Ian's muscles began to ache, but he didn't ease up.

At one point she might have gasped "stop," but it became another "don't stop," and her breath reeded in her throat, climbing up the register of need and pleasure and fulfillment. She lay beneath him, her face, throat, and chest wet as if she'd just come from a bath. The sounds of dawn—early work traffic, the fading music of night creatures, dedicated morning joggers—began to filter through the window; only then did Ian let himself go inside her. He lifted her leg and her ass until she was perfectly positioned for what he wanted. Her eyes opened even wider, and she growled. She actually growled. Ian wanted to laugh, but his dick had control of everything in that moment, and it only wanted to come.

His hips pistoned into the bed, and he let his voice loose, grunting and gasping as the feeling, leashed before like a captive lion, roared in his body until he was shivering with the electricity of it and his back ached and he was coming fast, fast, fast inside her pussy. He took her with him. Tam reached back to hold on to the scrolled headboard, her mouth opened, her back arched high off the bed, her hips jerking in perfect counterpoint to his.

"Fuck, yes!"

Their frantic breaths roiled against each other in the aftermath. Ian rolled over and brought Tam's unprotesting body with him to lay on his chest. Her breath still came heavily, her face buried in his neck, and the rest of her body draped over him. Their lazy sex smell tugged at him, inducing the beginnings of lethargy.

He blinked at her ceiling. Fuck. This woman *was* magic. Ian hadn't been able to enjoy himself like this in a really long time. He sighed and relaxed even deeper into the bed.

"You can't stay."

He looked down at Tam. She pushed herself up and away from him, separating herself from his body and then the bed. Her lovely ass, damp from their sex, sauntered to the other side of the room. She plucked her robe from the closet and put it on.

"Sorry." Her look wasn't sorry at all.

He sat up in the bed. "Can I take a shower first?"

"Sure."

Like everything else in this house, the bathroom was built for comfort. It had a roomy, glass-encased shower fitted with a radio, CD player, and mirror. The massive tub sat on the other side of the bathroom with various delicate-smelling, feminine things neatly tucked away on shelves within arm's reach. He climbed into the shower and turned on the water. Tam's dismissal aside, the night had been pure pleasure. He felt like he'd just come from a particularly good workout. His muscles pumped thickly with blood and were already aching. After a quick hair and body shampoo, Ian got out of the shower and toweled himself dry. In the mirror he was the same as before. Handsome face, cool eyes, body as strong as always, but inside was another matter. Inside he was weak and begging. But only for her.

He walked out of the bathroom and into her gaze. "Thanks for the shower."

She sat on the window seat, the same one she'd watched him from that first time, looking beautiful and sexy and in control in her flowered robe. But he didn't miss the way her eyes devoured his naked body, lingering only a little on his heavy cock that they both vividly remembered had been inside her only a few minutes before. He started to get dressed.

"So are we in one of those on-the-sly relationships, or will you come out for a drink with me sometime?" he asked.

"I don't go out for drinks."

He knew she was bullshitting, but didn't want to press the issue.

"Not even water?" Well, maybe just a little.

"Sometimes." A smile came and went on her face. "I do eat, though. Why don't you invite me to your place for dinner?"

So she *was* planning on keeping him secret. "When can you come?" he asked.

"Anytime."

That sounded promising. Ian felt his lips twitch. He picked up the pencil on her bedside table and, on the cover of her sketch pad, wrote down his address, phone number, and his name, too, in case she forgot it.

"My schedule is very flexible after six in the evening every day. I'm off on the weekends and Thursdays. And," he smiled as she glanced down at what he'd just written, "you don't have to call first."

"Are you sure about that?" She raised an eyebrow. "Doesn't a boy like you have at least a dozen little sex bunnies lined up to fill his evenings?"

"Maybe a boy like me, but this *man* doesn't."

Her lips pursed, and then she smiled. "Point taken." She stood up from the window seat. "I'll call you.'"

And, Ian thought with a wry grin, that was his cue to go.

7

He was surprised when she showed up on his doorstep the following Thursday bearing gifts.

"May I come in?" she asked as he stood there staring at her for longer than what was called for. She held a large picnic basket in front of her with both hands. It looked heavy.

"Please do," he said, regaining his equilibrium. This was definitely a surprise.

This was the first time he'd seen her in black. The slim-fitting, sleeveless dress skimmed down her shoulders over her pretty breasts and belly to swirl just above the floor and the silver sandals on her feet. As she walked past him into the house, the scent of green tea and rosemary floated up from her skin. He almost closed the door on his foot when he noticed the back of the dress. It was nearly nonexistent, revealing the subtle musculature of her shoulders and back as it dropped from the narrow shoulder straps to hug her high ass, hips, and thighs.

"Where's your kitchen?"

Ian pointed and watched as she walked toward it, her small but shapely behind twitching like a metronome. He looked on, amazed, as she unloaded her picnic basket on the counter. Damn. Tam took out a bottle of prechilled white wine, grilled salmon, asparagus, mashed potatoes, gravy, sliced strawberries, and two small cakes, all in their own separate containers.

"I thought since I didn't call to give you time to make dinner, I'd bring a little something." Tam turned and opened cupboard after cupboard until she found wineglasses. She took out two and began to set up the small dining table for dinner. "I hope you're hungry."

As a matter of fact, Ian was. He had also been about to go out for chicken wings and beer with his friends. But that was obviously not going to happen now.

"Just give me one second." He went into the bedroom to cancel on his friends. "Sorry, Eric. Something very unexpected came up. Tell the guys I'll see them on the court tomorrow night."

His friend made some noises of protest, but eventually said, "Cool," and hung up the phone. When Ian got back to the dining area, two places were already set, food on the plates, candles lit, and the wine poured.

"I'm normally much more domestic than this, but you'll have to take what you get tonight."

"I'm sure I'll be more than satisfied with your efforts," Ian said.

Tam snickered and invited him to sit down. "Come, before the food gets cold. I had to race over here as it is to make sure the steam was still on the fish." She glanced at Ian. "Oh, I forgot to ask, you do like salmon, don't you?"

He laughed. "Yes, I do."

They sat down at the table, facing each other like teenagers on a first date. She glanced at him over the flickering lights of the candles, smiling. The salmon was good, tender without being overcooked, and the butter-simmered asparagus melted on his tongue.

"Good choice," he said, indicating the wine. It was a vintage he had in his cupboard, a light pear-infused wine with just a hint of the fruit's sweetness.

"Thank you," she murmured.

They ate a few more bites, occasionally watching each other with nothing but the silence between them. Then Ian decided to break it.

"So, what brings you to my neck of the woods?"

Tam smiled. "Not too much. I was bored sitting at home by myself. Jasmine's off on a study date, and I can't focus on painting right now."

"I see." He wondered if this was a booty call disguised as dinner. Not that he had a problem with that.

Tam neatly sliced an asparagus stalk in two and then forked a piece to her lips. She licked off the butter, swirling her tongue around the abbreviated vegetable before sucking it into her mouth.

"So, tell me about yourself," she said. "I feel like I know a lot about you as a professor, but not too much about Ian Tate, the man."

"You know a lot about the man."

"I want to know more about you than the size of your dick and how many times you can make me come."

"Why do you want more than that? I thought all you wanted to do was fuck."

"You do get straight to the point, don't you?"

"I try to. It saves on all the excess bullshit."

Tam smiled again. "Well, I'm interested in you. Obviously." She paused. "We don't always have to get together for sex."

"Ah, I see. You think that just because I'm Jasmine's professor, things would get complicated. Well, your daughter doesn't have to know anything about us. Nobody does."

She tilted her head to look at him. "I'm not trying to keep you a secret."

"Really? Then why can't I take you out to dinner somewhere public?"

Tam blushed. It was the second unexpected thing from her tonight. Her skin darkened to an even lovelier shade, and she looked down.

"OK. Scratch that." She sipped her wine, waving the fingers of her free hand dismissively. "We're two reasonably mature people who enjoy each other's company. Can you just leave it at that?"

"I just want to be clear on what's going on here." Ian felt the need to keep this light. Their talk was getting much too serious much too quickly. "We can get together and fuck, maybe even have the occasional dinner. But if, say, I had a faculty party to go to and needed a last-minute date, I shouldn't bother calling you, right?"

"Something like that wouldn't be completely out of the question," she said just as facetiously. "Under some circumstances I would be able to go with you."

"That's a relief," Ian murmured, his tone dry as desert sand.

Tam rolled her eyes and laughed. They finished their dinner talking comfortably about nothing too important. Then she helped him wash the dishes before they went into his cozy bachelor's living room and sat on the couch in front of the darkened television.

"If this were a normal date, I'd ask you to watch a movie with me," Ian said.

"Who says this isn't a normal date?" She leaned over to look at his meager DVD collection stacked neatly under his IKEA coffee table. "You want to watch this one?" She sat back with a copy of *Coming to America* in her hand. It had been Zoë's favorite movie. And with such a simple thing, his wife's memory bubbled up in him.

"Sure," he said, clearing his throat. "You want some popcorn?"

She refused the popcorn, but he got up and went into the kitchen anyway to get them both glasses of water and a bowl of M&M's. Ian swallowed hard as he emptied the packet of candy into the clear glass bowl. When he walked back into the living room, she had the movie ready to play in the DVD player. Her sandals were off and her legs curled up on the sofa. She seemed innocent and young. For a moment it was easy to forget that this was the woman who had effortlessly given him the best sex of his life and seemed to have no problem with a no-strings-attached repeat performance.

Tam looked up as he neared the sofa; then she leaned toward the table to pick up the remote. Her bare back, slender and sleek, glowed briefly in the blue light of the television before she sat back in her seat. The earlier impression of innocence vanished when she turned toward him.

"Ready?" she asked.

When Ian sat down, she leaned into him, inviting him to slip an arm around her. Another surprising move, but he wasn't going to complain. Her skin, brushed with that same illusive green tea and rosemary scent he'd noticed when she first walked into his apartment, was soft and yielding beneath his hand. Tam pressed PLAY on the remote control.

The opening credits started, and, for a moment, it was easy to believe it was Zoë beside him on the sofa, saying for the millionth time how much she loved Eddie Murphy, although the *Beverly Hills Cop* series wasn't exactly her favorite piece of cinema. But his wife had never called it "cinema," and she never smelled like fresh growing things, and she never had bits of red paint stuck in the corners of her fingernails.

"Are you all right?" the not-Zoë asked.

"Yeah, just a little gas. No big deal." He lightly thumped his chest for effect.

"Too much asparagus, maybe," she said and rubbed the place over his heart. "Just don't burp in my hair."

"I'll try my best not to," he said. Then she draped an arm over his sprawled thigh, her hand hovering just above his dick. All thoughts of Zoë went flying out the window.

But Tam didn't go any farther. It was just her and her soft skin and the possibility of sexual contact that made him want to arch his hips to her hand or move his own hand to her breast just to take the night to its inevitable conclusion. They watched the movie in relative silence until it ended with the final happily ever after, and then Tam was yawning and stretching out her long legs.

"That was nice," she said. Her breath smelled like chocolates and near sleep as she leaned in toward him. "I'm going. Jasmine should be home by now."

His eyes searched her face for some hint that she might be joking. Did she really just come over here to tease him and then run back home? Her mouth settled on his, creating a light suction.

"Good night."

Before she could pull away he anchored her to him, opening his thighs wider and pulling her lips closer again. The chocolates were stale on her tongue and the sleep flavor bitter, but Tam was sweet. She twined her slim arms around his neck and pressed her breasts against him. His dick perked up, blooming full and hard against her stomach. Ian scraped his blunt fingernails gently across her back and felt pleased indeed when she arched deeper into him and opened her mouth wider for his kisses. Soon she was kneeling in the sofa, her thighs spread over him as she held his face and kissed him deeply, saying with her tongue and her hands and the trembling beginning of a moan that she wasn't quite ready to go.

Ian moved his hands to her hips, kneading her soft flesh. Her dress hiked up, and he was under it, exploring the pieces of string that made up her panties and then the skin beneath. She actually moaned when his hand brushed over her shaved pussy, and her mouth slipped away from him as she gasped. His fingers found her soaked lips and her clit and then lightly stroked the opening of her pussy. Tam's head fell back, and she pulled down the straps of her dress to reveal her breasts. Her nipples were as hard as the chocolate M&M's. They didn't at all melt in his mouth as his tongue moved over them, tasting and sucking them while his hand played with her soaking pussy.

He caressed her clit to the rhythm of his tongue on her nipples, and she rewarded him with a long, singing moan. Her wetness dripped over his fingers, washing over them like seawater. She was so slippery, so open he could slide his dick inside her now with almost no resistance. She would swallow him, hold him in the sultry vice of her pussy and ride him hard until they both collapsed with pleasure. The image of it made his dick throb even more. She gasped again as he slipped a finger inside her, still stroking her clit with his thumb. Tam raked her fingers through his hair and down his neck, feeding him her breasts, her nipples, the gift of her noises. He sped up the motion of his fingers, and she grasped his head to her chest, nearly suffocating him in the steamy heat of her breasts. Her hips started to jerk uncontrollably, her pussy snaked against his hand, and she was coming, gasping and shuddering in his grasp, her arms still holding his head tightly to her breasts.

"Shit. . . ." she murmured breathlessly against his hair.

"I'm glad you enjoyed it," he said with a soft laugh.

She pulled away from him, releasing his head to fall back and let the couch catch her full weight. From the deep olive green of the sofa, her body looked sated and soft. She smiled at him, taking a slow visual tour of his body, with a particularly long stop at the swollen ache in his jeans.

"So," she said. "What can I do for you?"

"Not a thing. I'm good."

"Really?" She looked at his dick again. It throbbed tellingly as she licked her lips and then slowly eased a finger between them. She sucked on the finger until it was wet and moving with liquid ease in and out of her mouth. His dick wanted to take the place of that finger; it wanted to jump out of his pants to slide deep into the damp cavern of her mouth. Ian knew he must look like he wanted it badly. He had that mouth-open, dick-hot-and-hard expression he'd seen reflected in her eyes a time or two before.

"No, it's OK," he said again. "I've got some papers to get to before tomorrow. If I don't do it now, it'll be the weekend. And I don't like working through my weekends."

Her eyes widened in surprise, and the motion of her finger stopped. "You're serious?"

"Unfortunately, yes," Ian said.

Tam pushed down her skirts and got up off the sofa. She settled the straps of the dress back on her shoulders and went into the kitchen to gather up her picnic supplies. From the dim light of the candles still flickering on the table, Ian watched the almost meditative way she moved around his kitchen until she had all her things in the picnic basket and was ready to leave.

"Thank you for a lovely dinner," she said. "And an even more . . . tasty dessert than I had planned." She stood in the threshold of his kitchen, basket held in front of her, boldly appraising him again. "I'm disappointed you didn't take me up on my offer, but I guess there's always a next time."

"I hope so." He really, really hoped so. Ian wasn't sure what he had been gambling on when he had pulled his dick away from Tam's mouth, but he hoped it would pay off. Soon.

He walked her to her car, where they exchanged a laughably chaste good-night kiss. It was early, not quite ten thirty. Yolanda, his neighbor on the other side of the duplex, hadn't even left for work yet. She worked at a classy strip joint, what they called a "gentlemen's club," in town. Yolanda's Saab convertible still sat in the driveway under its logoed tarp.

"Call me sometime," Tam said. "Maybe we can do that public dining thing you talked about."

"Definitely."

He stepped back as she pulled out of his driveway and, after giving him an awkward little wave, drove off down the well-lit street.

8

"So what, or who, did you stand us up for last night?"

"Did that dime next door finally let you hit that?"

"Please say she brought some of her stripper friends home and you all had a full on orgy."

"And just because you're our *very* good friend, you caught all the action on tape. Right?"

Ian and his basketball buddies battled each other in a good-natured game; the men laughingly overtook each other, tossing the ball back and forth and occasionally making a basket. None of the men took the game very seriously. They played to work out and talk shit. And the effects of their biweekly game and nearly daily workouts—strong physiques, easygoing temperaments, and effortless athleticism—were obvious in each man.

Troy, the investment banker and the only married man among them, loved to hear about his friends' single, and sometimes scandalous, lifestyles. He'd willingly given up his own bachelorhood nearly three years ago to a little sous-chef at a local four-star restaurant. He was too happy to even contemplate cheating, still, he liked to hear about his boys and their seemingly endless parade of pussy.

"What did I tell you boys about neighbors?" Ian asked, laughingly sweeping the ball from Eric's hands and darting behind him to run for the basket. He shot and missed. "Shit!"

"Exactly. Don't shit where you eat. Common sense." Eric threw himself after the ball that was heading dangerously out of bounds, easily fending off the efforts of his two friends on the opposite team. "But that woman is a fine, fine thing." Eric ran down the court, bare torso gleaming with sweat, the rivulets running down his slim but muscled back to dampen his dark blue shorts. He threw the ball toward Rashawn, who ran with it toward the basket and scored.

Troy caught the ball as it fell out of the net, dribbled, and then shot it toward Ian. "Just please tell me you got some footage," he said. His friends laughed.

"You know Ian is not going to play some girl like that. Unless, of course, she wants to play like that," Rashawn said, intercepting the pass and then darting toward his basket. Ian blocked him, stole the ball, and, for the first time that night, made a basket.

"About time," Ian said.

"So when are you going to tell us, bro? Don't keep us hangin'."

"It wasn't much," Ian said. "A friend came over unexpectedly and—"

"I knew it. Pay up, Shawn." Eric laughed. "I told you it was a woman."

Ian threw the ball at Eric, who laughed again, caught it, and tossed it up to easily make a basket. "Thanks, man."

"So, was it good?" Eric asked.

"Oh, yes."

Troy caught the ball on its rebound from the basket and

slowly dribbled it backward toward the opposite basket. "Yeah?"

"Oh, yeah. Maybe one day we can do that double-date thing with you and Tania," Ian said to him and then turned to his single friends. "You fellas need to find some respectable women before you can come. Strippers you get from the club don't really count as dates."

"Fuck you," Rashawn said and stole the ball from Troy.

They all knew about Ian's wife. It was a sad story he'd told one night three years ago when he was too drunk to know any better. They knew how she died and how much he missed her. The fact of his grief never stopped him from fucking nearly every willing girl when he first moved to Irvine. Now Ian was a little bit more discriminating in his tastes in one-night stands. And before Tam, that's all any of them ever were, whether the sex lasted for one night, one week, or one month.

"I still think you should hook up with that fine ass next door," Rashawn said. "Regular pussy just a doorbell away."

Eric made a rude noise. "Yeah, another stalker just a doorbell away."

"You got that right."

Although attractive Cali men were scattered everywhere like sand, when Ian had first arrived in Irvine, the girls had flocked to him as if he was the only one. The first woman he'd slept with here turned out to be one of those "America's Most Wanted" kind of stalkers, showing up at Ian's favorite bar every day, even following him home to beg for another date. Ian didn't give her any hints to get. He straight up told her he was interested in her only for the sex and maybe a drink outside of that. She hadn't appreciated his honesty. He ended up paying almost five hundred dollars to get his keyed Honda Accord repainted. That psycho hadn't been the last.

"Since you're so focused on Yolanda, why don't *you* try to get up in that?"

Rashawn sucked his teeth. "Right. Like I know where that pussy's been. Half the damn strippers I know suck dick on the side. The rest of them turn up their assholes for a gold chain and a free meal."

Ian laughed. "You would definitely be in a position to know."

They had all been there when Rashawn went through his hyper-sexed phase and blew an indecent amount of money on strippers and porn. His friends had all laughed at him before finally staging a minor intervention that set him straight and gave him a different perspective on things. These days he was mostly celibate, with the occasional girlfriend who invariably ended up looking like a hooker straight out of *Pretty Woman,* the X-rated version.

Rashawn sucked his teeth. "Fuck off."

"Come on, fellas." Troy laughed and palmed the ball. "This game is tired. Let's go grab some beers."

And that was the end of that.

"He doesn't have office hours right now."

Ian looked up from the sheaf of papers on his desk at the sound his the secretary's voice.

"It's OK, I'm not a student. This is a personal visit."

"Oh, in that case—" Before Ella could finish the sentence, Tam knocked on Ian's half-open door and walked in.

Ian leaned back in his chair. She smiled at him.

"Surprise. Again."

He hadn't seen her in almost four days. The night after their "movie date," he called the number she'd scribbled on his refrigerator and left a message. Instead of returning his call, she'd now showed up at his office.

"Busy?" she asked, coming deeper into the office and closing the door behind her.

"Not too much to talk to you."

"That's very gallant of you to say."

"I'm sure you're used to men being gallant and chivalrous as well as everything else just for you. Even the assholes."

"Unfortunately that's not quite true." She sat down in the chair across from his desk, looking very much like one of his students in her tight blue T-shirt and a skirt that fell away from her knees as she crossed her legs. "So, what are you up to?"

"Not too much. Looking at my midsemester student evaluations."

"I thought profs only gave those out at the end of the semester."

"I don't see any point in doing it then. The students are in the class now. If I can make their learning experience better while I still have them as students, then our time together will be more productive."

Tam nodded. "That makes sense." She tilted her head to the side in that appraising look he was coming to know very well.

Ian pushed aside the evaluations to give her his full attention. She looked fresh today, a lovely blend of innocent womanhood and coy coed. Funny how that never seemed appealing in the dozens of younger girls who'd sat in that same chair in the past.

"I could get used to these visits of yours," he said.

"Don't." Tam smiled as she said it. "I like the surprise of you. Of us."

His eyebrow lifted. "I didn't know there was an us."

"Mm-hmmm. And isn't it a nice surprise, like flowers on a nonspecial day or sex in the afternoon?"

"I'll take your word for it."

Her nipples were hard under the tiny shirt, and Ian was trying not to stare. Then he shrugged and let his eyes drink their fill. If she hadn't wanted him to look, she wouldn't have worn the shirt. Tam must have known that her breasts were like succulent little plums peaking under the blue material, just begging for a brush of his hands. He remembered how sensitive her nipples were, how she hissed from the barest touch of them, how she couldn't seem to come without him sucking or playing with them. Tam shifted and dragged his gaze back up to her eyes.

"So, when are you going to be finished?" she asked.

"It's hard to say. I have office hours beginning at two." It was almost one thirty. "Do you have anything particular in mind?"

"No. I just wanted to enjoy your company for a few minutes before heading back home to do some work." Tam uncrossed her legs. "And I do, you know. Enjoy your company." She stood up and walked around the desk to where he sat. Her scent, that same green tea and rosemary blend, teased his nose as she stepped closer. Tam sat down on his desk, clearing a path for her bottom with a careless sweep of a hand behind her. Papers fluttered as they slid over the desk's surface and then fell to the floor. Her breasts settled close to his mouth. She looked down at him, bracing her sandaled feet on the arms of his chair. "Do you enjoy my company?"

"Very much."

She wasn't wearing any underwear. The intimate smell of her pussy, wet and in need of attention, brought him instantly up and hard, nearly bursting out of his pants. Tam saw that. She didn't miss much. With a curling, catlike smile, she leaned closer and braced her hands on his shoulders. "I was hoping you'd have time for me this afternoon."

Ian groaned. He could see where this was going. This was to pay him back for the other night when he didn't fuck her like she wanted. As much as the idea of those kinds of games usually turned him off, he was more than ready to play this one. He wanted to be available for her. But he had at least two students signed up to see him this afternoon, and the last thing he wanted to do was have one of them walk in on him having sex with Jasmine's mother.

"Why don't you come by my place tonight?" he asked, pitching his voice low. "We'll have the evening all to ourselves, and I can fuck you for as long as you can stand it."

She actually pouted, and he laughed. Her face flexed, and she looked . . . hurt. Tam pushed away from him and stood up, putting away her gorgeous pussy.

"I don't think so." She walked to the door. "Since you don't have time for me now, I'm going to leave. Don't call me."

Ian watched her close the door quietly behind her.

He spent a few seconds trying to figure out what had just happened before he jumped to his feet. "Shit."

His secretary looked up as he burst into the little reception area, her eyebrow rising to her hairline.

"Where did that woman go?" he asked.

She pointed to the stairs leading down and out of the building. Ian flew after Tam, banging open the door leading to the stairs. His tennis shoes slapped against the steps as he raced to find her. He saw the flash of dark blue and the lighter blue of her skirt.

"Tam!"

She stopped on the flight of stairs below him and looked up. "What do you want?"

"I want to talk to you." Ian slowed down but kept walking steadily toward her.

"What about?" Her hand landed on the railing, holding lightly to it as her foot hovered above the next step.

"Your childishness." He stopped on the stair above her.

She turned fully to face him. "You laughed at me."

"No, I didn't. I laughed at the situation, not at you."

"I *was* the situation," she said petulantly but turned into him only to smile at his exasperated expression. "Jasmine ran me out of the house today. She said I was being hormonal."

"Are you?"

"Hell, yes."

He chuckled.

"So, what are you going to do about it?" She trailed her fingers up the smooth metal railing until they lay next to his. Quicksilver-fast mood swings. That was one thing he'd forgotten about being with a woman for longer than a few sex-filled nights.

Ian brushed his hand over her hair and down her long neck to the warm, slight weight of her shoulders. "What do you think?"

She chuckled and took the last step to push them together. Desire slammed between them and ignited like nitro. Her mouth devoured his, opened wide and hungry. Tam gripped his shirt and popped one button and then two. Her fingernails scraped down his chest, bringing up goose bumps and his dick, hard and harder against her belly.

"Fuck!"

Her hands dived to his pants, quickly freeing his dick. She held him between her hot palms and dropped quickly to her knees.

"No." He swept her back up and against his chest. "I don't want that. Not now. Not here."

Her look was questioning, but when he pushed her backward and turned her belly against the railing, a pleased sound vibrated in her throat. He kissed her from behind, tangling their tongues together as her head turned over her shoulder, her neck twisting back. Tam straddled and, tilting up her bottom, bled "yes" from her every pore. And Ian was pushing up her skirt, ripping her panties out of the way, and then sinking into her gratifyingly wet pussy.

They both groaned. The lust and want rose up in Ian like a tsunami until he had no control over his body and certainly not his mind. They froze for a moment like that, pleasure so intense immobilizing them on that railing, in that stairwell, breaths rubbing raw against each other. Then Tam arched her back and grunted, pushing back against Ian. He sighed and eased even more deeply inside her comforting warmth; as he moved faster, the comfort burned away and the heat became consuming and they were back to frantic speed again, gasping and groaning in the narrow stairwell, their noises echoing back at them, the sweat soaking their clothes. Tam reached back and up to stroke his face. The simple pressure of her fingertips against his cheeks stoked Ian's fire even higher. Her pinkie dipped into the parted hollow of his mouth, sliding against his tongue as he fucked her.

Ian heard foreign noises, the door upstairs banging open, and then voices. It only made him grasp her tighter, fuck her harder. The voices came lower, and then another door banged open as the intruders disappeared onto a higher floor. Some part of him was relieved. He didn't want anyone to find him like this, his pants hitched under his ass, his dick buried to the hilt in the hottest woman he'd ever known. But part of him didn't care. It just wanted to feel. It wanted to feel her.

He reached around for her swollen, pulsing clit and took it between his fingers, stroking her hard just the way she liked it when she was close to coming. Her mouth opened, and she cried out, gasping with each thrust, her glorious loudness music to his ears as she lost her control to him, flinging her pussy back against him as she held on tight to the railing with one hand and guided his fingers on her clit with the other.

"Fuck. Yes. Fuck. Yes." He was nothing and everything inside her, incinerated and coming and exploding and dying all at once.

She came around him, screaming into the palm of his hand. Tam bit him, and Ian groaned. The pain sent more shock waves rolling through him, and his hips jerked against her ass. Another set of voices flowed down the stairs, this time definitely heading toward them. Ian hurriedly tugged up his pants and put his dick away. Tam groaned and staggered off the railing to tuck down her skirt and wipe her hands across her sweaty face.

"Come." Ian tugged her out of the stairwell and into the bright sunlight. The door closed behind them, locking them out of the building.

Her breathing wasn't quite under control when the two students came through that same door only moments later, but by that time she and Ian were far up the path, heading to the front door of the Humanities building.

"Well," Tam said. "That was interesting."

"Very."

They walked silently to the parking lot toward the conspicuous blue of her car, with its gleaming chrome wheels and a giant wrapped-and-tied rectangular something, a painting, Ian assumed, sticking up from the backseat beyond the lowered convertible roof.

"Listen," he said. "I want to give you something." He reached into his back pocket for the piece of paper in his wallet he'd been carrying around for the better part of a week. "I wanted to give you this in case we got even more . . . involved."

"Yeah, I think today counts as more involved."

It wasn't that she had come to see him at school, or even that she'd been emotional with a man she had no intention of making her boyfriend. It was simply that they'd fucked, hard and hot and well. And recklessly without a condom.

"I'm clean," he said, handing her the piece of paper, his STD test results.

She blushed and wrapped her arms around herself. "Thanks." Tam cleared her throat and looked down. "I guess that was really careless of me, to let things go that far and not know . . . Shit." She looked up at him. "I'm clean, too, Ian. That I can promise you. So that you don't have to trust what I say, I'll bring my paperwork to you later. OK?"

He smiled at her, feeling a sudden tenderness for her well up inside. "OK."

She cleared her throat again. "I think you better go now. You'll be late for your meetings."

"Fuck." He looked up and around toward the gigantic campus clock that was visible from most places on campus. A few minutes after two. "Yes." He backed away from her. "I'll call you after my meetings are over. Can you come see me tonight?"

She nodded, still wrapped in the protection of her arms. "Yes."

"Good. Talk to you later then." Then he was jogging back toward his office, his skin still hot and smelling like her.

9

"I just got into an accident," Tam said as soon as Ian answered his phone. "Can I meet you at your house later?"

Ian froze. "Where are you? Do you need a ride home? Are you hurt?"

"No, no. I'm fine." Her voice was firm, if a little preoccupied. "Let me just finish dealing with these cops, and I'll call you when I'm on my way." She hung up before he could ask any more questions.

It was just after four o'clock. If she was caught in an accident now, it might be until well after six before she escaped from the traffic. He thought briefly about calling Eric and asking his friend to use his connections in the sheriff's department to find Tam's location. But that would be a little bit too much, to show up at the scene of her accident trying to be her knight in shining armor when she didn't even want to be see in public with him.

At home Ian had a Scotch-and-soda dinner and then sat down to watch TV. But not even his favorite porn channel with its constant parade of uninhibited women could take his mind off Tam and what she could be going through right now. When the doorbell rang a few minutes after eight o'clock, he catapulted off the couch.

"Hey," Tam greeted him with a forlorn look and an unsuccessful attempt at a smile.

"Hey."

They stared quietly at each other for a moment; then Ian looked beyond her to the car sitting in his drive. It was obviously drivable. The convertible top was up and intact, but the front end of the Mini wasn't. The front grille with the Mini Cooper insignia and license plate was crushed in about three inches, and one of the front lights winked with bits of broken glass. But the car was otherwise fine. It dripped wet on the driveway's concrete.

"I just took it through a drive-through car wash. I thought it would look better." She sighed. "Take me inside. I don't want to see it anymore."

Ian opened the door for her to step inside. Tam headed straight for the bedroom, dropping her clothes—sandals, handbag, skirt, blouse—on the floor as she went. Without a word, she climbed into the bed under the covers.

She curled into herself and stared at him. "I wasn't paying attention."

Ian sat on the bed beside her; then, at Tam's wordless invitation, got in under the covers with her.

"I wasn't paying attention," she said again. "After I left the gallery I went home to get my STD test results." She put a cool hand against his chest. "I knew better than to call you and drive at the same time, but that didn't stop me from doing it. I was halfway through dialing your number when I felt the car jerk and I heard that fucking loud noise. Shit." She bowed her head. He touched the delicate curve of her neck and stroked the fine hairs he found there.

"Sorry, Tam."

"I should have fucking known better," she hissed into his chest.

"It's all right, baby. We can fix it."

She sniffled and then sank deeper into the bed.

"We can fix it." He continued stroking Tam's neck, calming her until the sound of her deep, even breathing hovered in the room and she fell asleep.

He was in heaven. A hot, humid heaven that smelled like mouthwash and rosemary shampoo and Tamarind. His body felt awash in sensations, liquid heat dancing through his veins, the cool AC humming across his bare chest, and his dick swallowed by someone who knew exactly what she was doing. Ian groaned and arched himself deeper into Tam's wet mouth. The same mouth that had tugged him from a dream of zooming across a California beach in an intact Mini Cooper with a smiling woman by his side.

In the dream he had looked down in consternation as his dick rose up between him and Tam in the car, tenting under his loose, linen pants. Then she was reaching for him, not paying the slightest attention to the sandy road ahead. Her mouth tugged him from that dream, and he opened his own mouth to say something and groaned instead. She swallowed him up in sweetness, sliding him ferociously against the back of her throat, in the hot tundra of her mouth, until his body was a hot, hard, yearning instrument with only one explosive purpose.

Her head nodded over him, telling him yes, it was all right, even as her fingers caressed his balls, played with the super-heated cum that was ready to anoint her mouth if she let it. He watched the length of his thickly veined dick impossibly appear and disappear at the gateway of her mouth; then she was telling him "Yes, faster," and he couldn't watch her anymore because his head fell back and his whole world was going up in flames behind his tightly closed eyelids.

When the planet rearranged itself, he opened his eyes to her straddling his belly, her damp pussy a hot exclamation mark against his skin.

"Morning," she said.

"Is it?"

"Yeah, it's a bit past six." Her face swam in pleasure as she rubbed her pussy against the hard muscles of his belly.

She shifted over his skin again, and he watched as she pleasured herself, using his body like an oversize dildo.

"Let me help you with that," he said and then pulled her up until she was crouched above his face and her shaved pussy was open to his seeking mouth. Damn, she was wet. At the first touch of his tongue, she shuddered.

Her hands grasped the headboard, her fingers fitting neatly around the dark cherry bars as she settled herself more comfortably on his face. Heavenly. She was heavenly. The soft weight of her thighs caressed his cheeks, pointing up to the wet center of her that at this very moment claimed all his attentions. Tam smelled like sleep and wonderful awakening. The deep pink of her pussy captivated and aroused, making his mouth salivate for another taste. He licked her again, and she hummed. The soft licks became greedy slurps, and he fit his mouth on her—like she was made just for him—sucking and licking her creamy pussy while she danced on his mouth. Her breasts bounced and trembled with each snakelike undulation of her body. He reached up to grasp her nipples and breasts, gradually tightening the pincers of his fingers until she moved faster, her slow belly dance giving way to the hectic salsa-and-sweat-fueled merengue, and she threw her head back, breathing heavily, gasping, both hands holding on to her head as if she was afraid it would fly off.

"Ia—" His name broke off with a wailing groan and then another. He held her hips as she came, even when she pitched sideways to the pillows next to him, her hips still jerking as his mouth lightly soothed her clit.

"No, stop. . . ." She moaned. "Too much." Her trembling hand pushed him away.

He released her, pulled her down and over to him, watching her soft, sweating face as she wiped a limp hand over her eyes and forehead. "Damn. You give amazing head."

"It is one of my many skills."

She opened an eye to check to see if he was joking. Tam laughed at his smirking face and then closed her eyes again. "That was so lovely."

"I could say the same to you. That mouth of yours should be insured."

"We're quite a pair. Maybe we should go into business together?"

"That's all right. I like my current job, thanks. And I suspect that you like yours too much to give it up for a nine-to-five sucking dick and taking home your pay in cash." Ian considered it. "Your mouth would get rubbed raw and tired, wouldn't it?"

"For you, I can go all night," she murmured, watching him for some response.

"I might give you a chance to prove that statement."

"Anytime."

Now was as good of an "anytime" as any. But five seconds after the thought floated through Ian's mind, he dismissed it. He didn't want her to suck his dick all morning, he wanted to make love to her. Although, she wasn't really into that. Fucking was all she was in this for.

"I have a better idea of something you could do with your mouth." He nuzzled her throat and the hot space between her collarbones. "Tell me what you want me to do for you. Tell me, what's your pleasure?"

She laughed as he nibbled on her shoulders. "You're off to a pretty good start." The laughter became a groan when he licked her breasts, teasing the stiffened nipples with his tongue and teeth. Tam sighed and moved restlessly against the sheets.

"So, tell me what you want."

"I want," she sighed again and arched her breasts against his mouth, grabbing his head to hold him to her, "I want this."

"Be more specific." He spoke around the swell of a nipple. "Tell me everything you want. Everything."

"I . . . I want . . . I want you to lick my nipples hard, just like you're doing now . . . and I want your fingers in my cunt. I want you to fuck me with your fingers. You're really good at that." She squirmed against his fingers. "Yes, just like that . . . only my clit, yes, touch my clit. Ah . . ." Ian heard the smile in her voice.

He caressed the soft, slippery bud between his fingers, teasing it gently and then slowly building the pressure until her breathing came erratically and she was pressing her thighs open wider for him.

"Put your fingers inside. Yes . . . yes. Just like—Ian, yes. . . ." She made a wordless noise, thrusting her hips faster until the bed was singing with her movements and Ian worked beside her, his dick a hard weight pressed against her thigh. His hand ached, but still he fucked her, fucking her greedy pussy and stroking her clit.

"Fuck me, please don't stop that . . . please!" Her back arched abruptly from the bed, and her arm flung out. "Ian!"

Her pussy seized rhythmically around his fingers, and her juices poured out. He continued moving, rubbing his dick against her thigh, pumping his fingers inside her. She twitched, gasping.

"I came," she said into the quiet room.

He moved steadily down her body. "Are you sure?"

"Yes, I'm sure—oh!" She lost her breath and arched up, caught unawares by his mouth on her pussy.

Ian chuckled. With a low sigh, he dove into the loamy wet of her, delving his tongue into her pink heat, licking and sucking the slick pussy lips that fanned out like taffy. Tam was the sweetest woman he'd ever tasted. He could eat her pussy all day and never be full. She arched against his mouth.

"I want to see your face," she murmured. "I want to watch you while you fuck me."

He needed no other invitation but that. Her pussy welcomed him, opening up and swallowing his entire length. Then he was the one gasping. He plunged deeply inside her, the pleasure building even higher with her eyes on his face. Ian groaned, and he lost control of his hips, sinking into her again and again. He burst inside her.

"Oh, god, Tam . . . Tam."

He must have blanked out for a moment. The next thing he knew, Tam was gently rolling him off her and then snuggling against his chest. She sighed, all quiet and soft, like she'd just discovered something wonderful and was still taking time to sort it all out.

Tam was a puzzle. Not quite the mysterious and hard woman he'd taken her for in the beginning, but not exactly the accommodating, ever-sexed creature in his dreams either. She lay in his arms, a kitten with her claws firmly sheathed, practically purring in his bed and cuddling up to him. He could definitely get used to this.

"Who is that in the picture?" She wriggled her bottom against him as she pointed to an old photo of Zoë. It was the one of her in front of the dojo where she had taught tai chi and practiced capoeira. Zoë was smiling, looking shy as she half turned away from Ian's camera, peeking at him through her hair.

"My wife." Tam stiffened in his arms. Before she could say anything, Ian touched her gently on the shoulder. "She died almost five years ago."

"Oh. I'm sorry. I had no idea."

"Why would you?"

She looked at him. They hadn't shared very much with each other beyond their bodies and some test results. So far, all he knew about her was that she loved to paint and was good enough at it not to have to make money doing anything else. He knew how she liked to fuck, how she sounded when she came, but those were things strangers could know, too.

"Do you miss her?"

"Sometimes. Less and less these days." He left her to interpret that any way she liked. Ian glanced at the clock. "I have to get ready for work. You want to shower with me?"

"No, go ahead. I'll be here when you get back."

He took his time in the shower, massaging the water into his sore muscles and over the scratches she'd left along his back, shoulders, and arms. She had been more uninhibited this morning than she'd ever been, not that he had much of a basis for comparison. But Tam had been loud, clinging to him and then flinging him from her with a wildness he hadn't experienced with her before. He knew she had bruises, too. Ian walked into the bedroom, drying himself. She was exactly where he had left her, lying on her stomach in the bed. Her head turned to watch him.

With quick, efficient movements, Ian rubbed the last of the moisture from his body and then put on boxers, socks, and jeans.

"You're a gorgeous man," she said.

This was the first time she'd called him a man and not a boy.

"You mentioned that when we first got together. Does it bother you?" He turned, shirtless, to her.

She smiled. "Not anymore."

He looked at her, at her legs swaying to and fro in the bed, her back lovely and bare in the late morning light. "That's not usually something that makes most women uneasy."

"I'm not most women."

"True, that." He pulled a long-sleeved shirt from the closet. "That color looks really good on you." She turned over, and the sheet fell from her, showing off her beautiful throat and breasts. "Red doesn't do it for every man."

"I'm not most men."

They both chuckled. Ian watched her as he buttoned his shirt. She seemed especially comfortable and in no mood to leave the cozy confines of his bed. It was easy to imagine staying in bed with her all day, fucking and talking and fucking some more. But he had students, and they paid tuition so he could come to class and pass on his pearls of wisdom, even if they had been scattered beyond recovery by Tam and her amazing pussy.

Ian put on his loafers and then took a few quick passes over his hair with the brush. When he walked near the bed, her eyes, lit with a soft, appreciative light he could definitely learn to get used to, followed him.

He opened the drawer to the bedside stand and took out his spare keys. "Take these, and let yourself out whenever you're ready. The alarm code is one-two-four-four. Punch it in, and then hit ENTER before you leave. Same thing when you come in." He leaned down and kissed her forehead and then her slightly open mouth. She tasted like sleep and cum. "I'll talk with you later."

For most of the day his mind was back at home with her in bed. All the while he was talking about Dorothy West and Angelina Grimke, he was inside Tam, ramming his blood-filled, straining dick into her from behind as she urged him on with her hoarse shouts and held on to the bars of the headboard, their breaths sounding harsh and loud in the air. While his students dissected the lyrics to the music of the Harlem Renaissance, he heard the symphony of their voices from this morning, Tam's husky voice telling him to fuck her and make her come and eat her pussy and go deeper and don't fucking stop!

Ian taught most of the class from behind the shield of his desk, only rising once near the end of class to write the next homework assignment on the board. By then the throbbing size of his dick had subsided enough for it to be not quite so obvious. He used his hour break between classes to call her.

"Where are you?" he asked. Ian wanted to fuck. He wanted to fuck her. Badly.

"Nowhere near you." She laughed at the need in his voice. "When are you done?"

"Not until after seven. Maybe even eight. I have a meeting."

"Call me when you're finished. Maybe I can meet you somewhere."

"Sounds good."

Ian tucked away his cell phone. *Get ahold of yourself. This woman is not feeling you like that. Chill.* But neither his dick nor heart was paying attention.

When Ian walked into his office at half past five, his secretary covered the mouthpiece of the phone. "I have good news for you," she said. "Your meeting for tonight got canceled."

"How did you know that's good news for me?" he asked, not bothering to hide his smile.

"Just a hunch." She laughed and went back to her phone call.

During his lunch break, Ian had read the local independent paper and was surprised to find a nearby gallery with a list of familiar area artists showing through the end of the month. Tamarind Hannah's name was on the list. The gallery, Epoch, wasn't far from his house, so Ian decided to make a quick stop by there on the way to his favorite Thai restaurant to pick up dinner for him and Tam.

Although it was relatively late in the evening for galleries on this side of town to be open, there were still a fair amount of cars in Epoch's parking lot. All of them high-end rides, including a tricked-out Corvette and a silver Bentley. Ian pulled his Honda Accord into the lot, feeling more than a little poor. Tam's accident-ravaged Mini was nowhere in sight.

He got out of his car to walk across the street to Epoch, waiting by the parking meter on the curb to let the last of the evening traffic pass. Epoch's building was elegant and stood out nicely from its neighbors with its glass and steel facade and the exotically colored orchids lining the bottom of the glass walls like scented sentries, their heads bowing gracefully toward anyone passing by. From the street he could see that there were more than a few people inside, all staring round-eyed at the art around them.

As he was getting ready to cross the street, a familiar flash of blue and then brown caught his eye. The elements coalesced into Tam, lovely and springtime in a flowing blue skirt and a white halter top that clung to her. Ian smiled. He lost the smile when she touched an unfamiliar man. She smiled up into his face and slipped a hand in his. The man bent his head to kiss her, and Tam turned away coyly, her eyes looking down and away in a way Ian had never seen. The stranger drew her face to his with one fingertip under her chin and then kissed her hard on the mouth.

A car honked its horn and screeched on its brakes, jolting Ian from his near sleepwalk into the street.

"Sorry, man," he said to the driver and held up an apologetic hand. "Sorry." He walked back to his car and sat behind the wheel.

That wasn't right, whatever he just saw. His eyes were playing tricks on him. Ian made to get out of the car again and then stopped himself. Cool it. Drive. Go home. He started the car, pulling out carefully into the street and turning the opposite way from home, just so he wouldn't have to drive past the gallery. He passed the restaurant where he was supposed to get their dinner. Nothing special, just some salad, sweet tofu bites, and fruits she liked—small things made especially for lovers so they wouldn't be too full to have sex and then eat and have sex again. Now the sight of the restaurant's red door made him feel sick. And angry.

Ian wanted to call her, wanted to curse and drink a tall glass of Scotch and shake her and ask her what the fuck was going on. But he didn't like to drink on a school night, and he'd never shaken a woman in his life. His eyes felt gritty and dry, as if the sand off the beach had blown up to blind him or make him see things that weren't there. Like her faithfulness or what he thought was her growing infatuation with him. Why the hell was she in another man's arms when he was making plans to romance and woo her? Why was he the fool?

He drove back to the gallery. By the time he pulled back into the space he'd vacated before, most of the cars were gone. Only one, a sleek, two-door Bentley, remained in its spot. He locked the car and walked to the front doors of the gallery. The lights had dimmed, but he tried the door anyway. It was open. A melodious, electronic chime sounded as he walked inside.

Tam appeared from a hidden back room. "I'm sorry, we're—" Her words fell away when she saw him.

"Where's your car?" he asked.

She shook her head as if to clear it of an illusion. Of him. "It's in the shop. The one you saw outside is a loaner."

A loaner Bentley. Impressive. Her new man (or was he an old one?) must be rolling in the dough.

"I didn't know you worked here," he said.

"I don't. Epoch belongs to a friend of mine. I'm minding the store until she gets back to town."

He nodded but didn't say anything, merely watched her as she walked to the front door to lock it but not before peering into the street, first in one direction and then another.

"Expecting someone?"

"No, just checking for customers."

"I thought this place was closed."

"It is."

She turned to face him. "How did you find me here?"

"By accident. I was heading to Bangkok House when I stopped by to check out some of your work. The paper said you and a few other artists had work showing here."

"Oh."

"Why did you ask me how I found you? Did you think I was stalking you? Or that I found out something you didn't want me to know?"

She crossed her arms over her chest and stared at him, but her look didn't affect him like before. The cracks in her facade were laughably apparent, especially from this distance. "Like what?"

"Don't be coy, Tam. Like your other lover. The guy whose dick I saw you practically sucking in front of everybody in this damn gallery two hours ago. I didn't know you had another toy on the side." He circled her, coming gradually closer. Her arms shifted over her chest, but otherwise she didn't move. Her expressionless face made his anger flare even higher.

"So this guy I saw you with, what's his name?"

"Garrett." She sighed. "His name is Garrett."

Ian nodded as though giving thoughtful consideration to the name of the guy she'd been fucking the whole time they were together. "Is he the 'friend' who owns the beach house you took me to that first time?"

Her cheeks darkened, but she didn't drop her gaze. "Ian, don't make a big deal—"

"Is he?"

She sighed again. "Yes."

"Was he watching us have sex the whole time? Did it turn

him on to know that my dick was inside your pussy, the same pussy he was going to be drinking from later that day?"

She flinched. "No. I'm not sure what he saw, but . . . but I really do feel for you, Ian."

"Feel what? Feel your pussy get wet every time you see me? I already know that. And you and I both know that's nothing special."

She had the nerve to look hurt.

"Don't goddamn get that look on your face." The look pierced him and made him regret his hard words, but she was just playing him. Again. Ian moved toward her anyway, touching her face and bringing her close. "Shit." She kissed him. "Shit."

He tasted tears in her open mouth. She held his cheeks tight between her flattened palms. "I'm sorry," she said between their kisses. "I am. I'm sorry."

What the fuck did that mean? That she was sorry he found out and put an end to her playtime? Ian tried to pull gently away, but she slipped her hands behind his head and held him close. Her teeth scraped against his closed lips, nibbling, biting, hurting. He wrenched himself away.

"Stop it."

She came toward him again, and he had to grab her shoulders to hold her back. "Stop fucking with me, Tam. I think you've had your fun. We're finished."

She wriggled and flailed in his grip.

"Isn't that what you wanted?" he asked. "Isn't this what all your advance-and-retreat bullshit was about? You wanted to fuck me but not get too involved? Well, you've already had your fuck, and I'm leaving. All you had to say was 'it's over.' What's so fucking hard about that?"

"This is not over," she hissed.

"Just because you say so?" He laughed. "You're a fucking—"

She twisted from his grip and spun close, slamming into his chest. "You know it's not over between us, Ian. You know it." She pressed her hand against his chest. "This doesn't lie. Neither does this." Her other hand on his dick froze him. It wasn't her boldness that held him immobile. No, it was because his dick, like an obedient dog, rose on command for her, stiffening behind the thin cotton of his slacks and pushing back against her hand. Ian swallowed.

"Stop it," he hissed again.

But she didn't stop; instead she stepped closer, pushing at him, assaulting his senses with her body's perfume and the intoxicating pressure of her hand against his dick. Her touch grew more certain the longer he stood there, unmoving. He could never say no to her. And a part of him asked now; why did he have to? She pressed back at him until his back was to the wall and his dick was throbbing just for her and his heart was a jackhammer in his chest. Did she even realize how far gone he was?

Ian grasped her shoulders again to hold her back from him. Her eyes were certain of his surrender, on her terms. Fuck that. Ian leaned in and kissed her like this was the last time he was ever going to taste her lips. He devoured their pouty curve, their damp insides, and sucked hard on the tongue that flickered and writhed against his. She moaned and pressed her body to him. They were in a duel of wills, each wanting to dominate the other, each expressing it in the same way, but Ian was fueled with anger and lust and frustration. He lifted her, draped her unprotesting body over one of the exhibition pieces, a hip-high wooden carving with a dipped curve that fit her back perfectly. It was just long enough to fit her hips and back while her head dangled over the edge. She lay on it, trying to find purchase with her hands, but the wood was too smooth and her body was just beginning to sweat. He tore away her skirt and underwear, leaving her lower body completely exposed and her bare,

damp pussy gleaming in the gallery lights. With one quick movement of his hand her camisole was on the floor. The dark tips of
her breasts jumped with each quick breath.

Tam fumbled for Ian's belt, but he pushed her and her hands
back, still kissing her mouth, her chin, her jawline, biting her
smooth skin until she flinched with pain and pleasure, her body
floating up and down with each touch of his teeth. He combed
his fingers through her pussy lips, coating them with her slick-
ness. This was going to be the last time for them. This was it.
His chest tightened, and his heart raced faster. Ian slid his fingers against her clit, massaging her pussy until she gasped and
moaned, a surging symphony of sex that reminded him too
much of this morning's pleasure. He tasted her with his fingers
and found she was wet inside, drenched and ready for him.

Tam surged up again, still trying for his belt and his stiff
cock that begged shamelessly for her touch. Ian pushed her
back but didn't stop there. She obviously wanted something.
He was going to give it to her. The belt left their loops with an
audible slide. He loosened the top button of his pants and
pulled down the zipper but that was all. When Tam reared up
again, he captured her hands in the noose of his belt, pulling the
leather through the buckle until her wrists were snared together. He fit his hips into the vee of her thighs.

"What—what are you—uh!"

He surged into her. She fit around him like hot, molten mo-
lasses, thick and engulfing, swallowing up all his senses. This
time he wasn't worried about the buildup, he wasn't worried
about her orgasm, only that she felt his need, all his desperation
for her that had come to nothing.

"What does he do for you that I can't?" He fucked her. "Is it
the money? Is it that overpriced car? Or is it the way he treats
you like shit because you always come back for his scraps?"

He fucked her hard against the sculpture. Her body slid
back and forth across the smooth surface, but only as far as his

pounding hips and the tightened belt held in his fisted hand would allow. Her body was an erotic arc of leaping breasts, liquid cunt, and heaving belly. A Venus hewn in onyx and stretched to its very limits under the gallery's soft lights.

His mouth opened in that sweltering O of desire. His hips pistoned, his body tightened. All his muscles leaped toward Tam and her weeping pussy, toward her writhing body and the siren call of her wails under him.

"Does that feel good?" He gasped the question, although the liquid slide of his dick and her gasping cries made the question moot.

As she gasped a yes, he twisted his hips, changed the angle until she was crying out. He grabbed her thigh and threw her leg over his shoulder.

Everything bubbled up inside him then, his stupid love for her, his tattered pride. It didn't matter who saw them through the gallery's clear glass windows—all that mattered was her, under him, telling him yes.

"Fuck me!" She panted. "Harder. Yes. Yes!"

He gave her everything she asked for and more. Winding his hips, twisting her nipple, sweating above her until a high, keening wail announced the beginning of her come.

"Oh, God! Oh—fuck! Don't stop, don't stop!"

He didn't stop. He could never stop. Even after her body shuddered and clutched at him—once, twice, three times—Ian kept on going. He pounded away at her until he was coming, too, throwing his head back and thrusting into her, jerking her sweat-slick body across the sculpture. He was dying. Jesus! He was dying.

"It's OK, baby," she said. "It's OK."

His body shuddered and gave up the last of its seed to her, and then he was pulling out of her and turning away. He covered himself with the tail of his shirt and pulled his pants quickly up. With a disgusted sigh at himself, he wiped his hand across his face, and then he reached over Tam to retrieve the belt he'd used to restrain her.

"I've got to go," he said, buckling his belt. He backed away as she sat up. "I'll see you around."

"That's it?" She looked stricken and breathless, like a well-fucked woman who wanted more.

"That's it." Ian unlocked the gallery door and walked away from Tam without looking back.

10

"I wish things didn't have to be like this." Jasmine looked at him with pleading eyes.

"It's all right, Jasmine." He tried to smile. "There's nothing to worry about. Your mother and I are finished."

The clock above his office door ticked away the eighteenth minute past two, almost half an hour since Jasmine had walked into his office and told Ian she knew what had happened between him and her mother.

"She can be really thoughtless sometimes. I'm sorry about whatever it was that she did. But she misses you, I think. She's just too stubborn to say it."

Ian shifted with impatience as each word Jasmine spoke poked at him, made him remember and cringe with disgust at the fool he'd made of himself over Tam. "Whatever your mother and I had is in the past. Let's just leave it there."

Jasmine looked down. "Sorry."

"No, don't be sorry. None of it's your fault." But part of him did believe it was her fault. If it weren't for Jasmine, he wouldn't have met Tam. Then again, if it hadn't been for his dick, he wouldn't have gotten into her car that first day, he wouldn't have fucked her on the beach, and he wouldn't be in the frozen hell he was in now. "It's not your fault," he said again.

She didn't come to him in dreams anymore. Ian didn't know whether to be grateful or pissed off. He did the same things he did before, went to work, ate, slept, saw his friends. But underneath it all lay her nagging absence. Thoughts of Zoë no longer comforted him. He couldn't even rely on the old pain of missing her to take his mind off Tam. Something inside him had finally put Zoë to rest.

Although it was only a small comfort, he knew that Tam was thinking about him. She tried to call. He saw her name on the caller ID when the phone had rung once and then stopped. But he wasn't going to call back and make it easy for her. Obviously whatever she had to say to him she also knew he didn't want to hear.

"You look like shit," Eric said, sitting down next to Ian on the bar stool.

"Thanks," Ian muttered. He knew his exhaustion-ravaged face and disinterested expression weren't the sexiest things to bring to the bar, but that was all he had today.

"Did that woman come back to you yet?"

"She's not coming back, and I don't want her back."

"That's bullshit, and you know it." Eric signaled the bartender and ordered a Corona and lime. "If she walked in here right now and dropped to her hands and knees to beg, you would gladly take that bitch back." Eric nodded his thanks to the bartender and passed her his credit card. "Start a tab for me, honey." He turned back to his friend. "In fact, I can't think of any circumstances in which you wouldn't take her back. You're pussy whipped."

Ian had told Eric about Tam over a month ago, even shown his friend a photograph of her. That was before they had stopped seeing each other, when things had been at their most explosive. Eric was all sympathy and voyeuristic interest. Of all Ian's friends, he was the one who understood about the sheer power of lust and its ability to blast away all reasonable thought and need. When Ian told him about the other man, Eric had shrugged philosophically. "A hot woman like that, of course she has some on-the-side dick, which, by the way, might have been you."

"I *was* whipped," Ian said in response to his friend's earlier comment. "Now I'm over it."

"Right." Eric took a deep drink of his beer. "What would you do if you saw her right now?"

"Don't fuck with me, Eric. I'm not in the mood."

"You better think about it, because your hot piece just walked in here with some other Negro. Don't turn around, fool. Be cool."

But Ian was past the point of trying to be cool. He was ice cold. His friends may be able to tell that the woman had taken everything when she left—his heart, his balls, even his libido—but to the rest of the world, he was the same as usual. He watched her in the mirrored wall behind the bar.

She was in his bar with someone else. Not the one she'd left him for. Tam was all over the guy, leaning into him as they walked around the bar looking for a place to sit. When they sat down on an overstuffed couch in the corner, she tucked herself into the crook of his arm like a child. The man teased her, played with one of her pointy ears, trying to get her to laugh. But he was nothing to worry about. Tam obviously wasn't his type.

"Oh, honey, please!" the man trilled. "Butch up, and get over it."

"Never mind," Eric said. He went back to sucking on his beer.

But Tam was now firmly in Ian's mind. He watched as Tam's companion left her to get drinks at the bar near where Eric and Ian sat. The man's eyes passed over them with casual interest before leaning in to kiss the bartender on both cheeks. They chatted as the woman made his drinks. He didn't say anything about Tam. Ian was listening while his eyes stayed firmly locked on Tam in the mirror. Her gay boyfriend went back to her with drinks, and she thanked him with a smile and that familiar coy tilt of her head. Ian knew the exact moment when she saw him.

She froze and almost spilled her drink. He took a large swallow of his beer and watched her in the mirror, daring her to look away. Tam looked tired, like she'd been spending some long, hard nights fucking her sugar daddy. But she was still beautiful.

"Hey, sorry we're late," Rashawn said, breezing in with Troy. "That traffic from downtown's a bitch."

"It's cool," Eric said. "You didn't miss anything except Ian's little girlfriend loving on some gay boy over there in the corner."

"Serious?"

"Not really. I think she's just trying to take her mind off our boy. Look at her." Eric nodded toward Tam. "She can't keep her damn eyes in her own business."

"Shit, then let's give the bitch something to look at."

Before Ian could tell Rashawn to cool it, his friend wrangled a trio of cuties, what used to be Ian's type—slim shoulders, big asses, and tiny waists—to entertain the boys for the evening. Although Rashawn's brawny athlete's physique and easy charm got them over there, the moment the girls got a good look at Ian, they forgot about everybody else.

"If I wasn't trying to make this fool feel better, I'd push him

276 / Fiona Zedde

out of this bar so the rest of us can get a little piece of the action," Rashawn said.

"Speak for yourself. I've got no problems getting mine," Eric said.

"Whatever, man." Troy laughed. "Don't work too hard to convince yourself."

The girls slid up to Ian, each trying to get him to notice her over the others. The winner made herself at home in the vee of his spread thighs. Her friends gave up the fight and turned to Eric, Troy, and Rashawn to make halfhearted conversation.

"Hey," the bold one purred, rubbing her palms up his thighs, "my name is Tanisha. What's yours?" Never mind that Rashawn had introduced everyone not five minutes before. Was this girl deaf?

He told her his name, wondering how far she would go with her hands before she struck gold.

"What a coincidence," she said. "I have *I*, *A*, and *N* in my name, too." She chuckled and leaned closer. "I'd love to have a little more Ian in me." Tanisha laughed at her own joke and brushed her breasts against his chest. Her hands gripped the tops of his thighs, pressing up the material of his pants to emphasize the shape of his dick under the cotton.

"Excuse me." Ian looked up, surprised, when Tam came over. "Can I talk with you for a minute?" she asked.

"Go find your own man, honey." The younger woman gave Tam a dismissive once-over. "This one's taken for the night."

Ian shook his head and forced a laugh. Tam didn't look too happy, but it could just have been the inconvenience of having to deal with someone like Tanisha. "Give me a sec," he said, pulling away from the girl. She reluctantly released him while keeping a jaundiced eye on Tam.

His ex-lover guided him away from the main part of the bar

to one of its quieter rear lounges. There were couples seated back there and a few threesomes, too, leaning close and talking intimately together. She sat down on one of the deep purple velvet love seats and invited him to do the same.

"It's good to see you," she said.

"Is that what you called me in here to tell me?" He could feel himself weakening, feel her scent twine around his senses, pulling him back to where he was almost a month ago.

"No." She looked into his face as though she was searching for something. "No." Tam bit her lips together and then clasped her hands in her lap. She sighed. "I've never had to beg a man for anything in my life. Never."

"I don't want you to beg me for anything."

"Are you sure about that?" She shook her head. "No, I'm sorry, that's not how I wanted this to go. Just listen." Tam sighed again. "I miss you. I want to see you. I want us to be lovers again."

"Are you still seeing that other guy?"

Tam pursed her lips. "Yes, I am."

Ian held himself still, willing the disappointment not to show on his face. "This conversation is over. It was good seeing you." He stood up.

"Ian, please. You don't understand."

He looked down at her. "Don't beg me for anything, Tam. If you want me, here I am. If you want him and me and every other piece of dick that catches your eye, then you can beg until your tongue falls out and your tail wags off. It's not going to happen. I would say 'sorry,' but I'm not."

He forced himself to take a step, and then two, away from her. "Enjoy yourself tonight. Enjoy your life. I hope you find whatever it is you're searching for."

No matter how many times he did it, walking away from

Tam never got any easier. Ian went back out to the bar, wiping his face clean of any real emotion. Tanisha was more than happy to reclaim her place between his thighs, and he let her, even buying her a drink to make himself seem more welcoming. He never noticed when Tam left.

"The royal penis is clean, your highness."

Ian couldn't even smile as he watched one of his favorite parts from *Coming to America*. Truth be told, he didn't understand why he was torturing himself by watching the movie. The phantom scent of warm, rosemary-flavored Tam snuggled up against him on the couch, making him long for her even more. She had laughed at that line in the movie and then turned to ask him, "Would you like someone to wash your penis?" The question had been more of a suggestion than a real query, and Ian had gotten instantly hard, ready to ask her if she would use a washcloth or her tongue. A loud knock on Ian's door jolted him out of his memories. He got up to answer, wondering who it could be at this time of night.

Another knock sounded at the window, and he heard Rashawn shout, "If you're in there jacking off, wipe it up and put the dick away! We don't want to see that shit!"

Ian opened the door.

"We could hear you moping all the way from Long Beach."

Eric nudged Ian out of the way to walk inside the house. "Get dressed. We're taking you out."

"I personally have had enough of this pining bullshit," Rashawn said, coming in behind his friend. "You need to get back on that horse and ride it till everybody's satisfied."

"Uh-huh." Ian eyed Rashawn with a jaundiced look.

"I think you'll enjoy this party we're taking you to," Eric said. "I know I will."

After Ian reluctantly got dressed, they piled into Eric's Range Rover and took off. When the truck finally stopped a half hour later, it was on the side street of a neighborhood Ian had never been to before. He and Rashawn got out of the truck and followed Eric down the street and up the nondescript-looking walkway to a red door. It was the entrance to a traditional-looking three-story house, not at all out of place in the suburban neighborhood, with its colorful garden and periwinkle exterior paint. They could hear faint strains of music coming from inside the house, something slow and mellow. At Eric's knock, a woman came to the door. She smiled warmly when she saw them.

"Aren't you boys just looking fine tonight?"

The woman kissed Eric on both cheeks and tugged him inside along with his friends.

"I haven't seen you here in a long time," she said to him. Her pretty chocolate skin glowed from beneath a thin golden sheath.

"I've been a little busy," Eric said. "You know—life."

"I understand." She chuckled. "You know where everything is and how to maximize your good time. If you have questions, you ask Alee at the bar."

Eric squeezed her arm in thanks and then nodded at his friends to follow him up the winding staircase. Ian was beginning to see what kind of party this was. Although the people downstairs were all fully dressed, they were relaxed and laughing with their drinks cupped loosely in their hands as other hands casually caressed them, either playing with hair or touching innocuously bared body parts. As though they were warming up for some main event.

"Is this a whorehouse?"

"I'm shocked and disgusted that you even think I'd take you to such a place." Eric's offended tone didn't fool anyone.

Rashawn snickered.

"No, my friend," Eric said, raising his voice to be heard above the growing noise. "It's a party. A place where people come to have a good time."

Rashawn laughed again. "And keep on coming again and again."

"You are so fucking corny."

More people leaned against the railing that ringed the entire second floor to watch the byplay going on downstairs and pick who and what they wanted for the night. The anticipation of sex was thick in the air.

Ian glanced at Rashawn. "Are you OK with all this?"

His friend nodded, taming his smile. "I'm good. No worries."

With an answering nod, Ian turned back to his contemplation of the crowd. "I'm not really feeling this, fellas," Ian said.

"We know, but you will soon."

Eric always talked about these kind of parties. Parties where the women were willing to do anything just for the fun of it. And most of the men, too. If a guy wanted to do another guy for the night, that could definitely be arranged. He knew Rashawn indulged occasionally. "No big deal," his friend often said. Whatever got him off.

"Pick what you like," Eric said to Ian. "It's all fun tonight."

Rashawn nudged him. "And don't try to push up on someone who looks just like that broad you're trying to forget."

No one could replace Tam or even look like her. That was

one of the things he'd found so appealing. The woman in his dreams and the woman who'd eventually found her way into his bed were the same. And unique. He'd never find someone like her again.

"Look at that," Eric said, pointing to an open alcove a few feet away that had its own little show going on. "That guy's having a little too much fun with that ass."

Ian looked despite himself. And instantly regretted it. Heinrich, his colleague from the university, exerted himself over the pert, pale rear end of an ecstatically crying woman. The sweat dripped down his face as he effectively wielded a paddle, swinging it through the air before connecting it sharply with the reddened bottom turned up over his knee. The wet crotch of the woman's panties clearly outlined her juicy pussy lips.

Heinrich looked up as his new spectators approached. A few already gathered around him wandered away, sufficiently warmed up to stage their own show elsewhere.

Jesus! Ian did not want to see this. "Hey, Rick."

"Ian." Heinrich stopped in midswing to mop at his face with a white handkerchief. "I didn't know you indulged."

"I don't. My friends dragged me here."

Rashawn turned an incredulous look to Ian. "You know this guy?"

"He teaches at the university."

"Damn! Now I know you're the most uptight guy at that place."

Eric stepped back, holding up his hands. He was staying out of it.

"Why don't you try not to be an asshole tonight?" Ian suggested, baring his teeth.

"I'm just trying to help *you* out." Rashawn grinned.

"Uh-huh . . . right."

His friend dismissed the subject with a shrug. "She's nice,"

Rashawn said then, gesturing to the girl over Heinrich's knee. Ian hadn't even seen her face.

"Yeah, she is." Heinrich smiled up at the taller man. "Want to share?"

"If ever a question had an obvious answer."

The two men smiled over the bright red bottom just as the woman turned to them both and added her own smile to the grinning twosome.

Eric exchanged a glance with Ian. The two men turned away and left Rashawn to his games.

"I need a drink," Ian muttered.

They got drinks at the bar and fought their way through the crowd to find a space on the oversize couch in the second-floor living room. The couple next to Eric tongued each other down, sucking at each other's faces until the noises they made started to turn Ian's stomach. Or turn him on. He wasn't quite sure which. The woman's hand snaked out to stroke Eric's thigh. Her long burgundy-tipped fingers spread over Eric's trousers and then dipped between his thighs. Eric lifted her hand as if he wasn't quite sure where it came from and then dropped it back on its owner. He scooted closer to Ian.

Ian grinned. "I thought that was the kind of thing you wanted here."

"Not when I'm talking to you. That's a little freaky. And before you ask, yeah, *too* freaky for me."

Ian smiled and put the beer to his lips.

"So, is this doing you any good?" Eric asked.

"What? Sitting next to a couple that's going to be fucking any second now on top of a sofa with a higher sperm count than my ball sac?"

"Yes."

Ian smiled weakly. "It isn't. But I still gotta thank you fellas for trying."

"She's really got you bad, huh?"

"Yeah, real bad. I've never had it like this before. Not even . . ." Ian thought carefully before he finished saying what was waiting to burst past his lips, "Not even with Zoë." He swallowed.

"Shit." Eric stared at his friend. "Are you serious?"

Ian didn't say anything. He just stared out at the decadent sprawl of bodies before him. "Have you ever had it bad for a woman?" he asked.

"No. Never. I get inoculated against that kind of thing."

The couple next to them stretched out even more on the sofa, and the woman's leg flung out over Eric's thigh. She moaned as her lover cupped her pussy through her slacks. Eric arched an eyebrow and then, almost as an afterthought, leaned over to watch the action. Having lost his audience, Ian adjusted his position on the couch to do the same.

The woman who was stretched out had her hair cut in a sleek bob that made a blade of her already narrow face. Her lips parted to moan when her partner for the evening tugged down the zipper of her pants and slowly worked slim fingers inside. Her breasts were out. They were full and had tiny nipples like Hershey's Kisses. The lover feasted on the small dark nipples, flicking a quick pink tongue over the hard nubs until the woman groaned and churned her hips against the couch. Eric held on to the leg thrown casually over his.

Ian couldn't see her pussy, but he could smell it. The hot, musky scent made him rise full and hard in his trousers. His body was ready to fuck, but he wasn't. He wasn't the least bit interested in fucking her or anyone else at this party. He appreciated his friends for wanting to distract him from his pathetic situation, but it was too soon for him to get into anything like this. But he could see that Eric was becoming interested in the current proceedings. Very interested.

The woman on the sofa was quiet. But her lover wasn't. He made appreciative murmurs as he suckled the thick breasts, growling low in his throat when the woman widened her legs even more to receive his fingers deep inside her. His teeth tightened on her nipples, and the woman threw back her head, gasping silently. The fingers worked in her pussy, thrusting in a quick rhythm while her hips bucked against the couch and her leg flailed in Eric's grasp. Ian watched her mouth. And she watched him.

"Fuck, yeah," she mouthed as her eyes locked with his. "Fuck my pussy. Yes."

Her teeth flashed as she quietly snarled the last word. Her partner's fingers moved faster, and her hips bucked harder. Eric rested his hand on his thigh, very near his stiff dick, but he did not touch himself. Ian watched her and tried to imagine Tam doing something like this. He couldn't.

The woman apparently came. Her leg flailed one last time, and her hips abruptly pushed into the air, arching into her lover's hand. Then she was still. When the guy raised his head from her still hard nipples, they saw that he was a woman. Eric licked his lips.

"That wasn't too bad," he said.

"I've seen better," Ian said with a slight smile. He sipped his beer, but the damn thing was almost hot. "I'm going to grab another beer. Want something?"

"No, I'm good."

Ian got up from the couch and went for the bar. On his way back from the bar with a cold beer in hand he saw that Eric had joined the amorous couple on the couch. He had more than the woman's leg in his lap now and seemed very happy indeed to be getting her attentions. Ian shook his head and then backed out of the room that was rapidly filling up with an audience for the event taking place on the couch. He swam through all kinds of offers—to have his children, suck his dick, give him a hand job, hold his beer, be his cum rag for the night—just to get to the back door. The deck was relatively empty except for a lone man jacking off as he watched two men and a very greedy woman go at it on a blanket in the grass below. The man stood, a sweating glass of Scotch in one hand, his purple-headed dick in the other, methodically stroking himself as if he was alone in his own bedroom.

Ian walked down the deck's stairs to sit under the large maple tree in the backyard. He missed Tam. Honestly and completely. Even in the midst of all this mindless fucking, he wanted her. Not necessarily to fuck. Just to talk to. To see. To ask if she was into this kind of thing.

The man on the deck finished up with a splash and a re-strained groan, but the threesome on the grass kept on going. One of the men lay on his back under the woman's spread thighs, sucking on her pussy while the other man worked hard at trying to give her a pearl necklace. Her thick, cum-slicked breasts and his long straining dick made the likelihood of success very high.

Ian sipped his beer, felt it sweating and cold in his hand. The tree was rough against his back, his dick a limp weight in his trousers. Sounds washed over him—moans, sighs, the liquid slap of flesh against flesh—and he felt dirty, in need of Tam's cleansing presence. Then he saw her. It had to be a trick of the light or of his second beer on an empty stomach. She looked so different hovering above him at the railing in her hip-hugging short skirt and the blouse that lifted and separated her breasts, offering them up like ripe fruit for anyone near to pluck. She looked . . . common. The trick turned and laughed with some-one beyond Ian's sight. Her long silver earrings danced in the air as she turned her head. Then the trick pushed away from the railing and disappeared inside.

Ian realized then that it wasn't the light or his beer. It was Tam. She moved with that unmistakable grace, that sense of owning the room, the space, even the universe she occupied. Ian hesitated only a moment before following her. The grass slid wetly underfoot, but he quickly regained his balance, crossed the yard, and ran up the wooden stairs.

Ian followed the flashing earrings and tightly girded ass, watching to see what she would do. Her escort—the man from the gallery—tugged her along while his eyes took in everything around him, devouring all the different types of sex taking place in the house. Tam watched, earrings dancing, as her head moved from side to side, her gaze flickering over the multiple visual stimuli. When someone touched her, she looked at them but kept moving. They paused to see what they could of the action taking place in the built-for-three space behind the stairs.

A woman appeared at Tam's side and lazily caressed her ass. Tam's lover looked immediately interested. But when he touched the stranger, the woman dismissed him with a cool shake of her head. Tam wasn't tempted, so shook her own head and watched the woman go without the smallest sign of regret. A man approached them, then another, and another, then a couple. All were refused with Tam's smiling dismissal. Her companion was interested, but she was not. *If she wasn't interested in fucking any of them, why was she here?*

Ian followed them, sipping his beer, until Tam's lover was lured away by a barely dressed set of twins. Tam looked around her, seemed lost for a moment, and then took a deep breath and walked toward the bar. She collided with Ian on her way there.

"Excuse me," she said, recoiling from his body.

Ian knew when she realized it was him. Her hand grasped his biceps, and she inhaled quickly, filling her nose with his scent.

"Are you following me?" he asked before she could completely get her bearings.

Her hand tightened convulsively on his arm before letting go.

Tam smelled potently like herself, of rosemary and green tea. The scent took him back to the night in her bed, the lushly colored pillows, the soft weight of her breasts against his chest, her pussy eagerly swallowing him.

"I didn't know this was your kind of place," she said, ignoring his question for the foolishness it was.

"There's a lot you don't know about me."

Their shoulders brushed as they walked toward the bar together.

"Apparently so." She nodded at the G-stringed bartender. "Long Island iced tea, please."

Tam made Ian reckless enough to signal for another beer. Before she could get out her money, he paid for both their drinks.

"Does all this make you wet?" he asked, putting his wallet away.

It all seemed so surreal, the two of them walking through the house full of gyrating, fucking, and sweating bodies, talking calmly after an absence of weeks between them. Tam looked down at the thick bulge straining against his jeans.

"Does all this make you hard?" She didn't bother to hide the sneer in her voice.

You make me hard. Ian cleared his throat. "Your friend seems into it."

"He is. He wanted to see if I could get into it, too." She sipped her drink, took a larger gulp and then another.

They stepped out through the front door, ignoring the interested looks and grasping hands. The night air was cool on Ian's face. As soon as the door closed behind them, the droning hum of voices disappeared. It could have been just the two of them on any suburban street, even Tam's, with the quietly winking stars above, the scent of night-blooming flowers from the garden, and the comforting silence.

Ian was buzzed enough to admit to missing Tam, even enough to admit it to her face. But he didn't. He drew in a deep breath of Tam-scented air. "Feel like taking a walk?"

"Sure."

He took a deep swallow of his beer before putting the bottle between stalks of daffodils and the stone walkway. The last thing he wanted to do was get arrested for drinking alcohol on the street. Tam didn't seem to care. She took another big sip of her drink as they strolled down the walk. The sound of her ridiculous heels was loud on the concrete sidewalk, a porno soundtrack to the twitch of her ass and the exaggerated sway of her hips.

Tam sucked her teeth. "This goddamn skirt." She pulled down at the offending garment. "I don't even know how people find this shit sexy."

Ian smiled. Plucking at the tiny piece of leather, she seemed once again like the alluring creature he met two months ago. But he knew she wasn't. Not really. Tam was fucking someone else. Someone who didn't even value her enough to keep her for himself.

"Are you satisfied with your choice?" he asked.

Tam looked at him but didn't say anything. She knew exactly what he was talking about.

"I've missed you," she said finally, curling her mouth around the edge of the plastic cup containing her drink.

"I've missed you, too."

Their meandering footsteps took them to a playground perched safely in the middle of the neighborhood's tiny park. Tam sat on the swing and anchored her drink deep in the sand before grasping with both hands the metal chain suspending the seat of the swing. Ian stood nearby with his hands in his pockets and watched her pump herself in the swing. The skirt rode all the way up to the tops of her thighs, revealing her pale blue panties. *Who else wore sensible panties to a sex party?*

He suddenly wanted to drop to his knees in front of her and lick that blue cotton until it was soaking wet inside and out. Ian adjusted his sneakered feet in the sand and cleared his throat.

"Because of you"—she said matter-of-factly, her earrings fluttering in the breeze with each back-and-forth pass of the swing through the air—"I can't enjoy other men."

"I can't do anything with that." Ian murmured. "You're not making too much sense to me right now."

"Yeah, that's my problem, too."

She seemed far away and emotionally remote as she swung back and forth in the silence. But she was closer to him now than she had been in the past few weeks, and so he savored her presence. He wanted more. Much more.

If he was drunk enough he would have asked her to suck him off one last time. To take out his already hard dick and cover it with kisses, lick its seeping head, and take him deep into her mouth. And she'd probably do it, too, in her own way, working his dick until he came and then swallowing every ounce of his juice. She'd lick her lips, catlike and sweet, and ask if he had any more cream. But he would have to shake his head, because it was his turn to sate a long-denied hunger.

This hunger would lead him to sniff her pussy, to slide off her heaven-colored panties and lick the salty musk of her and dive deeply inside her with his tongue to imprint her smell all over his face. If he asked nicely enough, she would grasp the back of his head like she used to; she'd buck against his face while he fucked her with his tongue and pounded her clit with his nose. She'd come and wail and shower his mouth with quick squeezing kisses from her pussy lips.

But Ian wasn't drunk enough for that. He was aware enough to know that he would hate her and himself afterward if anything happened between them.

"You ready to go back?" he asked.

They walked back to the house in silence. It was a particular kind of torture, being so close to her, smelling her, knowing that she wanted him as much as he wanted her, yet not being able to have her. Ian rotated his shoulders to loosen the tightness in his chest.

As they approached the house, a couple walked down the driveway toward them.

"Party over?" Ian asked.

"Oh, no, honey," the more slender of the two men said. "Things are just starting to get interesting."

Ian could only imagine what other "interesting" things could happen in that house tonight.

"Have fun," the two men chorused as they ambled down the path, holding hands.

"I bet Garrett is right in the middle of whatever that is," Tam said, wrinkling her nose.

"I'm assuming you'll want to jump right in there with him."

"That's not a good assumption to make," she said.

He held open the front door for Tam, and, almost against his will, his eyes dropped down to the rocking bridge the leather of the skirt made between her ass cheeks. *Maybe there's some appeal to this getup after all.*

Stale air from inside the house blasted Ian in the face as soon as he stepped inside. The place reeked of sex. The hour or so they had been gone had cleared Ian's senses, but now he felt dirty again. He wanted to pull Tam out of there, tell her to go home to her daughter and her rosemary-scented bed.

A man emerged out of the morass of bodies to grasp Tam's arm. "I was looking for you."

She seemed surprised to see him. Ian pulled the door closed behind him and turned to leave, but Tam tugged at his hand. He stayed. Her boyfriend looked like he was high, with his unnaturally bright eyes, too-wide smile, and blood-flushed lips.

"Why?" Tam asked him. "You were obviously having a good time."

"Are you jealous?" The man chuckled like he'd just made a good joke. "I see you found somebody you like." His eyes casually appraised Ian. "You look familiar. I didn't know Tamarind liked the pretty-boy type." He chuckled again. "No offense." He offered his hand to shake. "The name is Garrett."

Ian took it and immediately wanted to wipe his off. The man's hand was damp. Tam slowly released his other hand. This was what she had given Ian up for? He turned deliberately to the woman who still owned his heart.

"Enjoy the rest of the party," he said to her. "I'm heading home."

She opened her mouth to say something but closed it again. "It was good seeing you," she finally said.

Ian nodded once and then walked off to get his friends. This "party" was over. He found Rashawn in an upper-level bedroom playing the voyeur to an enthusiastic orgy on the shag-carpeted floor. He looked up when Ian walked into the room.

"Is that your ready face?"

"Yup."

"No prob. Eric is downstairs getting to know that cute little bartender a little bit better. I think he's just killing time."

"Good. Let's go."

Rashawn stood up and followed him from the room.

"I saw you with that woman," Eric said as soon as he saw Ian.

"Fuck." He wasn't in the mood to talk about this.

"Did you?"

"No."

They walked out of the house, with Rashawn looking at them both. "What happened?"

The Range Rover chirped as Eric opened the doors with the remote. "He was cuddling up at the bar with that old chick who stole his balls."

Rashawn looked at Ian. "No shit?"

"I think you two just arrange to bump into each other in public for dramatic conversations." Eric started the truck.

"Fuck you."

"Don't look at me for that, bro. I know *she's* the one you want."

Rashawn chuckled and fell deeper into his sprawl in the corner of the truck. Ian halfheartedly punched Eric in the shoulder. His friend was right. Tam was the one he wanted. And, right now, he couldn't do a damn thing about it.

"Just take me home," he said.

12

She smelled like sunlight and sex. Grass stains marked the
crinkled white of her skirt that they were laying on. Her face
was rapture in the breeze, her lips parted and wet as he slid easily inside her cunt, moving in a nearly frictionless rhythm. She
was incredibly wet. He could feel the sun on his back, its heat
trailing each muscle, sinking into the sleek flesh of his ass as he
moved inside Tam. Her pleasure was absolute; it was tied un-
breakably to him, and he was all she wanted. She called out his
name and smiled, rising up in her dream orgasm to fling her
arms around his neck and clutch him tighter. Her pussy swallowed his aching dick; his body felt full. He was going to come.
Ian opened his mouth. An alarm sounded, discordant and loud,
jerking him out of his dream.

"Fuck!" He turned over and slapped at the inconvenient
alarm clock. Or, at least, he tried to, but a heavy weight pinned
him to the bed. It smelled like sunlight and sex.

"Do you want me to turn that off for you?"

He lay back against the sheets, drinking in the vision in his
bed.

"Sure."

Tam stretched across him, her bare body, breasts, belly, thighs elongated in the sun toward the clock. Then it was off, its shrieking silenced, leaving only the sounds of their quiet breathing. She had him trapped between her thighs and under the steaming heat of her pussy. His dick was hard and stood up between them, pre-cum glistening on its head. She didn't touch him.

"I don't want anybody else," she said. Before Ian could speak, she put a finger to his lips. "Just let me finish, OK?"

He nodded.

"For a long time now I've known I wanted you. But I had some crazy ideas about having the freedom to fuck whoever I wanted, whenever I wanted. When I saw you the other night, I finally had to put the bullshit aside."

Ian knew he should have been surprised, maybe even angry, at her presumption to barge into his house the morning after they'd met at the party and slip into his bed. But all he felt was relief.

"What about your rich boyfriend?"

"Garrett isn't my boyfriend. For a long time he was just convenient."

"And now?"

"And now he's not. If you still want me, there's only you. Is that OK?"

It was. He nodded, and she fell into him, drowning him in her scent and in the skimming heat of her hands.

"Please," she whispered, moving up and over him. "Make love to me."

Ian lay under her, entranced. Tam sheathed him in her moist heat, rising up like a siren on the surf, her back arched and her mouth wet and open, to lure him once again beneath her waves. And, this time, he wasn't dreaming.

Have passion, will travel.
Let your fantasies be your guide as you embark on adventures that will take your breath away. All it takes is a soft whisper and a flash of skin to scale the heights of ecstasy. . . .

Wild Thing
Maggie Hamilton's current Mr. Right Now leaves a lot to be desired, so when she sets sail on a singles' cruise, her expectations are high. But a booking error lands her in honeymoon hell. Good thing the stunningly handsome cruise director makes showing Maggie a good time his number-one priority. And soon they're both riding the waves of desire. . . .

Hold Me, Thrill Me
Most people would think of a tropical island as paradise. But to Ryan Holmes, it's a prison. Her ex-boyfriend left her stranded there, and now she's waiting tables to make enough money to get back home—and satisfy her lust for vengeance. Meanwhile, a French waiter is satisfying her body's deepest cravings—and leaving her hungry for more. . . .

Light My Fire
Emily Mitchell has finally convinced her workaholic boyfriend to take a vacation. Too bad it's to a ski resort—in August. His lack of attention is leaving Emily cold anyway. Until she falls into her neighbor's hot tub—naked. Now Emily's feeling the heat—under the stars, on horseback, and in every place imaginable with a man who can't get enough of her. . . .

Pack your bags, rev your engines, and get ready to visit a place that will exceed your wildest expectations. . . .

Please turn the page for an exciting sneak peek of P.J. Mellor's GIVE ME MORE coming next month!

Maggie sniffed and wiped her nose with the tissue stuck in the belt of her once-white slacks and tried to rinse the grime from the washcloth. Sweat trickled between her breasts, making her wish she had never invested in the new instant-cleavage-enhancer bra model. A lot of good it did her.

Hunched over the miniscule sink, she rubbed at the dust-streaked terry held under a flow of water that was one step above trickle status. When it became obvious that most of the dust was embedded for eternity, she twisted the little pointed knobs to turn off the water and made her way back into the living quarters to resume her cleaning, careful to avoid poking her eye out on the colorful beak of a stuffed bird next to the "grotto."

An hour later she stretched and rubbed the small of her back while she looked around at her progress. All one and a half plastic bushes of backbreaking progress.

"This won't do."

She walked to the wooden box housing the phone and called the concierge.

*   *   *

Ten long minutes later, a timid knock sounded. She fought her way through the vinyl, slid back the bolt, and opened the door.

The small man from the deck stood, all but quivering, in the hall, his clipboard clutched to his scrawny chest.

"Ms. Hamilton?" he called above the jungle sounds. "I'm Otto, the purser. Front desk said you had a complaint."

"Yes, Otto, I certainly do," she shouted back and motioned him inside. "Come in."

Just when she wondered if she'd have to resort to dragging him bodily into her suite, he stepped across the threshold.

She waved her hand in the direction of her personal jungle. "I'm afraid this just won't do. I feel like I need a machete to even find my bed! Plus, I'm very allergic to dust." She pointed at one particularly fuzzy example, in case he failed to notice. "And the noise is, well, you can hear for yourself. I need to change rooms."

The poor man seemed to cower. "I—I'm afraid that's just not possible, M—Ms. Hamilton. All the other books are roomed." He stepped back, his knuckles white where he gripped his clipboard. "I mean, all the other rooms are booked." He reached back and opened the door, his intent on escape clear.

"Wait!" She lunged toward him, eliciting a startled whimper from the man. "Please. I'll take anything." She sneezed and focused her teary eyes on him. "Please. The dust is killing me."

His lips disappeared into a tight line. He stood a bit taller. "I'll speak to the cruise director, but I doubt he can do anything."

He hurried out and closed the door with a snap before she could think of an argument.

"Great," she murmured, swiping at a particularly obnoxious split-leaf elephant ear that had been whacking her head in the air-conditioned breeze. "Just how I wanted to spend my first day at sea."

She'd just dragged out her portable air cleaner and located a plug—no easy feat, given the decor—when a knock echoed in the little jungle.

She crawled out from under yet another fake palm and got to her feet, brushing the dust bunnies from her white slacks as she walked toward the door. It no longer mattered that her door did not have a peephole. Jack the Ripper could be on the other side, and if he offered her a clean room, she'd gladly follow him anywhere.

Her pile of dust-gray cleaning rags caught her attention. Keeping up appearances was a necessity. In a swooping motion, she bent to scoop them up as she walked by. Her bare foot hit a wet spot on the edge of the grotto. Her mind registered the cool, slick feel of the porcelain "beach" a nanosecond before she slid with a scream and a splash into the churning water.

The woman's scream from behind the locked door made Drew's blood run cold. Even the ridiculous jungle sounds couldn't drown out her distress. It was bad enough to be assigned to the honeymoon cruises for his final season. He'd be damned if one of his cruises would lose a bride.

Hands shaking, he fumbled with his set of master keys before he found the right one and got the door unlocked.

He saw her immediately.

She sat chest deep in the grotto, little islands of what looked like dirty washcloths floating around her. One small hand covered her left eye and forehead.

"Are you OK, ma'am?" He pocketed his keys and moved to the edge of the water.

She didn't blink. "My eye hurts," she said, the husky quality of her voice slipping down his spine like a seductive fingernail. Great. Finally his libido kicks in and it's with a newlywed woman.

"What happened?" He scanned the room for her husband, ready to personally throw the bastard from the ship. Men who abused women were lower than a snake's armpits, as far as he was concerned.

"I slipped and fell into the water."

Sure, you did. He reached out a hand to help her stand on what he knew to be a less than skid-free tub bottom. "I've got you. Just take small steps, and then I'll help you over the rim. Do you need to see a doctor?"

She shook her head, her short curls sticking to her skull. Wet, her hair looked almost translucent, so he'd bet she was a blonde.

The silk shirt sticking to her like a second skin most likely was yellow. He tried to avert his eyes from the scrap-of-nothing bra revealed by the wet fabric but couldn't seem to drag his gaze away from the tempting sight. Lordy, it was enough to make a grown man weep.

Once-white pants clung to world-class legs, leaving little to the imagination. Why were all the good ones married?

Her hand felt tiny within his grasp. He resisted the urge to pull her close. Barely. Damn, what was wrong with him? Maybe he'd been out to sea too long. He was definitely drowning in the clear turquoise of her bloodshot eyes. Why do women stay with bastards who make them cry?

Wow. Maggie looked up—way up—into the blue eyes of easily the most handsome man she'd ever seen. *Now this is more like it.* Tan, with golden-brown hair and mile-wide shoulders, dressed in a white uniform shirt and Bermuda shorts, he looked good enough to eat.

Dang. She realized she was holding his hand like some starstruck teenager. She dropped it and took a step back.

Unfortunately she was a bit too close to the edge of the grotto.

Arms flailing as she again fell backward, she grabbed for the first thing her hands came in contact with . . . his shirt.

With a huge splash, they landed chest to chest, heads banging together. Maggie tasted blood at the same time she realized she was held underwater by the weight of the man. Shoving him aside, she broke the surface and gasped for air, trudging toward the water's edge.

"Did you have to land on me?" Sputtering and coughing, she turned on him.

He lay facedown in the water.

"Shit!" She plowed against the force of the jets and grasped the back of his uniform collar to haul him above the surface of the water.

Her arm around his neck, she dragged him to the edge of the whirlpool, grunting with effort.

Good thing she was a lifeguard.

Beneath her palm, his heart beat a strong rhythm. He was breathing. Breathing was good.

"Lets get you out of these nasty wet clothes," she whispered, flicking open one gold button after another. She'd sworn to be more aggressive on her cruise, and fate had dropped the hunk in her arms. True, he was unconscious, but that wouldn't last for long. Who was she to buck fate? Unfortunately the man's forehead was rapidly growing a nasty goose egg. Before her eyes, it darkened to a deep cherry red right before the skin split from the immediate swelling.

Having her way with him would obviously have to wait.

With a grunt, she rolled him to his side and thumped his back.

He coughed a few times and wheezed as he struggled to sit up.

Shoot. Mouth-to-mouth would not be needed.

"Are you OK?" His voice was croaky. He cleared his throat and looked at her through sinfully thick, blond-tipped lashes. The once-over from his baby blues had her sitting back on her heels in an effort not to squirm.

He traced the tender skin next to her eye, where she'd bumped her head in the first fall, leaving a trail of fire.

Forcing back a wince, she reached out to touch the now huge bump on his forehead. It was hot.

His breath hissed. He leaned back a bit. "Ow." He probed the bump. "I really whacked my head." He glanced up. "Are you sure you're OK?"

"Fine." More than a whisper seemed inappropriate, for some reason.

He broke whatever connection they had and stood, helping her to her feet. "Thanks for dragging me out of the water." He scanned the room. "Where's your husband, Mrs. Hamilton?"

"Ah, it's Miss. Or Ms." Her skin burned with his scrutiny. "I mean, I'm not married."

"Excuse me?" She couldn't have said what he thought he'd just heard. He wasn't that lucky.

"I said I'm not married." She frowned and brushed at her wet, see-through pant leg before meeting his gaze. "Wouldn't that defeat the purpose."

"What purpose would that be?" Somehow his shirt had become unbuttoned, so he began working the sharp buttons through the wet fabric. No need to get excited, despite her claim. Newlyweds often forgot they were married at first. Probably a tough acclimation.

"The purpose of the cruise, of course."

The woman sounded annoyed and looked a little agitated.

Maybe it was best to humor her. "I suppose different people take cruises for different reasons." Although why a single person would take a honeymoon cruise was beyond him.

He gave her another once-over. She sure was a looker, he'd give her that.

She flashed a little lopsided smile that sent heat zipping through him.

Too bad she was married. And lied about it. Not to mention the fact she was more than a little wacky.

He turned toward the door. Best to cut his losses and get on with his day.

"Wait!" She grabbed his arm, the warmth of her palm doing funny things to his heart rate. "I don't even know your name."

He glanced at her hand and then back at her red-rimmed eyes. Their clear color seemed incongruous with the almost-painful-looking redness surrounding them.

"Drew. Drew Connor." He extricated his arm and offered his hand. "Cruise director."

She slipped her hand into his in what felt like an oddly intimate gesture.

Get a grip, Connor! The woman is just returning your hand-shake.

"Maggie Hamilton." She shrugged and removed the temptation of her hand. "But I guess you already know that."

"Ms. Hamilton?" He tilted her chin with his fingertip.

"Maggie," she said on a breath. "Call me Maggie."

"Maggie." Despite his best intentions, he leaned closer. "Think hard. You're not really single, are you?"

Her brow wrinkled. She stepped out of his reach and heaved a sigh. "Why are you having such an issue with my martial status?" She threw up her hands and strode to the side of the bed before turning on him. "Don't you think I would know it if I'd married someone? What? Do you think I'd forget something like that?"

Maybe she was telling the truth.

Fists on hips—very shapely hips, he might add—she glared at him. "Why are you grinning like that?"

He took a step toward her.

"Mr. Connor—"

"Drew." He took another step.

"Drew." She held up her hand. "OK, you can stop right there, *Drew*." He took another step. "Why are you looking at me like that?"

He closed the distance. Practically chest to chest, he felt the heat. He knew she felt it, too.

"You're really single, aren't you?" He raised her limp left hand and surveyed her ringless finger.

"I—" She swallowed and looked up at him with her incredible eyes. "I already told you that."

Damn, this was stupid on so many levels.

He put his arms around her, half prepared to be kicked or slapped.

She reacted by encircling his neck with her arms.

OK. Let's think about all the reasons why this is a bad idea.

He pulled her closer.

One: it's against company policy.

He leaned down, feeling the exciting warmth of her breath against his lips.

Two: even if she isn't married, she should be off-limits, due to reason one. Plus, if she isn't married, why is she on a honeymoon cruise? Maybe she's an escaped criminal. Maybe she's the female equivalent of a gigolo, who preys on married men.

The last idea fueled his excitement. He ground his already rock-hard erection against her.

She smiled and ground right back, eliciting a moan he hoped sounded more like a growl. Growls were more manly.

Three: stop reacting with your body, and listen to your mind, stupid! You don't even know this woman. This isn't some singles bar. You're going to get caught.

He glanced down at her. The heat from their wet clothes practically made steam. Her incredible eyes were heavy-lidded. She licked her lips, and he was a goner.

Four: time to score.

Maggie looked up at the man holding her in his arms and felt her knees go weak. If he didn't kiss her soon, she might just climb up his hard body and have her way with him right here, right now.

"Kiss me," she said on a breath, his mouth poised mere millimeters from her own.

"Oh darlin', I plan on it, I definitely plan on it." His husky whisper vibrated her lips an instant before settling in for the duration.

Whew! The guy sure knew how to kiss. She wouldn't be surprised if she had steam coming out of her ears.

He nibbled the edge of her lip before swooping in for another toe-curling, bone-melting kiss.

Her knees threatened to buckle. She couldn't take a deep breath, even through her nose.

He shifted position slightly, deepening the kiss she swore couldn't get deeper. Who needed to breathe anyway?

"Our clothes . . ." she finally managed to whisper against his lips.

"What about them?" He nuzzled her neck.

"They're wet." Her teeth closed around his earlobe.

He shuddered. "Well, we'll just have to get out of them," he returned.

His hands bracketed her waist, pushing the wet silk of her top ever upward while he continued to feast on her lips and neck. He paused a moment at the front clasp of her intensifier bra before popping it open with a flick of his wrist.

She held her breath. Would he notice the disparity in size once he palmed her actual flesh?

Then his hands cupped her, and she released a sigh. Who cared? As long as he kept doing what he was doing.

Her top came up and over her head, his mouth scarcely leaving hers.

Breaking contact, he knelt at her bare feet, peeling the wet linen of her pants down her hips and then balancing her while she stepped out of the sodden fabric.

A hot trail of kisses tracked his progress up her body until they again stood chest to chest. Well, actually more like chest to abdomen, since he was a good foot taller.

His mouth once again took possession of hers while he slipped her bra straps from her shoulders and down her arms.

She rubbed her pebbled nipples against his firm chest, loving the friction.

In response, his hips bucked against her while he deepened the kiss, all but lifting her from her feet.

She wrapped her arms around his neck, swallowing a tiny gasp of excitement at the feel of his fingers hooking in the sides of her thong. The wet string dragged along the skin of her hips and then rolled beneath her buttocks to scrape down her thighs. When it fell to her knees, she was forced to break the kiss and step out.

Somewhat of a klutz under normal circumstances, she didn't want to risk tripping on her own underwear during what might easily be the most awesome sexual encounter of her life to date.

His gaze left a trail of fire down to her toes and back up again. Beneath her palm, his heart pounded while his breath came in harsh drags of air.

"This is nuts," he said on a breath. "Tell me to stop." He nibbled the edge of her lip. "Are you sure this is what you want?"

She nodded. Karyl wanted her to walk on the wild side. Maggie glanced at her personal jungle. It was about as wild as she was going to get. "I want to do something wild to celebrate my first cruise." She hoped her smile was more assured than she felt. "Let's make love in the water."

His eyes widened, and then a slow grin revealed a set of blinding white teeth and a lethal dimple. "Anything the lady wants . . ."

He made short work of stripping—dang, she didn't get a chance to check him out—and then scooped her up in his arms and stepped into the grotto.

She gripped his shoulders to keep from drifting away from the delicious heat of his hard body.

"Wait." He reached for a boulder at the edge of the waterfall. It opened. He pulled out what looked like a small foam Boogie Board and positioned it at her back.

"Lay back. Relax," he instructed. "Let me do all the work."

It was difficult, but she managed to somewhat relax while Drew caressed her legs from ankle to thigh. With each pass of his hands, her muscles grew more pliant.

He stepped into the vee of her legs.

Warm water lapped at the juncture of her thighs. She resisted the urge to clamp them together and squirm.

"So pretty," he said in a low, husky voice, his breath telling her he was oh-so-close to her most private place. "So smooth. Soft." His lips whispered over her, causing her to arch in a silent plea.

Water sloshed in her ears, but she was beyond caring.

He licked and suckled while his fingers played with her flesh, which was spread before him like a sexual smorgasbord.

Good thing she'd indulged in a Brazilian wax, she thought, and swallowed a giggle when Drew lapped at her and then flicked her nub with the tip of his tongue.

Her muscles twitched before taking on the consistency of wet spaghetti. She clamped her legs around his head, anchoring him in place.

Shudders rippled through her. Arching her back, she gasped in her effort not to scream.

It worked. Unfortunately the action plunged her head beneath the water, and she managed to suck in about a gallon of water.

Great. Attempts to cough were moot, with her head still below the surface of the water. Her body twitched. Whether it was from the earth-shattering release or impending death was a toss-up.

Just her luck. The most powerful orgasm of her life was obviously going to be her last.